On the Air

On the Air

Geonn Cannon

P.D. Publishing, Inc.
Clayton, North Carolina

Copyright © 2007 by Geonn Cannon

ISBN-13: 978-1-933720-32-6
ISBN-10: 1-933720-32-8

9 8 7 6 5 4 3 2 1

Cover art/design by: Barb Coles/Stephanie Solomon-Lopez
Edited by: Nene Adams/Medora MacDougall

Published by:

P.D. Publishing, Inc.
P.O. Box 70
Clayton, NC 27528

http://www.pdpublishing.com

Acknowledgements

I'm not going to go on for pages and pages like some people do, but there are a few people who do need to be acknowledged and, without whom, this book would not exist. This book is dedicated to Debbie, my first and most ardent fan, and to Christy, without whom I would never have come up with the idea for this book. Also, to Stephanie, who decided this story was worth her time and effort.

Also, to Chris Baty and National Novel Writing Month. This book would definitely not have been written without the draw of this wonderful writing community. If you want to write a book, any time of the year is fine. But only in November will you have such a wonderfully insane and dedicated support group waiting to lend you a hand. Visit them at www.nanowrimo.org.

Chapter One

"KELF, the island's number one place for the hits!"

Nadine Butler leaned forward as soon as the station identification finished playing and smiled at the microphone. "Welcome back, my little ones," she said. Turning her gaze toward the window set in the wall across from where she sat, she admired the crystal blue glare of the harbor and marina. Through the latticework of sailboat masts, she saw the large Washington State ferry easing its way through the calm waters.

"I can see the first ferry of the afternoon through my little window here. Hello, to all you newcomers. Hello, to everyone coming home after a journey. For those meeting me for the first time, I am Nadine Butler, the Pixie of KELF AM 1220, and I am here with you for another three hours or so. We're taking requests right now, so if you're a tourist, give me a call at 232-KELF and I'll do my best to make your stay on our little island as memorable as possible. Coming up, we've got the Eagles, Jackson Browne, and Fleetwood Mac. Stay tuned!"

For each of the ferries that arrived during her show, she had a special introduction that was especially welcoming to the last of the summer tourists who visited the tiny northwestern island of Squire's Isle, thirty miles off the coast of Washington. Some of the tourists were from Seattle or Vancouver, but the vast majority came from all over the country to see a real American small town...her town.

Nadine's broadcast booth was a nondescript closet-type space dominated by the semi-circular table that held the various odds and ends necessary for radio broadcasting. A stack of CDs and tapes towered to Nadine's left. Just over her right shoulder, a wide picture window overlooked the bullpen and the sea of cubicles KELF called its business offices. As Nadine finished her welcome message, she hit the button that would begin a pre-set block of commercials and turned her attention to the phone banks.

The button for telephone Line Three had been flashing since the end of the last song, so she depressed it first. "This is Nadine Butler, and you're on the air with the Pixie. Tourist or local?"

"Um...tourist," replied the uncertain male voice. "Is this really on the air?"

"Live on tape, honey," Nadine said. She rested her elbows on the table and leaned toward the microphone. It increased the volume of her voice, and listeners had told her it sounded more intimate, like she was physically in the room with them. "What's your name?" Nadine asked.

"Robert."

"And what can the Pixie play for you, Robert?"

"You got any Springsteen? *Born to Run?*"

She glanced at the stack and saw a Bruce Springsteen's *Greatest Hits* CD within easy reach. Stretching her arm out, she plucked the CD off the rack, withdrawing the disc as she spoke into the microphone. "Robert, that is one of my all-time favorite Springsteen tunes, and I *do* have it right here. I'm gonna play that for you the first chance I get. All right? Thanks for tuning in to the Elf! Have a great trip, okay?"

"All right."

Smiling, Nadine disconnected the call. She glanced at the clock to see how much time was left on the commercial before she moved her finger to the next flashing phone light. "You're on with the Pixie," she said to the caller. "Tourist or local?"

She answered the next three calls, got a request from each of them, and seeded the songs into her already-planned play list. Running her finger over the list of song titles, she frowned. With this list plus the commercials she was obligated to play during this hour, she was still going to run a little short on air-time. Nadine pulled the headphones from her ears and hurried to the door of the booth, opening it and sticking her head into the bullpen. She glanced around until she spotted an older black man pushing a mail cart between the desks. The man she knew only as Billy — the resident "mail boy", janitor, and jack-of-all-trades — appeared to be in the middle of handing out the day's memos. She whistled, making him lift his rheumy eyes to hers.

"I need just under three minutes," Nadine said.

Billy leaned against his mail cart and drummed his long fingers on the handle. His eyes danced back and forth across the carpet as if reading something written on the hardwood underneath. Suddenly, he smiled, pointed at her, and proudly said, "*Gypsies, Tramps, and Thieves*, two minutes and thirty-six seconds."

"Cher?" Nadine asked, wrinkling her nose in displeasure.

He shrugged and gripped the mail cart's handle tightly. "I like 'er. Nice voice."

Nadine held her hands out in surrender and said, "Then Cher it is. Thank you, Billy."

She returned to her seat in the booth just as the ad for Gail's Seafood Restaurant ended. She put the "cans" back over her ears and depressed the broadcast button with her pinky finger. "Gail's Seafood Shack, man...talk about some good eatin'!" she said into the microphone. "If you haven't been there, it's just the greatest seafood you will ever eat. And to prove it to anyone out there who doubts their Pixie, I have a coupon awarding dinner for two to Gail's if you can answer one extremely easy trivia question. Trust me, with food this good, I'm all but giving this prize away. Here's the question: who, in 1966, said his band was bigger than Jesus? Give me a call at 232-KELF with the right answer and you'll be eating very, very well tonight.

"Right now, though, I'm sending this one out to Robert, a newcomer to our fair shores. Robert, I hope you have a great time on Squire's Isle and that you don't feel the urge to run." She snickered and said, "Yeah, I know how bad that was. This is the Boss from 1975 — it's *Born to Run* on KELF."

As the song started, she saw that the phone lines had all lit up once more. It was a typical reaction when she ran a contest, especially an easy one, so she ran her fingers over the three lights and pressed one at random. "Hi, KELF. You're on with the Pixie."

"Hey, this is Tony. I just came over on the ferry and I wondered if I could request a song...?"

"Sure thing, Tony! What do you wanna hear?"

"*Me and You and a Dog Named Boo*, by Lobo, I think...?"

"Oh, I adore you for requesting that, Tony. I've loved that song since I was a little girl, so I'm going to give you a special prize," Nadine said. She loved being able to randomly give prizes to people who were not expecting to win; it was a genuine bright spot that never failed to lift her spirits. "You're my tourist of the day! What that means is that you can come by the station — we're just south of the ferry lanes, just ask if you can't find us — and pick up a coupon for two free ice cream cones from Sandy's Dee-lights. Sound good?"

"That sounds great!"

"If you're happy, I'm happy, Tony. I'll get that song on for you ASAP, and be sure to come by and get your coupon before five."

"Okay! I'm making my way over to, uh, the, uh..."

"Sholeh Village for the whale-watching?"

"That's it!"

"Well, then, you're in for two treats today, Tony. I'll move your song up to make sure it plays on your way out there, all right?"

"All right!"

"Tony, I am going to send you away with good memories of Squire's Isle if it's the last thing I do. Keep it tuned to KELF, and I'll get some 'bright red Georgia clay on your shoes'," she said, quoting a line from the song.

"Well, all right."

She thanked him for calling and went on to Line Two. "KELF, you're talking to Nadine."

A woman meekly asked, "You have a winner for the trivia yet?"

"I don't! You wanna make a guess? Who said that his band was bigger than Jesus?"

"I *think* it was John Lennon..."

"That's right!" Nadine hit a button that caused a noisemaker to sound loudly. "Oh, no, there's confetti all over my booth!" she exclaimed. "What's your name?"

"Sara."

"Well, Sara, are you a local or a tourist?"

"Born and raised here on the island."

"Well, that is fantastic! So you've been to Gail's before, I assume."

"I have."

"Good! You know what you're in for. Get something really good, and think of me when you're eating, all right?"

"Okay!"

Nadine chuckled. "Okay, I'm going to send you to the secretary now. She'll get some information from you, and then you can pick up the coupons anytime before five this evening. Sound good?"

"Sounds great!"

"Glad to hear it. Sara, who is hooking you up with a free dinner?"

"The Pixie," Sara answered with a touch of laughter in her voice.

"That's right, your Pixie Godmother never lets her children go hungry. Keep listening to 1220 KELF, and you have yourself a great dinner."

"All right."

"Bye-bye, Sara."

There were still two minutes left on the Boss' song, so Nadine decided to answer Line Three. "KELF, this is the Pixie."

A man asked, "You have a winner yet?"

"Oh, sorry, we just got one."

"Ah, nuts." The caller sounded disappointed. "Thanks anyway!"

"You got a song you want to hear?" Nadine asked.

"*Norwegian Wood* by the Beatles."

"Oh, no, you're a real Beatles fan, huh? You probably knew the answer right off."

"Yeah, I did."

"Aw, well, better luck next time! I promise you at least one more easy Beatles trivia sometime this week, okay?"

"I'll train my dialing finger."

"Don't give me *too* much information, honey," Nadine laughed. "I'll get your song on for you as soon as I can, all right?"

"Okay!"

Nadine disconnected the call, saw the phone lights were dim at last, and rolled her chair around to face the stack of CDs next to her. She ran her fingers down the spines and pulled discs of the Beatles and Lobo. As she was searching for Cher, there was a tap on the glass behind her. She turned her head; through the picture window, she could see Miranda Powell, the station manager, standing in the bullpen. Nadine waved in acknowledgment, and Miranda motioned for her to come out. There was not enough time before the end of the song for a conference, so Nadine pointed at the CD and held up two fingers to indicate two minutes. Miranda nodded and crossed her arms over her chest, clearly prepared to wait.

Nadine leaned forward, bracing her elbows on the table and wondering what Miranda wanted. The woman was the "messenger" who usually passed down bad news from the station's owner; she was mostly hands-off when it came to the talent, so it would have to be something of semi-importance to get her to interrupt a show. All Nadine could think of was there had been a complaint. "I said Jesus on the air," she muttered to herself. "The Satanists must be demanding equal time."

When the song ended, Nadine hit a switch to transfer the feed back to her mic. "Hey, everyone out there, be you tourist or native, whale-watcher or sight-seer, friend or foe — I'm Nadine Butler, the Pixie, and we have a winn-ah for the dinn-ah at Gail's." She hit the replay button and the recorded call with Sara's voice began issuing from the tape deck.

She set the requested Lobo song to play as soon as the winning call ended and stood up. Hanging her headphones on the edge of the desk, she went to the door and opened it. "I've got three minutes and some change," she told Miranda. "What's up?"

"You're not in trouble," Miranda said immediately.

"Uh-oh," Nadine said. She could feel her bright mood in danger of fading. She braced herself for the worst as she slumped against the door and shook her head. "Now I'm *really* worried. What's wrong?"

Miranda reluctantly said, "Hoagie...he has a conflict this weekend. I'm sorry."

"Oh, God," Nadine groaned. "Can that man *ever* fulfill an obligation? What is it this ti—" She froze when she remembered the commercial the station had been playing endlessly that week. "Oh, no. Not the fair. Please, Miranda, do not do this to me. Please!"

To her credit, Miranda looked uneasy at making the request. She lifted her hand in a conciliatory gesture and said, "I'm sorry, Nadine, but Hoagie can't host it this year. You're the best option for replacing him. You're the most popular DJ we have and you...I'm sorry, but you *are* single."

Ah, Nadine thought, *that old chestnut. Miranda thinks I'm single and therefore, I have no life.* "Hoagie is single," Nadine argued. "So is Leah."

"Hoagie has plans on the mainland this weekend that he can't back out of," Miranda said, "or so he claims. And I'm not sure I could trust Leah for this. It *is* a family-oriented sort of thing." She hesitated and then said, "To be honest with you, Nadine, I would hate to think of you sitting at home by yourself this weekend."

Nadine sagged in defeat. Miranda was, in her own misguided way, just trying to be nice. She shrugged in resignation but asked anyway, "Can I say 'no' without it affecting my job here?"

"Well, we won't fire you, if that's what you mean," Miranda replied, smiling broadly, "but you'd really be helping us out. Most of the people going to see Hoagie would prefer to see you, anyway. It wouldn't affect ticket sales; we'd probably get even more ticket sales because of the switch. You'd be saving the day, Dean."

Oh, not the nickname! Nadine thought. *That's really playing dirty.* She closed her eyes and reluctantly accepted that her weekend off was a lost cause. Waving her hands, she muttered, "All right, yeah. Fine. But remember this the next time we talk about raises, all right?"

"You got it. Thank you, Nadine. You're the best." Miranda pulled a folded piece of paper from her pocket and thrust it at Nadine. "Since the fair is this weekend, I'm going to need you to announce the change as soon as possible."

"Make Hoagie do it during his show. Make him explain why he's backing out."

"Don't make Hoagie the bad guy, Dean."

"Stop calling me Dean," Nadine said. She was not really angry, just frustrated. She snatched the paper away from Miranda and said, "This is the last time this quarter, all right? The last time I host one of these stupid galas, the last concert, the last last-minute switch. Deal? From now on, when I have a weekend off..."

"It will actually be a weekend off," Miranda said, nodding. "I got it. You're a dear for putting up with it this time."

Nadine sighed and waved the woman off. She went back into her booth, reading over the copy as she sat down and replaced the headphones. She flipped a switch and tried not to let out an annoyed sigh into the microphone. "That was Lobo with *Me and You and a Dog Named Boo* and those St. Paul wheat fields. Ah, gotta love that song! Just makes you want to hop in the car, pick a direction, and keep on driving. Don't try it here, though; can't drive too far on an island unless you're going around in circles.

"Anyway, enough of my nonsense. Or maybe more of my nonsense because I just got handed a note," Nadine crinkled the paper between her fingers so the crisp sound would be heard over the mic, "that says I am going to be the hostess with the most-est at this year's Squire Days. That's right, this weekend's Renaissance Faire will be emceed by yours truly. I'll be out there broadcasting live for most of the weekend, so why don't you come by and see me, okay? We'd love to see you all out there in your nice tight tights and big fluffy dresses! Coming up, we've still got the Eagles and a few more requests from those tourists, bless their pointy little heads. Keep listening to your favorite Pixie on 1220 KELF AM."

She pulled the headphones away and glanced at the phone lines. Sure enough, almost thirty seconds after she went to commercial, Line Three lit up. She glanced through the glass, saw that Miranda was gone, and answered the call. "KELF, this is the Pixie."

"So it *is* you," a quiet female voice said. "Not some...I don't know, lying body snatcher or anything?"

Nadine winced. *Well, isn't this going to be awkward?* "Hi, Kate," she said, trying to sound apologetic. "Look, there was..."

"You're working this weekend? *All* weekend?"

"That's what it looks like," Nadine said. "Only a couple of hours each day, but...yeah, it might as well be all weekend. Ruins our plans, at any rate." She checked the counter. There was a minute and forty-five seconds left on the commercial. "I...I don't really have time to have this argument..."

"It's not an argument," Kate replied. Her reasonable tone made the back of Nadine's neck prickle in alarm. "I just want to make sure I have all the information so we can have a fully informed fight when we get home," Kate went on. "So you're working all weekend? And when you're not working, you'll probably be too tired to do anything else. That's the situation?"

"I know, I know," Nadine sighed. "It was my idea, you cancelled a bunch of stuff to clear the weekend so we could go, and now I'm reneging and..."

"Okay," Kate interrupted. "That's all I needed to know. Have a good rest of the show."

Kate hung up abruptly, and Nadine resisted the urge to throttle her mic. She mimicked Miranda's voice, giving her a nasal quality the real woman did not possess. "You *are* single. You *are* the most popular DJ here. You *are* the biggest pushover on staff." Nadine knew she could tell Miranda and her co-workers that she was seeing someone and just leave it at that, ignoring gender and the whole furor it would cause to know her significant other was a woman. But she had been around long enough to know that her lover's identity would not stay secret for long. It was easier to just say she was single...in theory, at least.

Nadine was torn. On the one hand, it would solve a lot of problems if she just said she was with someone, if she admitted she had plans over the weekend and could not possibly fill in for Hoagie. The odds were that Miranda would back off without an interrogation. On the other hand, if Miranda pressed for information and Nadine was forced to out herself, that would cause a whole new can of worms to be opened. Her closet was the rock, her work was a hard place, and she was wedged firmly between them.

She sighed again, tucked a stray lock of hair behind the ear of her glasses, and hit the broadcast button. "Welcome back," she said, forcing her voice to its accustomed, cheerful tone. "You're still listening to KELF, I'm still Nadine Butler, and our songs still rock." She transferred directly to the next song in the play list and sat back in her chair. Looking at her watch, she groaned.

Three more hours on the air.

More than enough time to brace herself for a fight with her girlfriend.

At 4:58 p.m., Nadine switched off from commercial and said, "Well, folks, that's going to do it for my show today." She looked over her shoulder and saw Hoagie making his way through the bullpen. "Joe 'Hoagie' Hogan is making his way to the booth right this minute, so he'll be with y'all right after Jackson Browne. This is Nadine Butler, your KELF Pixie, saying good-bye for another day. Thanks for letting me spend the afternoon with you. And remember to tune in tomorrow; I'll be lonely if you don't."

She switched on Jackson Browne's *The Load-Out* and stood up. It was a nice, slow song, a perfect capper to her show. Plus, when partnered with the song *Stay* as it usually was, the song was long enough to give her time to get out and let Hoagie into the booth for his show. She looped her scarf around her neck and put her play list into a desk drawer so it would not get in Hoagie's way.

Hoagie Hogan sidled into the booth. He was a full foot taller than Nadine and probably more than a foot thicker. He always wore jeans and flannel shirts. His curly blond hair hugged his head tightly as if afraid of the long fall if he went bald. The man shed his denim jacket and tossed it over the back of her chair.

Nadine rounded the table and let him take her place in the nerve center. Bending over, she opened the fridge that was tucked beneath the desk. After locating the last can of Pepsi near the back, she straightened, leveled a glare at him, and said coldly, "Joseph."

"Joseph? You sound like my mother when she's about to let me have it. What'd I do?" Hoagie asked, having the nerve to look somewhat aggrieved behind a day's worth of beard stubble.

Nadine was unmoved. "You cancelled the Renaissance Faire."

"Oh," he said, shrugging casually. "Yep, I did."

She resisted the urge to chuck her Pepsi can at him only by reminding herself that it was the last one. "You know what this does to my schedule?" she asked.

He scoffed. "What schedule? Come on, Nadine, we both know you're the most popular DJ here. I'm just giving the people what they want."

Nadine sighed, straightened up, and popped open her Pepsi can. "Popular or not, you owe me."

"Yeah, yeah, I'll find some way to pay you back."

Nadine squinted at him suspiciously. "It worries me, the way you said that."

He waved her away. As she slipped out of the booth, she heard him trim off the end of *Stay* and say on the air, "Welcome, welcome, welcome, I am Joe Hogan, you can call me Hoagie. I'll be here with you until you're sick of me."

"Too late," Nadine muttered.

She walked to her desk and took a seat, looking over the memos Billy had left. She managed to get the stack of incoming mail sorted and a handful of it read before she finished her drink. Crushing the empty can and slipping it into her coat pocket, she looped her leather satchel's strap over her head and across her body, then went down the narrow staircase to the ground floor.

The building's design was staggered so that the second story looked down over the first. The receptionist was on the ground floor, separating the "celebrities" of KELF Radio from the outside world by means of a huge circular desk. Nadine rounded the edge of this barricade, giving a friendly waggle of her fingers to Sue, the secretary on duty.

"I loved your show today, Nadine," Sue said, exactly the same as every day.

Nadine still appreciated the appreciation. "Thank you, Sue. See you tomorrow."

As she stepped outside, a brisk wind blew off the harbor and hit her head on. She paused, her body bent against the wind, and fumbled with the buttons on her jacket. The lank dark hair that had been mashed by headphones all day was stirred by the chill wind and began lashing at her face, though her eyes were protected by her glasses. She turned and walked over to her bicycle, holding her coat shut with both hands.

By the time Nadine undid the lock and chain and threw her leg over the seat, the wind had died down enough for her to find her balance. Riding toward Spring Street, she could see the line of cars in the ferry lanes and wondered how many of the people waiting there had called in song requests.

She turned onto Spring Street; from here, it was nearly a straight shot to her apartment, but it took about five minutes longer than the alternate, winding route. However, the fewer turns she had to make, the more time she had to think. The more time she had to think, the easier the upcoming fight with Kate would go. An added bonus was that her route took her past the newspaper offices where Kate worked. Speeding by, she straightened her back and peered through a window. Kate's desk, near the back of the brightly lit room, was already vacant.

Probably already at the apartment, stewing, picking her words carefully. Nadine sighed. She would just have to make Kate see that there was no way around what had happened. It wasn't like she was scrapping their plans because she'd changed her mind. It was work. She would just have to make Kate understand that.

She had met Kate three years earlier when the woman had been doing a fluff piece for the newspaper —Celebrities of Squire's Isle — and rather than interview the mayor, Nadine had been tapped. Coming from a raven-haired beauty like Kate, the request had been a hard one to turn down. Their first interview had gone well and transformed into dinner; dinner had gone even better and transformed into a night of sex.

They had been together ever since, two relatively visible women in a small town, both still closeted and butting heads about it. Kate was firmly in the closet and willing to stay there as long as she could. Nadine was wishy-washy on the subject. On the one hand, she would love to be out, would love to tell people that she was in a relationship for a number of reasons, not the least of which was the fact she could finally tell Miranda that she could not do things like the Renaissance Faire because she had plans with her girlfriend.

Nadine rounded the corner to her apartment building and stopped her bike in the courtyard. The Blair Idyll Apartments was shaped like a U, three sections surrounding a small courtyard with a neatly tended garden. Nadine tended the flowers herself in return for a break on her rent. As she walked her bike up the concrete walkway, she took a moment to look over the planting beds, which had been mulched over for winter.

She pushed her bike into the foyer. Her apartment was on the ground floor in the center section of the building, to the left of the entrance. She only had one neighbor who lived in the apartment directly across from her. A flight of stairs that started just outside her door led to the second floor, which had an identical floor plan and an open-air landing. Nadine remembered when she and Kate started sleeping together, they had been forced to sneak around as much as possible in order not to alert their respective neighbors. When Nadine's second-floor neighbor moved out, they had struck on the brilliant idea of Kate moving into the postage-stamp apartment above Nadine's. That way, they effectively lived together without raising any eyebrows or having to use stealth tactics like they were secret agents.

After chaining her bike to the stair railing, Nadine went into her apartment. "Kate?" she called. She withdrew the crushed soda can from her pocket and dumped her scarf and coat on a convenient chair. Her apartment was not exactly messy, but it was small enough to look cluttered. A couch and two armchairs dominated the living room, facing the little television that stood on a small oak end table. One wall was filled with framed photographs, every one a cherished memory — whale-watching trips, Kate on the beach, her mother circa 1960 in a tremendously ugly hat. Nadine took two steps to the kitchen and tossed the crushed soda can into a recycling bin next to the fridge and moved through the living room to the hallway.

The living room and combination kitchen/dining room made up the front half of the apartment. A bedroom, bathroom, and den made up the other half and were connected to one another by a thin corridor that ran between these rooms and the living room. The bathroom and den were deserted. Her bedroom, bed-free since she moved in and more of a storage area where she stacked her excess junk, was also empty. After searching the entire tiny apartment, she knew Kate must be upstairs in her own apartment.

Which meant Kate was too mad to pick a fight right now.

Wonderful. She felt relieved that the fight had been postponed, giving her a little more peace before the explosions started going off, but she kind of wished Kate had been there, just to be done with it.

Nadine dropped onto the couch, which doubled as her bed due to the cluttered bedroom, and found the remote amidst the clutter on the coffee table. She turned the TV on to the news, laid the remote on her stomach, and let the impossibly pretty anchors talk her to sleep.

Some time later, Nadine woke to the feeling of someone massaging her feet. She was momentarily disoriented, not remembering taking off her shoes or even laying down for that matter. However, the fingers working against her socks were so familiar that she kept her eyes closed for a few minutes and enjoyed the sensation. Finally, she sighed, pushed loose strands of black hair out of her face, realized her glasses were gone, and opened her eyes, struggling a moment to focus.

Kate was sitting on the other end of the couch with Nadine's feet on her lap, absently rubbing them while she watched a program with the volume turned down. Nadine scrubbed at her eyes, looked at the TV, and murmured, "What are you watching?"

"News. Late news," Kate answered. "You've been asleep about an hour."

"Mmm," Nadine hummed noncommittally. She knew the fight was still coming, but if she chose her words carefully, there was a chance she might be able to postpone it some more. Forget getting it over with, she thought. She liked peace and quiet. She liked watching TV and getting her feet rubbed. Nadine twisted to see the screen better but kept her feet planted on Kate's lap. "Anything interesting in the world?" she asked.

"Fire in Seattle, fire department got it under control...nothing big."

Nadine nodded.

After a brief silence, Kate said, "Squire Days, huh?"

Nadine groaned. *So much for putting it off...*

"I thought Hoagie was going to do that." Kate kept her gaze fixed on the television as she spoke, her voice remained steady and controlled, but Nadine knew the woman. She was just putting up a façade to keep from showing how hurt and angry she was really feeling.

"He said he would, but he had to back out. Family commitments, I guess. I didn't really ask."

Kate moved her hand to one of Nadine's ankle and squeezed it lightly. "You had commitments, too, you know. It was *your* idea."

"I know, hon." Nadine grimaced. They had had plans to drive to the mainland, see a couple of shows in Seattle, and have a real date for a change. To actually walk down the street and hold hands with each other...she had been looking forward to it for weeks, and so had Kate. "I'm sorry," she said contritely. "I know you had work and I know you had to cancel just for this weekend. I'll make it up to you."

Kate's hands moved to Nadine's calf and gently probed the muscle through the denim. "Really?" Her tone was quiet, playful and coy.

Nadine smiled, lifted her free foot, and pressed her toes gently against Kate's chin.

Kate laughed and tried to squirm away but managed only to lie down, her back against the sofa arm opposite Nadine's position. Nadine spread her legs apart, reached out, and gripped Kate's wrists, pulling the woman forward and on top of her. Kate chuckled as they embraced and she settled over Nadine's body. Their mouths met slowly, with the ease of familiarity. Kate's lips parted and deepened the kiss at just the right moment, and she moaned as Nadine fumbled with the buttons on her blouse.

"Just how do you plan to make it up to me?" Kate asked, undoing the button on Nadine's pants.

It took Nadine a moment to change her mental gears from sex to actual conversation. She stammered, "How...um, w-what do you want?"

"Will you dress up for the Faire? Will you dress up like a wench?"

"If it pleases milady," Nadine said with a sly grin.

Kate's answering grin was wicked. She slipped her hand into Nadine's pants, her fingers gliding lower and making Nadine gasp and curl her toes.

Afterward, naked and wrapped in each other's arms with an old quilt draped over their bodies, Nadine put her glasses back on and used the remote to turn off the TV. Settling down again, she combed her fingers through Kate's long, dark hair and stared at the window. The blinds were drawn, blocking what they had just done from the outside world. Nadine frowned. She felt trapped. Not because of Kate, but because she could not flaunt Kate; because they had to make sure the windows were closed before they made love; because they had to pretend they were just friends whenever they were out in public. She tilted her head and gave voice to what she had been thinking about for a while. "Maybe I should come out."

Kate did not register shock, nor did she blink her hazel eyes. Her gaze remained focused on the wall. When she spoke, she sounded calm. "You don't think it would affect your show?"

Nadine shrugged. It was their most-quoted reason for not coming out. Nadine worried about people refusing to listen to a gay disc jockey while Kate's fear was that the newspaper editor would suddenly start calling for the cancellation of her column. "I'd like to say no," Nadine finally said, "but truthfully? Hell...I have no idea." She checked her watch and patted Kate's arm. "Dinner?"

"I ate before I came downstairs." Kate curled closer and kissed the back of Nadine's neck. "Sleep upstairs with me tonight."

"I have to get up early," Nadine said. She hated to kick Kate out after sex, but if they slept in the same bed, she would not get any sleep at all. "I should stay down here."

"You sure?" Kate asked. "A warm bed instead of a couch...a warm me..." She slipped her hand around Nadine's waist and cupped her breast.

"I'd love to, but no, honey."

"All right," Kate said, nodding. She shifted off the couch to gather her clothes. Nadine watched as Kate dressed, keeping her gaze fixed on Kate's breasts until the shirt went on, looking at her ass until the tight jeans were pulled up to cover it. Despite the fact they had just had sex, Nadine felt another rush of desire from simply watching Kate's body. She gave herself a mental shake and told herself that sleeping alone was her idea.

Kate glanced around and stuffed her underwear into the back pocket of her jeans. She bent down and brushed her cheek across Nadine's. "Okay. See you tomorrow?"

"Mmm-hmm." Nadine stroked Kate's cheek with the backs of her fingers and went on, "This is our best fight ever."

Kate chuckled and touched Nadine's hair. "Sleep tight."

Nadine waited for Kate to leave before she got off the couch. As soon as Kate was gone, she felt lonely. Her nudity had been part of the afterglow of lovemaking, but now it was just making her cold. She rooted around in the bag next to her armchair until she found one of Kate's baseball jerseys, old and washed to a comfortable softness. She was petite enough and Kate lanky enough that the jersey reached to mid-thigh on her, leaving her decently covered. She buttoned it as she walked into the kitchen in search of sustenance. After scrounging around in the fridge for something to eat, she found her supplies were severely lacking.

She was about to call Kate and ask if her invitation was still open when there was a knock on the door. Nadine paused, aware of how naked she was under the jersey and equally aware that her underwear was draped over the top of the television set. She went to the door and called, "Who is it?"

"It's Kate," came the muffled answer.

Nadine opened the door, letting Kate step into the apartment. She was carrying a covered dish. Holding it up, Kate explained, "Last night's meat loaf. I looked in your fridge before you woke up; you don't have anything to eat for dinner."

Nadine was touched to the point of being speechless. After a moment, she smiled and took the dish out of Kate's hands. "Thank you."

"No sweat," Kate assured her. She kissed Nadine's cheek and gave her the once-over. "You look really hot in my jersey." She touched the white-and-blue shirt's hem and bit her bottom lip. Ducking her head and looking at Nadine through her eyelashes, she continued, "You sure you don't want to come up?"

"Less sure than I was earlier," Nadine admitted. "But yeah."

"Okay. Don't stay up too late. Good night, sweetheart."

"Good night," Nadine said. She watched Kate go out of the apartment and head toward the staircase before kicking the door shut and carrying her dinner into the kitchen. As she sliced off a piece of meatloaf and put it into the microwave, she smiled at the thought of Kate coming back downstairs for her. "I knew you didn't have any food," she had said. It was obvious that Kate cared about her and that was a warming thought.

Still, we've been together for three years. Nadine expected to feel something other than sweetness and the physical satisfaction of occasional — okay, pretty frequent — romps in the sack. If they eliminated the sex, what would they have? *A good friendship. Leave the sex in and we have a really* great *friendship.*

Nadine snickered and popped open the microwave. As she carried her food to the dining room table, she pushed her worries out of her mind. So what if all they had was a good friendship and really great sex? Relationships had been built on less, right?

Besides, she thought bitterly as she dug into her reheated dinner, *it's not like I have a ton of other prospects beating a path to my door.*

Chapter Two

In the five years she had been managing KELF, Miranda Powell had never been out of the front door before eight o'clock in the evening. She always remained in her office until Leah Nettles, the night DJ, arrived before she allowed herself to leave. Leah was reliable and had never been late, but Miranda liked to be prepared for every eventuality. She did not want to leave Hoagie alone to deal with a no-show if something unexpected happened. Leah and Hoagie traded places in the booth at nine, and Leah usually showed up anywhere from ten to thirty minutes early.

When Leah arrived at 8:55, Miranda was still on the phone, scribbling on her blotter as the station owner, Thomas Dugan, barked instructions at her. "Yes, sir," she said. She looked up when Leah appeared in the doorway, waved hello at the woman, and began gathering her things together. "Yes, Mr. Dugan," she said as he rattled on non-stop. "I wanted to talk about...yes, sir. No, I wanted to talk about..."

She leaned back in the chair and rubbed her temple with two fingers, trying to stave off the migraine she felt growing. "Yes, Mr. Dugan." She put the phone down and cursed. It was almost impossible to get a word in edge-wise with that man. She had called him with a distinct purpose in mind, but somehow he had managed to shift the conversation to budget and advertising and the various little day-to-day things he liked to hear about. Miranda was sure it made him feel like a part of the business, but it ate a hole in the end of her day, every day.

She jotted down a phone number and pushed away from her desk. Grabbing her purse and coat, she headed out into the bullpen. Leah was leaning against one of the desks, watching Hoagie through the window. Tonight, Leah was wearing a torn denim skirt, fishnet stockings, and a bright purple blouse that Miranda thought might actually look nice under the proper blazer.

"Is he having a good show?" Miranda asked as she joined Leah at the window.

"I don't know," Leah said. "I just like watching him. It's like the zoo."

Miranda smiled and caught a glimpse of their reflection in the glass. Like one of those magic eye pictures, it was hard to ignore once she noticed it. Standing next to Leah, she looked like a modern high school principal — cool, well-polished, and professional. She buttoned the coat around her floral-printed blouse and straightened her shoulder-length blonde hair where the phone had mussed it.

"I'm going to head out," Miranda said. "Have a good show."

"Okay, Miss Powell."

Miranda headed for the stairs and nearly made it before Hoagie called after her to wait up. She paused. He hurried to catch up, working his arm into the sleeve of his jacket as he moved.

"I'll walk you out," Hoagie said. He followed her downstairs, through the darkened and deserted lobby and out to the cold street. He waited while she tested the front doors to make sure they were locked behind her. Leah could still come out, but no one would be able to get in until she showed up in the morning to let in Willa Lamb and Simon Clark, the morning DJs.

She turned and, as she suspected, Hoagie was still standing there, waiting for her. She forced a smile and rubbed her hands together. "Cold out here," she said.

Hoagie nodded. "Yep. You need a ride someplace, Miss Powell? My car is..."

"I'm fine, Hoagie. I've got my own car in the garage."

"You want I should walk with you? You never know what could happen."

"It's December Harbor, not New York," Miranda said gently, not wanting to hurt his feelings. She had been born and raised in Manhattan, but Squire's Isle was physically and metaphorically about as far away from the Big Apple as she could get and still be in America. "I think I'll be okay. Thank you, though."

"No problem."

He stuffed his hands into his pockets and started to walk away, looking so dejected that she felt the need to offer the poor guy a little bit of consolation. "It was a great show tonight, Hoagie," she called after him.

He turned and smiled at her, a flash of teeth in the gloom. "It sure was. Good night, Miss Powell."

Miranda waited until he disappeared around the corner before she started walking toward the parking garage. Hoagie was sweet, but she would have to do something to dispel the unfortunate crush he seemed to be developing on her.

She found her car in the first space, unlocked the door, and dumped her things in the backseat. When she started the car, the radio came to life. It was, naturally, already tuned to KELF. Employee loyalty aside, it was really the only station that got any decent reception on the island.

"Good evening, owls and owlettes. This is Leah," the overnight DJ's sensuous voice informed her. "I'll be with you from now until the wee dark hours. So settle in, get comfortable, and get ready to feel the day melt away because I promise, I will not play anything that will make you jump out of your shoes. Your pants, on the other hand..."

Miranda smiled and made a mental note to officially chide Leah the next day. Sexual innuendo was fine as long as it was kept to a minimum, but lately Leah had been treading just a little too close to that fine line.

As Mick Jagger began his plaintive call to Angie, Miranda pulled away from the parking garage with Nadine Butler on her mind. So what if Nadine didn't have plans for the weekend? It was not fair to make her responsible for broadcasting a live show two days before the Faire started. The fact she was saddled with it just because she was single, and that Nadine *knew* this was the reason, could potentially be a problem. Miranda frowned. Nadine could sue them for discrimination, for a start.

Nadine never would sue, of course, she reassured herself, but it gave Miranda an idea. She stopped the car at a four-way stop next to the ferry lanes and drummed her fingers on the steering wheel as two cars crossed in the other direction. While she waited, she took the time to script the call she would make to Dugan first thing in the morning. This time, she was sure their conversation would go a *lot* differently.

The notion made her smile.

Nadine took a shower after dinner, made up the couch, and crawled under the covers in her pajamas. Picking up her work satchel, she dug around in it until she found the notes Miranda had left for her during her show. The first note read: *Think of medieval-type songs to play during the fair,* which was not very helpful. She scribbled down *Scarborough Fair* by Simon and Garfunkel in the note's margin, considered other possibilities for a moment, and shook her head. She would think of more, she was sure. If not, Billy could lend a hand.

Leafing through the other notes, she saw their purpose was to let her know about some of the acts that would be performing at the Renaissance Faire. Miranda had given her names, pronunciations, and a brief overview of what they did so Nadine could talk about them during her broadcast. Jugglers, swordfighters, jousting tournaments, belly dancers...she raised an eyebrow at that last one and thought maybe this assignment wouldn't be so bad after all.

The last post-it was a note that stockades would be employed during the Faire should any "dastardly evil-doers" need to be contained. Nadine smiled and said, "Please let me put Hoagie in the stocks. Oh, please, oh, please." A reflected beam of car headlights sweeping across the wall broke her concentration. She glanced at her watch; it was nearly eleven o'clock. She put aside the notes and dropped her satchel on the floor as she slipped down on the couch cushions. Despite the cancellation of their trip to the mainland, she was actually starting to look forward to the Faire. Maybe she could get Kate to dress up as a "fair" lady. It had been a while since they had played dress-up.

Speak of the devil, she thought, hearing Kate's familiar shuffle-step on the ceiling above her head. She knew from experience that Kate was walking from the bathroom to the bedroom. A few more steps and there came the quiet squeak of springs as the woman got into bed. Nadine loved being so close to Kate, to know she was safe in bed even though they were physically apart. It was the closest thing, she thought, to actually living together.

Hearing Kate go to bed reminded her how late it was, and she decided it was time for bed. Nadine reached up and turned off the reading lamp that curved over the couch and threw an arm over her eyes to protect against any more light that might reflect through the living room window and wake her up. She fell asleep shortly afterwards.

The next morning — Friday — was the day before the Squire Days festival officially began.

Nadine was up at eight o' clock and did a bit of research online. She managed to find only one more medieval-themed oldie, *Knights in White Satin* by the Moody Blues, and answered emails until ten o'clock. Two were from Kate — "I forgot to tell you twice, so I might as well email you while I'm thinking about it" sort of messages — and the rest were fan mail. She replied to as many as she could before it was time to go to work. She shut down the computer and headed upstairs to Kate's apartment. There was no answer to her knock, so she assumed Kate had already left for work.

Retrieving her bike and walking it to the street, Nadine got a good running start before she jumped onto the seat and headed across town.

Spring Street was the main thoroughfare of Squire's Isle; it started at the ferry lanes and cut straight through the heart of town. The first few blocks were home to the usual stretch of tourist traps, restaurants, and novelty stores. Once past the tourist façade, the more permanent mainstays began to pop up — a movie theater, a grocery store, a library. It was as if an invisible line had been drawn and the tourists knew not to go beyond it. *Here There Be Locals*, Nadine thought.

As she waited at the stop sign to cross Spring Street, a couple of people who recognized her from promotional material and newspaper ads called out hello and waved at her. She gladly waved back and thanked them for listening. When the street was clear, she rode across and turned south, a route which took her away from the radio station. She had left her apartment early in order to pass by the city park and take a look at the Squire Days festival grounds before she had to spend the entire day there.

Nadine parked her bike on the sidewalk and gazed out over the sea of colorful tents, the wooden fences that were being erected, and the three horse trailers already on site. She had a horrific image of the grass being festooned with steaming "presents" from the knights' rides and made a mental note to bring a change of shoes.

The park looked small as it was approached, but she knew the grounds spread out from the entrance. The KELF booth was usually somewhere near the front, but she could not spot it. Satisfied for the moment, Nadine climbed back onto her bike and rode the rest of the way to work. The roundabout trip had cost her almost an extra mile, and her leg muscles were burning from the effort. She was grateful, though; biking was pretty much the only exercise she got, so she liked to do it as much as possible.

She had to veer around a construction site at the corner next to the KELF building and waved an apology to the construction worker tearing up the sidewalk. He waved back, and she made it the rest of the block without running into any concrete chunks. Nadine chained her bike outside and stepped into the fantastic feeling warmth of the station's lobby. "Whoo," she exclaimed as she unwound her scarf. "I didn't notice how cold it was until I came in here! Morning, Sue."

Sue, the plump and perpetually smiling secretary, held up a sheaf of little yellow papers. "Morning, Miss Butler! Miss Powell wanted me to let you know about these memos. A bunch of people have been calling in about the Renaissance Faire. Turns out a lot of them decided to give it a chance just because you're going to be there. That must make you feel good, huh?"

Nadine took the memos and shrugged. "Kind of makes me feel bad for Hoagie," she admitted as she went through them.

"Oh. Oh, right," Sue said. Her smile faded, and she added, "Boy, I hope he doesn't get offended..."

"Ah, screw him," Nadine said, winking. "He left me in the lurch. I hope his feelings do get a little hurt."

Sue cackled and clapped her hands together. Nadine jumped at the sudden, sharp sound, but quickly recovered and laughed along with Sue. After a moment, Sue's laughs turned into coughs. Nadine moved to pat her on the back, but Sue waved her off. "No, no, you go on upstairs. You have to be famous!"

"Work, work, work," Nadine said. "See you in a couple of hours."

"Hear you before that," Sue said, pointing over her head and giggling.

Nadine went upstairs and dumped her things on her desk. She made her way to the back of the bullpen to Miranda Powell's office. Through the glass-fronted door, she could see Miranda talking into an earpiece connected to her telephone. Miranda glanced up just as Nadine was about to turn around and gestured for her to come into the office. Nadine stepped inside and waited for the call to end.

Miranda's office was the biggest in the building, but it had no windows. She had corrected this architectural faux pas by taking photographs of the town from the roof, having them professionally combined into a poster-sized panorama and hanging the picture behind her desk. In a lighted frame, it was surprisingly effective. The rest of the office was spartan — a desk, two chairs for visitors, and a couch next to the door. Someone had given her a plastic plant when she was promoted, but Nadine swore the fake leaves were drooping and the plant was near death despite its artificial nature.

She continued loitering by the door until Miranda finished her call and motioned at one of the seats. "Morning, Nadine," Miranda said.

"Hi, Miranda. What's up?"

"I talked to Thomas Dugan this morning."

Nadine tensed, despite the fact she had done nothing wrong. It was the equivalent of seeing a cop car behind her on the street; she always assumed she must be guilty of something. "The station manager?" she managed to say.

"The very same," Miranda replied. "I told him about the Squire Days situation, how Hoagie and I kind of left you in the lurch just because you were single."

"It wasn't *entirely* because of that, was it?" Nadine asked.

"No, the fact that you are our biggest celebrity did play a pretty big part. But you and I both know that the only reason I gave in to Hoagie so quickly is because you're single and you probably wouldn't have plans."

"Really?"

Miranda shrugged and leaned forward. "The fact is, it could look like discrimination. You *could* sue us."

Nadine sighed. "I would never do that. I might grumble and—"

"No, you don't understand," Miranda said. "You could sue us. I pointed that out to Mr. Dugan, along with the fact you often get saddled with crappy assignments, and he finally agreed that it wasn't fair. So, in order to appease you, you'll be getting paid time and a half for the Faire."

Nadine blinked in surprise. The Dugan family owned most of December Harbor and half the island, but they were renowned for having tight pockets and being reluctant to part with their wealth. Offering time and a half pay was unheard of. "Wow. Thanks, Miranda."

"I'm not done," Miranda said, giving her a perfectly evil smile. "I pointed out this was an ongoing thing. We get a job no one else wants, it generally goes to you. I pointed out that you're definitely the voice of the station, if not the face of it. Once again, he eventually agreed that you deserve a raise."

"A raise?" Nadine said. She was elated at the prospect, but tried to hide it and she failed. She was already smiling, leaning forward slightly. "That's...that's wonderful."

"I don't have the exact numbers yet; we're still haggling on that part. But I thought you should know it was in the works."

"Yes, thank you. You didn't have to."

"Consider it a thank you for being our sacrificial lamb for everything we ask of you. And hey, if it makes you smile a little bit at the Faire, all the better."

Nadine laughed. "You have my word."

She slipped out of the office and went back to her desk, walking on air and in a decidedly better mood. She took the memos Sue had given her and thumbed through them again — *looking forward to seeing you; I wasn't going to go but now I'm already buying the tickets*, so on and so forth. She smiled, still amazed after all this time that she was actually considered to be a celebrity on the island. An idea sparked, and she glanced around until she found Billy.

He was emptying a trashcan nearby. Nadine crossed the bullpen to meet him. "Hey, Billy, I might need your help a little more than usual today," she said. "Are you going to be sticking around?"

"Mmm-hmm, yep."

Nadine patted his arm and thanked him as she headed to the booth. She loved Billy; he had been homeless when he had been hired, living outside the station and asking people for lunch money. When Nadine actually saw him go into a restaurant and use the money for lunch — ordering a tall cold glass of milk instead of any of the various liquors the restaurant offered — she struck up a conversation with the man.

Billy had recognized her voice immediately. He loved radio, as she found out, and it was not long before he revealed his most astonishing gift — he could give the exact time, to the second, of any song she cared to name. After a few tests, she decided to take him at his word and convinced Miranda to hire him as the station's custodian on a freelance, day-to-day basis. Billy insisted they pay him only enough to buy himself dinner and lunch since he refused to get rich on a job he had not earned. As long as he was just working for food, it was better than begging as far as he was concerned.

He had been a constant at the station ever since, keeping the place tidy and helping the DJs arrange their schedule with the most amount of music without cutting off any commercials. Miranda had tried to give him a raise on several occasions, at least up to minimum wage, but he refused. One day Miranda had "slipped up" and given him a fifty-dollar bill instead of a five. An offended Billy had not come to work for a week after that and refused to return until they took the money back. He remained at the station working for his lunch and dinner, a storehouse of knowledge when it came to classic rock time limits, and Nadine was happy to take the credit for discovering him.

In the booth, Simon Clark and Willa Lamb were finishing up their morning show. Peering through the window, Nadine could see the shoulder of someone who was sitting across from them at the table, but she did not bother trying to identify the guest. She waited patiently for the DJs to play their farewell music, a medley of the word "Good-bye" from various songs, before she opened the door.

As she stepped inside, Nadine smiled at Willa and Simon and to her shock saw Kate rising from the interview seat. She tried to conceal her surprise but failed miserably.

"Oh," Willa said, raising her eyebrows as she looked from Nadine to Kate. "I was going to introduce you two, but...do you already know each other?"

"Uh-huh," Nadine said. She forced a casual smile to hide her confusion. "Kate is, uh, my upstairs neighbor, who didn't mention she was doing the show this morning."

Kate shrugged and said, "It was kind of a last-minute thing. They wanted to talk to me about that article I did on pollution and the orcas in the Strait." She unwound herself from the wires that were always draped over on-air guests. "While I have you here, are you free for dinner tonight?"

"Yeah, always," Nadine said. It was a battle to keep from looking at Willa and Scott for their reaction to the request. *It only sounds like a date because I know it's a date. They probably think it's totally innocent...*

"Okay," Kate replied. "See you at home."

"See you at home," Nadine echoed. She watched Kate leave and exchanged places with Willa. Simon pushed his own chair into the corner — the station had no other two-person DJ teams — and waved good-bye at her as he headed for the door.

"Have a good show," Willa said, closing the door behind herself.

"Thanks," Nadine said. Seeing Kate in her workplace, out of the blue like that, had been shocking. It was too close to being outed, in her opinion. She took her seat and rearranged a few of the items on the desktop to buy herself time until her nerves calmed. After glancing at the clock, she switched on the mic to begin her show. "Happy mid-morning, almost afternoon to all you lovely people in December Harbor and everyone across Squire's Isle. I am Nadine Butler, the Pixie, and I will be here until five this afternoon. Seems so far away, doesn't it? But I am here to take a little bit of the sting away because I am doing something special today.

"When I walked into the station, the secretary showed me all of these calls from people who were going to the Squire Days festival just to see me. That really touches my heart, truly, so I'm going to make you guys really happy." She picked up a random piece of paper and crumpled it next to the mic. "That was my play list for today, and I am throwing it out. Because all day today, I am going to be taking your requests. Give me a call, 232-KELF, tell me what you want to hear because you are taking over the radio station."

She scanned the actual play list and said, "For now, I'm going to be play-ing some of my favorites while I'm gathering up your requests. We've got Stevie Nicks coming up, some Jim Croce, and lots more that depends on you guys. Let me know what you want to hear." Nadine switched over to the CD and pulled off her headphones. She knew without looking that Miranda was standing outside the window watching her.

She stood up and opened the door. Sure enough, Miranda was standing right there with arms crossed, a disgruntled expression on her face. "All requests?" the woman asked.

"Billy will help me make sure we have time for all the commercials," Nadine said confidently. "We'll be fine. You worry too much, Miranda."

Miranda huffed and shook her head. "You have to do this to me right after I tease you about a raise."

"Teach you to tease a girl," Nadine said, grinning. She was well aware she was flirting with Miranda, but she did not care. What was the harm?

Miranda seemed to pick up on the flirting as well. She flushed. "All right, fine. All requests. Why not?" She motioned at the booth and went on, "Go! Take some requests. I'll accept all-request, but I won't allow dead air."

Nadine saluted, only half-mockingly, and went back to her seat. Once she was sitting down, she hit Line One on the phone and said to the caller, "This is the Pixie on KELF, what can I play for you?"

Miranda paused and watched as Nadine resumed her post. She loved the fact that the way the booth was configured, the DJ faced away from the window, otherwise she would hate to have to explain how often she found herself standing there, staring at Nadine's back and just...well, just staring. She loved to watch the woman work, loved how she leaned closer to the mic to make her voice deeper and more intimate.

And to top it all off, if she did not know better, she would have said Nadine was just flirting with her.

"'Teach you to tease a girl'," she muttered. "Sheesh. Like I don't have enough problems."

Billy came into the booth two or three times before he finally accepted Nadine's invitation to sit across from her. As she took requests, she wrote the titles and artist on a piece of paper. When she had a nice, long list, she would hand it to Billy and he would write the play times in pen next to the artist name. His tongue poked out of the corner of his mouth in concentration as he re-listed the songs in blocks of eight to ten minutes and handed the paper back to Nadine.

Meanwhile, Nadine kept taking requests and putting notations next to the song title to remember who had requested the song. She waited until *Guitar Man* ended and went back on the air. "This is KELF, I am the Pixie, and the radio station is at your mercy this afternoon, ladies and gentlemen. That was Bread with *Guitar Man* for Erin. Hope you enjoyed that, Erin. For now, we're going to take a little pause for a commercial break, and we'll be right back with more of your requests. Hang tight."

She cued-up a commercial and said, "Billy, you've been a godsend today."

"I aim to please, Miss Butler," he replied. He kept his eyes down and fiddled with the tip of his pen.

"I'm just telling you so you won't fight when Miranda tries to pay you tonight."

He shook his head. "I don't need nothing extra. Just..."

"Food money, right," she said. "You just want what's fair. Well, I wouldn't have been able to do this today without your help. You went above and beyond what you were hired for, and we're going to pay you appropriately. It's only fair. All right?"

He finally nodded his head — a quick up-and-down bob — making her smile.

"Good. Now..." Nadine was distracted by movement in the glass, just visible in her peripheral vision. She turned and saw Kate standing in the bullpen, waving at her through the glass.

"She was here this morning," Billy said. "Willa and Simon interviewed her."

"Yep, they did," Nadine murmured. She checked the counter on the commercial break and went quickly to the door. "Hey, hon...Kate." She glanced around to see if anyone had heard her slip. "What's up?"

Kate held up a couple of bags. "Since I was in the neighborhood, I thought I'd drop in and see if you wanted to have lunch in your booth."

"It's kind of cramped in there with Billy. And it's hectic today..."

Kate smiled. "I heard. All requests?"

Nadine shrugged but returned Kate's smile. "Thank you for the offer, though. It was really sweet."

"I do what I can. Well, you might as well take your sandwich." Kate handed the bag over and continued, "So I'll see you tonight."

Something in Kate's tone made Nadine take notice. Kate opened her mouth just enough so that Nadine could see the tip of her tongue as it rolled across her bottom lip. The promise in that slight peek was enough to send shivers down Nadine's spine. "Tonight," she echoed, nodding.

Kate winked and headed for the stairs.

Nadine watched Kate leave for the second time that day, then glanced toward Miranda's office. She almost had a heart attack when she realized the station manager was watching her.

Miranda came out and walked over to the booth, nodding at Kate's back. "Our guests usually don't come back until at least a day has passed," she commented, smiling. "What was her name...?"

Nadine felt like she had been caught with her hand in the cookie jar. "Kate Price," she answered nervously. "She works at the *Register*."

"Right," Miranda replied. She glanced into the booth. "I think your commercial is about to end."

Nadine gasped and ran back to her station. She slipped her headphones back on and said, "Hey, welcome back. How were those commercials? You going to buy any of that stuff? Who knows, right?" She glanced out of the small window that gave her a view of the harbor and saw a familiar green-and-white bulk sliding through the water. "Well, I can see the afternoon ferry coming in right now. All of you tourists need to know that K-E-L-F and the Pixie are having a very special show right now..."

"Okay, everyone, it's almost that time," Nadine said at the end of her show. "My wrist is sore from keeping track of all your requests, so I think tomorrow we'll be going back to the old-fashioned way, if you don't mind. My thanks to my timekeeper, Billy, my thanks to everyone who called in to make sure we didn't have dead air, and my thanks to everyone who listened today. Be sure to tune in tomorrow; I'll be lonesome if you don't. Good-bye, everybody."

She escorted Billy from the booth and stepped aside to let Hoagie in. "An all-request show?" the big man asked as he headed for the seat.

"It was to thank people for liking me better than you," Nadine said. Her tone was mocking, but she and Hoagie knew each other well enough not to take such gibes personally.

He scoffed and said, "Sure, Pixie, sure. You keep on believing that."

She playfully stuck her tongue out at him and went to her desk to retrieve her things. As she bundled up against the cold, Miranda left her office and handed Billy an envelope. The woman thanked him for his help, made sure he would actually accept the money, then went to Nadine's desk.

"Were you planning to dress up for the Faire?" Miranda asked.

"Do I have to?"

"No."

"Then definitely not," Nadine said, relieved. "I might wear something fancier than my jeans and sweatshirt, but otherwise..."

"All right. Hoagie was going to go the full court jester route. Tights, jingle-bell hat, pointed shoes...the whole bit."

Nadine cringed. "Another reason to thank our lucky stars that I took over for him."

Miranda snickered and said, "I'll see you tomorrow."

"Tomorrow?" Nadine repeated in confusion.

"I'll be at the Faire. Unofficially."

"In costume?"

"You'll just have to wait and see!" Miranda winked and went back to her office.

Nadine pictured Miranda wearing a wench costume and decided she would make a very nice wench, indeed. She chuckled and slipped the strap of her satchel over her head. Looking around for Billy, she saw that he was already back to work cleaning desks. "Thank you for your help today, Billy," she called.

"Happy to lend a hand."

She headed out, said good-bye to Sue as she passed the reception desk, and walked out into the cold.

Nadine had expected it when she got home, she just had not anticipated the ferocity of the attack.

As soon as she opened her front door, Kate was on her, all hungry mouth and wandering hands. Nadine managed to slam the door shut and glanced at the windows to make sure the blinds were drawn as she allowed herself to be pushed toward the couch. She sat down heavily, letting out an "oof". Kate's fingers went immediately to her blouse. Nadine sighed happily, leaned back, and let herself be undressed.

"How come you were at the station today?" she asked as Kate worked her pants button loose.

"Wanted to see you," Kate murmured. Her face was flushed, and she was almost panting with desire. A loose hair caught in her eyelashes, and she did not bother to brush it away. Nadine liked that; it made Kate look primal, a wild thing driven by passion.

Nadine lifted her hips to let Kate drag her jeans down her legs. She kicked them aside and closed her eyes as Kate caressed her naked thighs. "Just to...to spend time with me?" she asked.

"Yeah," Kate said, kneeling between Nadine's spread legs. She leaned forward and occupied her tongue for several pleasurable moments without speaking. Finally, she pulled away and asked, "Why?"

"Hm?" Nadine blinked, trying to gather her lust-scattered thoughts.

"Why'd you ask?" Kate enunciated clearly.

"Oh." Nadine cleared her throat. "I was just wondering."

"Well," Kate said, chuckling. She turned her head and kissed the inside of Nadine's thigh, a wet touch that made the muscle jump involuntarily. "To be honest, I kind of wanted to christen your booth."

Nadine had to laugh, a wild, warbling sound that was also kind of breathless because of the wicked things Kate was doing to her. "I think...you're going to have to give up on that dream, babe."

"A girl needs fantasies," Kate said, leaning forward again and licking her lips.

She did not speak for a long time after that; she did however spell a few words with the tip of her tongue, much to Nadine's delight.

Nadine took a shower when they finished and returned to the room to find that Kate had left without saying good-bye. She tried not to be hurt by her lover's quick departure, but after last night, Kate probably assumed Nadine wanted some privacy. She heard light footsteps in the apartment upstairs, confirming the woman's whereabouts. She put her glasses back on. "Guess the date is over," she muttered.

She sat on the couch, her hair wrapped in a towel and her body in a bathrobe, and turned on the TV, more for noise to fill up the silent apartment than for entertainment, letting the banal laugh-track of a sitcom wash over her. She pulled a notebook off the coffee table, found a pen that worked, and began scribbling down notes for banter she would use between songs in the morning.

"Fair days to all...thees and thous will probably be necessary..." She tapped her chin with the tip of her pencil, considered and rejected several possibilities, and went back to writing.

A few blocks away from Nadine's apartment, Miranda lived in the elite gated community of Sandpiper Condos. Her condominium was really a small living area ringed by the rest of the rooms, none of them very large. The truth was, no one lived in Sandpiper for the accommodations; they came for the security of the six-foot stone wall around the property. Even though break-ins were relatively unheard of on Squire's Isle, Miranda was still a product of an island called Manhattan and the stone wall had been *the* selling point for her. The owner had intended the wall to be more of a privacy feature, but it worked for her purposes.

Miranda had arrived home after leaving the radio station and gone straight to the bedroom. She undressed in the light of a single lamp and pulled a folded pair of pajamas from the dresser drawer. When she turned around, the outfit she planned to wear in the morning to the Faire caught her eye. She had not had any problem with the idea of Hoagie seeing her in it — other than the risqué innuendo she was sure to have been subjected to — but something about Nadine seeing her in the outfit gave her pause.

It was silly to be worry about it now, she finally decided, pulling on her pajamas. Nadine would not make any off-color jokes or inappropriate comments, but even so...the décolletage of the dress was awfully low-cut and revealed a considerable amount of cleavage.

Like she'll even be looking at your breasts, Miranda thought, impatient with her own foolishness. She climbed under the covers, turning to lie on her back. As she stared at her bedroom ceiling, she thought back to that lovely dark-haired woman she had seen Nadine talking to earlier. The reporter who had been interviewed on Willa and Simon's show... *What's her name? Kate Prince?* There was something about the way Kate and Nadine had been standing together, their body language with one another. She could not put her finger on what was bothering her, but the scene stuck in her mind.

Miranda shook her head and tried to dispel the images brewing there. Nadine and the reporter were just friends, that was all. Ever since she realized her attraction to women, Miranda had been seeing lesbian relationships everywhere. If half the women she suspected were actually gay, she would be very concerned for the fate of humanity.

She pulled one of the pillows out from under her head and smothered her face with it. Nadine was straight, her friend the reporter was straight, and every damn woman on the island was straight. There was no point dwelling on the impossible and the improbable.

Miranda relaxed her grip on the pillow and reached down to the waistband of her pajama pants. *Still,* she thought, *a little wishful thinking never hurt anyone.* She bit her bottom lip and pushed her hand lower. She touched herself through her panties and, after a momentary debate about whether it was tacky to masturbate about someone who worked for you, turned off the lamp to sin in private.

Chapter Three

It took Nadine a moment to realize why her alarm was going off on Saturday morning, well before noon. She stared blankly at the small clock on the edge of her coffee table. The blankets were piled on her body; she was cocooned in warmth, and her mind was still fogged with sleep. Nadine gazed at the time displayed in undeniable red LED numbers for an entire minute before she remembered her promise about the Renaissance Faire, then she covered her face and groaned into her cupped palms before kicking the blankets away.

She sat up and silenced the tinny, bleating alarm. Her glasses were lying next to the clock, but she did not bother picking them up. Nadine just stayed seated, staring at the blurred wall and rubbing her eyes until she completely woke up. She was naked from the waist down, tired and feeling completely used up.

After falling to sleep, Nadine had woken up a few hours later. The rest of the night was like that — falling asleep, waking up, and staring at the wall; falling asleep and staring out of the window until the sky turned violet and red as dawn broke over the horizon. She had been exhausted, but apparently her mind was too eager to turn over her relationship with Kate to allow her to rest. This weekend was supposed to have been a big step for them — going out in public, spending time together without sex entering the equation.

The only thing she had gotten from her insomnia-fueled ruminations was the start of a migraine throbbing behind her left eye.

She finally stood up and shed her T-shirt, stumbling to the bathroom. The shower was ice-cold, a common problem in an old apartment building with an inadequate boiler. The neighbors tended to use up most of the hot water before she was awake, so more often than not, she found herself blasted awake by freezing water. Not that she would complain. Today the chill was exactly what she needed to clear her mind.

When her teeth were chattering, Nadine got out of the shower, dried off, and wrapped the towel around herself in an attempt to quell her shivering. She sidestepped the clutter in the bedroom and dug through her collection of casual work clothes for something vaguely appropriate to wear in public to the Faire. She hated these "public display broadcasts". How many other professions would ask someone to climb on a wooden crate and perform their job for the masses?

Nadine finally chose a tweed suit that was just a little bit baggy. She added a rumpled gray dress shirt and a tie that she looped loosely around her neck for an appearance of formality without the choking. After getting dressed, she left the apartment and led her bike out of the building without looking up at Kate's apartment. She was not angry at Kate for leaving without comment the night before; she was just a little annoyed that Kate had left without even offering to stay.

As she walked outside, she was struck by how pleasant the day actually was. The sun appeared to be on a mission to disprove the "end a drought by throwing an outdoor festival" rule. There was not a sign of rain and the sheer brightness of the clear light made her squint. She left her bike leaning against a wall and ran back into her apartment to fetch a boonie hat she had been given by a fan. She put it on, hoping the hat would offer a little protection from the UV rays.

Her head protected, Nadine climbed back on her bike and checked her watch; she had a little over an hour to get to the park. She turned the bike in the opposite direction and instead rode into the heart of town. Turning the corner, she went past a row of restaurants that she often advertised on her show. They were family-owned and operated; no Mickey D's or Wendy's on this island. People seated at tables near the windows waved as she passed and, knowing the familiarity such a small town brought, she waved back and wondered how many knew she was on the radio.

Turning onto Front Street was like being transported to a completely new town. The stores here were kitschy little tourist traps filled with stuffed orcas and paintings by local artists displayed in the windows. Tourists rarely ventured past this strip mall area, the façade to the real-life town where people lived and worked. The sidewalks were already crowded with people who had arrived on the morning ferry and were waiting for the next one to take them back to the mainland.

Nadine paused before crossing the ferry lanes toward KELF. Instead of parking at the station, she angled her bike across the street, stopping in front of the building directly across from her place of work. She stared at it for a long moment. It was nothing special, just a small, one-story yellow brick building. The sign hanging in the front window said simply *Photos* over a neon yellow camera.

Knowing she either had to go inside or head to the park, Nadine leaned her bike against the wall next to the door and stepped inside. The bell over her head jangled. She brought a hand to the loose knot of her tie.

The wood-paneled public area of the store was tiny; a low counter ran parallel to the front door and offered little in the way of a waiting area. Nadine stood next to the cash register and gazed at the door that led to the photo-processing area. After a few seconds, the door opened and an older woman stepped out with an armful of photo packets.

"Just a second, dear," she said. "I'm..." She looked up and froze when she saw Nadine. "Oh."

Nadine smiled weakly. "Hi, Momma."

"Your father..." The woman looked nervously toward the front door.

"I know. He's never here on Saturdays. Why do you think I came now?"

"No, honey, he's down the street. He's buying..."

The front door opened behind Nadine and a gruff voice said, "Someone else in this town has a damned bike just like..." He paused and mimicked his wife's surprised reaction, then frowned. "Nadine's."

Nadine stayed put. Whether this was a conscious choice or forced by the fact that her father was blocking the sole exit, she was not sure. Her father was a block of a man, his arms thin but coiled with muscle. A brush of white hair capped his head. He looked at the world with his eyebrows knit together, his jaw caught in a perpetual clench. She thought he seemed willing to fight anyone and everyone who crossed his path.

Nadine fiddled with her tie under the force of his stare and finally glanced over her shoulder at her mother. Tamara Butler put down the photo packets she had been holding and rounded the edge of the counter. She went to her husband and forced a smile. "Nadine just stopped by to say hello," she told him.

Nathaniel Thomas Butler started to put his hands into his pockets, looked down at the bag of donuts he was holding as if it had simply appeared there by magic, and shifted his shoulders, frowning more deeply. "I thought I made myself clear." This was said to his wife, rather than Nadine.

"Sorry, Daddy," Nadine said. "I just wanted to make sure Momma was..."

He shoved the bag of donuts at Tamara and said, "I'll be in the back." He kept his gaze locked on the rear wall, away from Nadine, and added, "Call me if a customer comes in." He stormed around the counter and through the door Tamara had exited.

When they were alone again, Tamara put the bag down and gripped Nadine's arm. "Oh, honey, I'm sorry."

"What do you know?" Nadine murmured. Tears stung her eyes, but she refused to let them fall. "Still hurts."

Tamara bit her lip and looked down. "What did you want to tell me?"

"I'm broadcasting from Squire Days today and tomorrow. I thought you might want to come by and say hello. Maybe."

"I'd love to." Tamara rose onto her tiptoes to kiss Nadine's cheek. "I'll be there if I can."

Nadine smiled and hugged her mother, who was even shorter than her own five feet four inches. When they parted, Nadine glanced toward the back of the store and quietly asked, "Do you think he'll ever stop hating me?"

"He doesn't hate you," Tamara said. She straightened Nadine's blazer and tsked in disapproval. "I don't know why you have to dress like this all the time, Nadine. Honestly."

"It's fine," Nadine argued as she fended off the woman's fussing. She smiled sadly and kissed the top of her mother's head. "I have to go, Momma. I'll see you soon."

"Okay, honey. Be well." She tightened her grip on Nadine's hand before letting it drop.

Leaving the shop, Nadine took her bike by the handles and walked it to the corner, letting the tears finally fall. She had held on as long as she could and had thankfully managed to stay composed in front of her mother, but now that she was alone...she wiped her wet eyes before she climbed onto her bike and pedaled toward the park, her chest aching.

Her father had banished her from Butler Photography when she had broken the news to him. The hurt and pain in his face had been almost unbearable, like she had been denying him along with everything he believed in. He could not comprehend her decision, that it was her life and she was going to pursue a career on the radio. He was still pig-headed and stubborn about it.

"Fine!" he had snapped as he tossed her vocational booklet across the room. "Be a...a disc jockey." He had imbued such venom into the job title that she might as well have told him she was becoming a prostitute, and he had never forgiven her. Nadine understood why. She was his only child, the sole heir to Butler Photography, a business he had worked hard to build up and maintain. If the business was to live past him, she would have had to take over. Without Nadine taking her rightful place as his successor, the shop would either close down and be forgotten or have to be handed over to a stranger. Neither idea appealed to him.

During her school years, he had actively campaigned to have her return to the flock. Drop out, come home, and learn the ropes of photography and film developing while she was still young — that was his mantra. When she graduated, he made one last ditch effort to convert her. Nadine was implacable; she refused to give up her dream, and her father had literally turned his back on her. Since then, he had not spoken a word directly to her.

KELF was magic as far as she had been concerned. It stood directly across the street from her parents' photography shop. After one trip into the station's inner sanctum, Nadine had started sneaking over whenever she could. The DJs and the station manager grew to know her and anticipate her arrivals. They let her into the booth, showed her the marvelous things that let them speak to *everyone* on the island. What eight-year-old could have resisted being entranced?

As far as she was concerned, KELF was the be-all and end-all. Working in radio was like being God; a voice coming to people all over, in all moods. She could brighten their day just by being there. She could play music and make people dance. As soon as she knew what the words meant, she wanted to be a disc jockey.

It had cost her a father.

She wiped more tears from her eyes as she pedaled through the familiar streets of her home town. The worst part of it was that she would never come out to him, never let him know she was a lesbian. Her job choice had already demoted her to a non-entity in his eyes. The fact that his little girl would never give him grandchildren? She could not bear to think about how he would treat her in that case.

The Faire preparations she had seen the day before had not prepared her for the sheer extravagance of the final product. Even from a block away she could hear the droning wail of bagpipes. As she drew nearer, the music was joined by the bustling of the crowd and the sounds of several people singing. Nadine's headache throbbed as if to say, "oh, I will love it here" and she groaned as pain stabbed behind her eye.

She locked her bike to a tree and joined the sea of people heading through the front gates. When asked for a ticket, Nadine showed her KELF Employee ID card and the ticket-taker waved her through. Most of the people she saw were in full costume; a handful wore regular clothing, and there seemed to be a few people who had gone at least halfway with their outfits. A man wearing ratty slacks and a loose thermal shirt looked at least forty-percent authentic in her judgment.

Vendors shouted for her to try their mead — "Best in the land," they proclaimed when she passed by. A jester stepped into her path and thrilled her with his golf ball juggling. When she expressed her appreciation by clapping, he smiled at her sheepishly and said, "If I try with bigger balls, they bounce off my head. I figure it's better to be laughed at than dead."

Nadine chuckled and applauded his rhyme. Before she could even think about giving him a tip, he moved onto the next unwary pedestrian. She paused to watch a belly dancer enthralling the crowd from a small stage, applauded when the woman finished, and continued on her way.

She found the radio station's booth easily enough; it was situated at the end of the midway, slightly elevated to give her a nice view of the entire park. Two towers on either side of the booth held big speakers. A printed banner draped between the speaker stands announced "KELF RADIO, AM 1220, Broadcasting Live!!" Nadine briefly wondered how they had gotten the Faire organizers to allow this blatant anachronism, but it was not her place to wonder why. It was her place to climb up there and play music to entertain the crowds seething through the park.

"Great," Nadine murmured. "I get to play the great and powerful Oz. Pay no attention to the woman behind the microphone..."

She climbed the short staircase on the back of the platform and took her seat. The mobile radio station set-up was familiar to her, but she took a moment to reacquaint herself with the slightly different controls. As she was examining the dials, a hand fell on her shoulder, startling her. She turned her head and looked up into Miranda's steel blue eyes.

It took Nadine a moment to recognize the woman she had worked under for five years. Miranda's normally straight blonde hair had been transformed into ringlets that framed her face. She was wearing a flowing blue dress with a woven brown bodice that was tight and low-cut, revealing a rounded swell of breasts that was far more impressive than her business suits implied. Nadine found herself staring, transfixed by the sight. Fortunately, she caught herself before Miranda could notice.

"Everything normal?" Miranda asked, her gaze focused on the control panel.

Define normal, Nadine wanted to say. Instead, she simply nodded and said, "Looks like it."

Miranda nodded and knelt down, her décolletage with its amazing cleavage just inches from Nadine's face. Nadine swallowed hard and focused on a stack of rectangular blue stickers in a cubbyhole under the desk.

"Bumper stickers are here, the buttons..." Miranda opened a drawer that was stuffed with boxes of KELF AM buttons. "Hand them out at your discretion. We've got about eight million of the things. We've got about fifteen T-shirts you can give away in contests if you'd like. I think that's it."

Miranda squeezed Nadine's shoulder as she stood up. Nadine was painfully aware of Miranda's breasts being just one grope away. She had always found Miranda attractive, but she had also always managed to rein in her lust. This dress, however, was making things very, very difficult for her.

"Thank you again for doing this for us, Nadine," Miranda murmured.

"Just remember," Nadine said, raising her finger, "time-and-a-half overtime. Raise."

"Yes, ma'am," Miranda said. She started for the stairs and said over her shoulder, "I like your suit."

"I like your breasts," Nadine blurted before she could stop herself. Her face flushed hot, and she cringed, hoping Miranda had not heard her.

Miranda stopped on the top step and looked down, her hands smoothing the front of her dress. "Thank you. I bought it at a thrift store on the mainland. You really like it?" She glanced up and added, "My dress?"

Nadine nodded, eternally grateful for the out. "Yeah. I...it's gorgeous." *Full, firm, supple*, her mind went on. *Oh, shut up*, she told herself.

Miranda smiled her thanks and went down the steps. Alone again, Nadine turned and covered her burning face with both hands. "Wonderful, Butler," she growled, embarrassed by her slip. "It's not like you have to *speak* for a living or anything like that." She sighed and leaned back in her chair as she waited for the DJ at the station to turn the air-time over to her.

She bided her time people watching as the Looking Glass sang about *Brandy* over her head. She idly wondered why the band had not rewritten the song about *Alice*, going for the whole literary reference, but she figured they had known what they were doing.

The juggler she had seen earlier passed by, still tossing golf balls over his head but having added two or three to the rotation. He was bent almost backwards keeping track of them, but his hands were a blur. He glanced at her, and she smiled, applauding. He tilted his head in what she took to be a bow and walked on.

A few people saw her and stopped to ask for autographs. She signed bumper stickers and buttons, told them to keep listening for the T-shirt contests, and wished them a good day at the fair. As she was sending away the last of her admirers, she heard Ben, the weekend DJ, come back on the air. "That was *Brandy* by the Looking Glass, and that will do it for me here in the studio. I'm going to send it out to Nadine Butler at Squire Days right now. Nadine, you there?"

She leaned forward to the microphone. "I'm here, Benny. You oughta come out and see some of the stuff going on. We've got mead, we've got rhyming jugglers, we've got saucy wenches..."

"Sounds like my kind of place!"

"I'm telling ya!" Nadine chuckled. "It's a smorgasbord of ladies and beer. You should've gotten this gig for yourself! But Ben and Hoagie lucked out, and so did you, listeners, because I am going to be here from now until four this afternoon, keeping you company and keeping these lovely people entertained. Speaking of the lovely people, come on up and say hi! I'd be happy to play a song for you, and I've got bumper stickers and buttons to give away.

"Right now, we're going to start things off right with Mr. Simon, Mr. Garfunkel, and a little parsley, sage, rosemary and thyme."

She started *Scarborough Faire* and set up the next two songs on her play list. They were not particularly medieval...*but beggars can't be choosers*. She still had the Moody Blues song, but she was saving that for later. It was best not to blow all her tricks in the first few minutes.

More people were congregating in front of the booth. Nadine felt a bit like a judge as she rolled her chair to one side and peered down at them. "Hi! How are y'all?"

"Hey!" one guy said. "You really *are* the Pixie!"

She laughed and said, "I sure am. You guys got anything you want to hear?"

They gave her a handful of requests, which she scribbled down as best she could. "Okay, I'm definitely going to get those on for you!" She opened the drawer and grabbed a handful of buttons. "Anyone want a button?" She tossed them down, and people snatched them from the air. "Keep listening to KELF!" Her headache gave her a bit of relief as she smiled down at her listeners. This was the absolute best part of her job, despite her complaints; meeting the people who listened to her show was a great perk. She laughed and waved as more listeners approached. *Maybe it won't be such a horrible day after all.*

Miranda left the broadcasting booth, walked to a nearby concession stand, and stood in line for a turkey leg. As she waited, she looked down at her dress and noticed, for the seventieth time, how low-cut it was. It had been much more modest in the store. She was so anxious about how much it revealed that she had been sure Nadine had said she liked her breasts. *Wishful thinking, much?* she chided herself.

The person in the line in front of her walked away, and she stepped forward to the counter. "A turkey leg, please." She withdrew a leather wallet from the pocket of her dress and fished out two dollar bills.

"Dollar-fifty," the girl behind the counter said. "Your dress is really...like, really hot."

Startled, Miranda glanced up into the girl's eyes. "Really? You like it?"

The girl nodded, looked pointedly at Miranda's cleavage, and said, "Yeah. I really, really do." She handed over the turkey leg; a twist of aluminum foil was wrapped around the bone end. Miranda took it and held out the money to the girl. Their fingers brushed over the image of George Washington on the bill and the girl smiled. "I, uh...I'm just here for the weekend," the girl said. "Working for my uncle. I go to college on the mainland."

Translation — I'm over eighteen, if you're interested.

"Really," Miranda said.

"Really," the girl replied, nodding.

Miranda smiled. Maybe this was just what she needed. Hell, if she was hearing Nadine Butler come on to her, she really must need to get laid! After all...what good was a Faire without a one-night stand?

As the crowd of autograph-seekers dispersed, Nadine rolled her chair back to the controls and looked out over the crowd again. She was not searching for anything in particular, but she spotted Kate deep in the crowd. Kate was wearing a white blouse and slacks, her black hair loosely gathered under a brown newsboy cap. She was looking off to her left, her fingers lightly scratching her cheek. Someone came up next to her, and she laughed, looping an arm around the newcomer's neck and starting to walk down the grassy midway.

The woman with Kate was a brunette in a T-shirt and jeans. She did not snuggle into Kate's embrace, but to Nadine, it did not seem as if she was trying to escape, either. The mystery woman lifted a hand and pointed toward the booth. Kate nodded. Nadine watched as they made their way over. Kate waved when she saw Nadine looking at her.

When they were close enough, Kate called out, "Hey, Dean!" in a Jerry Lewis drawl. The mystery woman laughed, and Nadine instantly hated her.

Still, no need to be ugly about it. She forced a smile, waved back, and said, "Hey, Kate," as casually as possible. "Who is your friend?"

Kate gestured at the woman she was currently embracing. "This is Amy Wellis." Amy waggled her fingers and grinned. "She runs Coffee Table Books," Kate went on. "You know, that place downtown..."

"I know it," Nadine said. "So, ah...w-what are you guys up to today?"

"Just hanging out," Kate said. "Amy's been after me to join her baseball team. The Squire's Knights? Anyway, she's been pestering me for weeks to play in this afternoon's game, but up until two days ago, I had plans. When I found out you had to work, I called her up."

"How do you know each other?" Nadine asked.

"Kate interviewed me for this 'local celebrity' column she was doing," Amy said.

Nadine felt her hackles rise. It was the same subject Kate had been working on when they had gotten together. She fought to keep herself calm as Kate spoke again.

"Amy wanted to meet you and maybe get one of those KELF buttons...?" Kate asked.

Nadine opened the drawer and pulled out a blue and white button. KELF 1220 was scrolled across the curve of the button, surrounding "I listen to the Pixie!" in cursive writing in the center. Nadine wanted to add "And I sleep around with her girlfriend" before she tossed it into Amy's smug face. She refrained and rose from her seat in order to drop the button into Amy's outstretched hand.

"Thanks!" Amy said.

Kate watched as Amy fastened the button to her T-shirt — *Eyes off her chest, Price,* Nadine seethed —then smiled at Nadine. "Thanks, babe. The game starts around noon, so maybe I'll see you after?"

"Yeah, maybe," Nadine said. She glanced at the display and saw the batch of songs she had set to play was about to end. She gestured at the mic. "I have to..."

"Yeah, duty calls," Kate said. "Bye-bye!"

"Thanks for the button!" Amy called.

Nadine watched them walk off and switched her mic on. "That was *Black Water* by the Doobie Brothers. Coming up, we've got David Bowie, Billy Joel, and...a-and Paul Simon is up next." She went to commercial and searched the CDs for a certain song. She found it on a disc near the bottom of the stack.

50 Ways to Leave Your Lover. She kind of doubted it was at that point with her and Kate, but listening to the song would certainly help her mood. "Just duck through the gate, Kate," Nadine muttered as she slipped the disc in. She set it to play after the commercial break and watched her girlfriend walk away, arm-in-arm with another woman. Even though she knew she was being ridiculous, it felt like she was watching Kate walk away for the last time.

"Thanks for coming back," Nadine said a little while later. "In that last set, you heard Neil Sedaka's *Breaking Up Is Hard to Do,* The Bay City Rollers with *Bye, Bye, Baby,* and *Farewell* by Rod Stewart. And no, you don't win a prize if you call in with the hidden theme to today's show." She smiled, thinking about the number of people who had called in about the break-up theme and actually found herself a little cheerful about running an actual contest.

"But there *is* time for a contest right now," Nadine went on. "Who, of the following four, are not mentioned in the Joey Levine song *Life is a Rock (But the Radio Rolled Me)*? Remember, we're looking for the one who is *not* mentioned. Your choices are the Rolling Stones, Jack the Ripper, Elvis Presley, or John Denver. Be the first caller with the right answer, you could win a very snazzy KELF AM T-shirt. You can even get it autographed by me if you want. Let me hear from ya. Right now, we've got *I Wish It Would Rain* by the Temptations."

She heard footsteps on the stairs leading up to her platform and turned to shoo away what she figured was another teenager trying to be king of the hill. This time, however, it was Miranda Powell. The woman swayed a little when she reached the top and put her hand on the back of Nadine's chair to steady herself before she fell. "Hey," she said. Nadine detected a whiff of mead on her breath. "Good show?"

"Decent," Nadine replied. "Gave away a couple of T-shirts, about to give away one more if I get a winner."

"Good. I heard the trivia question. Is it John Denver?"

"No," Nadine said.

"Darn," Miranda said. She smiled and winked before moving her hand to Nadine's shoulder. She bent down to whisper in her ear in a conspiratorial fashion, "Maybe you could lay off the break-up songs for a while? It's kind of supposed to be a fun time."

"Yeah, okay," Nadine said. She smiled when she realized just how drunk Miranda was. *She's leaning down, remember not to look at her breasts.* Without her conscious volition, Nadine's eyes dipped down to Miranda's cleavage. *Idiot,* she chided herself.

Miranda followed Nadine's gaze and clapped a hand over her chest. "Oh, jeez. Giving everyone a free show, aren't I?" To Nadine's mingled pleasure and consternation, she straightened up and smoothed the tight-fitting bodice of her dress, which only emphasized her swelling bosom. She looked out over the Faire and said, "I'm heading home. Just wanted to stop by real quick before I left."

"You're not driving, are you?" Nadine asked.

"No," Miranda chuckled. "I found someone to give me a ride. You're sweet for worrying, though." She bent down and kissed the top of Nadine's head. "See you on Monday, Dean."

"Yeah, see you." Nadine felt heat rising in her cheeks; the spot Miranda had kissed tingled slightly. She flapped a hand in front of her face, hoping to cool off her blush. She could not help but wonder if her jealousy of Kate and Amy was anger at herself for lusting after Miranda. Kate and Amy had done nothing wrong, after all. Nadine was the one getting hot and bothered over her boss. After watching Miranda until the woman disappeared into the crowd, she turned back to her console and answered a phone line. "1220 KELF, you're on with Nadine Butler. You got an answer for our trivia question?"

Miranda found the girl from the turkey stand in the parking lot and said, "Thanks for giving me a ride. I think I had a bit too much mead." She wrapped her arms around the girl and squeezed her ass through the patchwork trousers she was wearing.

"How drunk are you, milady?" the girl asked.

She was at least half Miranda's age, but at the moment, Miranda did not care. Right now, all she cared about was getting satisfaction, scratching an itch that had been ignored too long. She put her arm around the girl and said, "Drunk enough. Come on. I'll give you directions to my place."

Finally, at 2:30 in the afternoon, the sun that had been relentlessly beating down on her head disappeared behind a cloud, a small mercy for which Nadine was grateful. The headache she had been nursing all day had spiked with a vengeance when she saw Kate with Amy. She was not sure if the majority of her headache was due to her sleepless night, the heat, or her encounter with her father, but she assumed the most insistent throbbing was caused by seeing Amy and Kate together. Her too-active imagination refused to stop manufacturing scenarios where the two women ended up in bed.

If the team lost, would they drown their sorrows in beer? If the team won, would they get caught up in the moment and share a celebratory kiss?

Nadine finally gave up thinking about it and gave away the rest of the T-shirts with insanely easy trivia, like: "Which member of the Beatles married Yoko Ono?" She also handed out every button in the drawer. When the bumper sticker pile started to dwindle, she had sought a new supply and found a stack of what had to be twelve thousand of the things stuffed in another drawer. She had yet to make a sizable dent in the stack.

At three o'clock, she transferred the feed to Willa Lamb back at the station, so that Willa could read the news off the wire. Listening to the other DJ with half an ear, Nadine watched the people wandering back and forth in front of her booth. A few of them reached up to shake her hand or paused to say hello. She signed a lot of bumper stickers — she refused to call them autographs, since in her opinion only famous people gave autographs — and wished them all a good afternoon.

When four o'clock finally rolled around, she wished everyone a "happy Faire" and began preparing to leave. She was not sure who was responsible for breaking down and putting away the broadcasting booth, but she knew it was not her job. She put the CDs and tapes into the safe and made sure it was locked tight before she climbed down from the platform.

Nadine paused to get something from a concession stand that proclaimed to be a turkey leg but looked like it had been taken from some prehistoric beast. Her stomach growled at the delicious smell. She had not had a chance to eat all day and was finally starting to feel hunger pangs. While she ate her snack, she wandered through the Faire, pausing to more closely examine some of the costumes that people were wearing. After a while, Nadine realized why she was delaying her departure — she did not want to go home and wait for Kate to stumble in, most likely with Amy in tow. God, she didn't want to face that.

But I have no choice, she decided. *Might as well go home and face the music, get it over with.* Her appetite gone, she dumped the remains of her monster turkey leg into a trash bin and went to find her bike.

Chapter Four

By the time Nadine arrived home, the headache had intensified until she felt as though there was a toddler beating the insides of her skull with a wiffle ball bat. She pinched the bridge of her nose as she unlocked the front door and failed to see the black duffle bag sitting on the floor in her way. She kicked it, cursed, and pushed it out of the way with her foot. As it fell over, a pile of sweaty baseball clothes tumbled out of the bag. *Guess that answers if Kate is here or not.*

Nadine stepped over the reeking clothes and headed toward the back of the apartment. "Kate? You left your stuff in front of the door again!" she called. There was no response, so she shut the apartment door and dumped her own bag on the couch. She heard the shower as she undid her tie, and her mind suddenly formed an image of Amy and Kate making out in the tiny stall.

No, you know for a fact that stall is too cramped to have sex in, she told herself. Still, she knocked on the bathroom door and hazarded a look inside. Through the steam, she saw Kate's familiar silhouette — thankfully just hers alone — behind the etched glass of the shower door. "Hey, Kate," she asked loudly, trying to be heard over the running water. "How was the game?"

"Good!" Kate said. "We creamed them." She pushed the door open and stuck her head out. "Amy wants me to sign up full-time. I'm actually considering it."

"Awesome," Nadine said without much enthusiasm. "I'll be out here when you get out."

"Okay."

Nadine closed the door and went into the bedroom. She undressed amid the crowd of boxes, broken TVs, newspapers, magazines, and other various things she had not unpacked after her move from college. She eyed the disorganized clutter warily, knowing it was a tinderbox, but the task of cleaning out was just too daunting. She sighed and turned her back on the mess. *Out of sight, out of mind.*

Pushing open the closet, she grabbed a pair of blue jeans. As she was searching for a T-shirt, the bathroom door creaked open and Kate stepped into the hallway. She was wrapped in a towel, her skin glistening with moisture from the shower. Kate saw Nadine in the bedroom and stepped into the doorway. Raising her arms, she hooked her fingers on the top of the doorframe, stretching sinuously. Nadine could not help openly admiring the way the towel rose up on Kate's hips, revealing plenty of firm flesh. Doubt was pushed to the back of her mind, and desire took control.

Kate's lips curled into a mischievous smile. "Well, damn," she said.

Nadine looked down at her boxer shorts and brassiere — hardly an outfit for seduction. "What?"

"I'm going to need another shower," Kate sighed. She dropped her hands from the doorframe and untied the knot of the towel between her breasts, letting the terrycloth drop. Nadine had just enough time to register the glorious length of her lover's lithe, toned body before Kate pushed her to her knees. Nadine went with the movement until she was lying on her back on the floor. Kate joined her in a moment, stretching beside her.

Kate removed Nadine's glasses, putting them down carefully an arm's length away. They kissed hungrily, intense and devouring kisses. Nadine's lips felt swollen and bruised by the time she opened her mouth to admit Kate's eager tongue. She felt Kate's hand on her belly, a thumb teasing her navel, then the woman's fingers slid lower until Kate was tugging on the waistband of her boxers. Nadine planted her feet on the floor, breaking the kiss and sighing as Kate sat up and slid her underwear off, tossing the boxers aside.

Okay, fine, Nadine thought, shivering as Kate settled beside her. The carpet was scratchy under her back, but she would not insist on moving to the more comfortable couch. *One last boff. One last roll in the hay before we have the Fight. God knows Kate's good at it.*

Relenting to Kate's sensual assault, as well as the insistence of her own body that this was a good thing, Nadine spread her legs apart, anticipation sending thrills down her spine. Kate moved her lips to Nadine's neck. The sharp edge of teeth in that ultra-sensitive area made Nadine groan out loud, her eyes squeezing shut as her nerves sang with blissful sensation. Her neck was Kate's favorite sweet spot to nibble and kiss, mostly because she knew how much it turned Nadine on.

Kate shifted, raising herself up on an elbow. Her slender fingers ghosted between Nadine's thighs, lightly caressing the tender, slick flesh. Some small part of Nadine wondered if Kate had ever studied the piano. Her fingers moved independently of one another when she was fingering Nadine, each one rising and falling, thrusting and stroking, seemingly playing out a song. Only Kate knew the tune, but Nadine got the benefit of her lover's dexterity every time.

Rousing herself with difficulty, Nadine unhooked her own bra and dropped it to the side, arching her back and deliberately drawing Kate's attention to her breasts, which were aching with need. Kate abandoned Nadine's neck, moving her head and capturing a pert nipple between her lips. She alternated between Nadine's breasts, sucking, nibbling, and licking around her nipples until Nadine was whimpering and arching her back even further, mutely offering her body. Kate chuckled and slipped her free arm around Nadine's waist, keeping her from squirming around too much. Nadine made a whining sound of complaint low in her throat, but Kate knew how much Nadine loved to have her breasts played with; she knew how sensitive they were and she used that knowledge like a secret weapon, much to Nadine's dismay and delight. They had once spent an entire night touching one another only above the belt, and Nadine had almost fainted from the orgasm she had when Kate finally went down on her.

The memory of that night, of Kate's long supple fingers stroking her nipples for nearly an hour, was what pushed Nadine over the edge.

Trying to speak in gasping, impatient sobs, she finally reached down and grabbed Kate's wrist, holding the woman's hand in place between her legs and squeezed her thighs together tightly. Kate knew the signs; she remained still as Nadine ground herself against the heel of her hand, coming so hard, it was like an explosion of pleasure inside her head. Gooseflesh rose on her breasts and arms; Kate gently kissed the pebbled flesh. Nadine trembled a last time, closed her eyes, and relaxed, sagging down onto the carpet.

Kate stretched up and kissed Nadine's lips, softly and tenderly, and cupped her breast, giving it a little squeeze. "That was wonderful," she breathed. She trailed her hand down Nadine's chest, stroked her belly, then started to sit up. "Can I assume you'll thank me later?"

Nadine frowned and opened her eyes. *Kathryn Price passing up instant gratification?* She rolled over on her side and watched in confusion as Kate got to her feet. "Why later?" she asked.

Kate gathered her towel and wiped her fingers on it. "Work. I have to cover tonight's Town Hall meeting." She stuck her tongue out, apparently at the thought of the boring night ahead, before she looped the towel around her shoulders like a scarf. "I'm covering the City Beat this month, so since I'm in town..." She shrugged and walked naked into the living room.

Nadine followed, also not bothering to cover up. She paused in the doorway and crossed her hands over her breasts. They were still sensitive, and she resisted the urge to shudder as she inadvertently brushed over her nipples. She was taken off-guard by Kate suddenly leaving. Despite the ill will she had been holding toward Kate all day, what they had just shared had gone a long way toward rebuilding their bridges as far as she was concerned. "Could I come with you?"

"To a Town Hall meeting?" Kate said with a disbelieving smile. "Are you sure you can handle the excitement?"

Nadine shrugged. "Come on. It'll be like a date. It'll make up for not getting to the mainland this weekend."

"I'm not entirely sure you understand what a Town Hall meeting entails," Kate said. "But yeah, come along. You can make fun of Mayor Dugan with me."

Nadine grinned. "Great! Just give me a chance to get dressed."

"Okay," Kate said. She loaded the duffle bag Nadine had tripped over and quickly dressed in her baseball uniform — *in case the neighbors were watching*, Nadine thought. "I have to run upstairs to change into something more appropriate anyway," Kate went on.

When Kate was gone, Nadine went into the bathroom to take a quick shower of her own. Her head was still aching, but the sex had actually helped take the edge off a little. She swiped at the fogged-up mirror and glanced at her reflection. Maybe she would not have to have the confrontation about Amy and everything she felt was wrong in their relationship. Maybe tonight was actually the first step she and Kate would take in becoming a real couple.

Nadine turned away, her smile fading. If she paid heed to all the obstacles in her path to happiness — the trauma of seeing her father and being snubbed by him, the anger she had been nursing since seeing Kate and Amy together in the park, the shame of being aroused when confronted by Miranda in her sexy low-cut costume — she would do the smart thing and hide under a blanket until Monday.

Instead, she got ready for her "date" with Kate.

The Town Hall was only a few blocks away, separated from her apartment building by a plethora of restaurants. When Kate came back downstairs in slacks and a white blouse, Nadine suggested they walk rather than take Kate's car. The weather had decided to turn chilly again, but the temperature was still comfortable enough that they would not need jackets. Kate agreed.

The streetlights glowed golden against the gloom. Nadine found the cool breeze blowing off the harbor was a balm after the unseasonably warm day she had endured in the booth. Nadine put her arm around Kate's waist without thinking and let herself be drawn into her lover's embrace. Their first date had ended with a moonlit walk, and Nadine smiled at the memory. *Our first night together, I gave her a flower*, she thought.

Nadine put her chin on Kate's shoulder.

Kate chuckled affectionately, squeezed Nadine's hand, and whispered, "All we need is a peony and everything will be perfect."

Nadine blinked in surprise. "I was *just* thinking that."

Kate smiled. As they passed through a shadowy patch between two streetlights, she kissed Nadine's cheek, an obviously daring gesture. Nadine felt her face flush and pressed against Kate's side. She was glad that Kate had seduced her before she could pick a fight. This was exactly what she had been aching for the past couple of months — a walk in the moonlight, a kiss on the cheek, being close enough to smell Kate's shampoo, enjoying each other's company like a real couple.

They walked in silence for a while. Finally, Nadine could hold her tongue no longer. "Is Amy gay?"

Kate did not hesitate. "Mmm-hmm."

"Are you..." Nadine was unsure how to phrase her next question without giving offense.

"Yes, honey, I'm gay, too."

Nadine chuckled. "No, I was going to ask if you were...if you were attracted to her."

"Why would you ask that?"

That's not a no, Nadine thought. *Why couldn't you have just said no, you stupid reporter?* She shrugged, trying to hide her dismay. "The way you guys were acting today, I just thought...I don't know. And there's the stupid article. It was the same article you were doing when you and I met."

Kate laughed. "Contrary to what you may believe, I don't use my job to pick up chicks." Nadine was glad it was dark so Kate could not see her blush. "I told you back then, I had a crush on you for ages." Kate stopped at the corner and turned to face Nadine. She stroked her cheek and went on, "Don't worry. Amy and I are just friends. I think she's seeing some butch cop from the mainland or something." She kissed the tip of Nadine's nose.

Nadine smiled, mollified, and nodded toward Town Hall. "Come on. Let's go get bored to tears. And then we can stop at one of these 'foine 'stablishments' and get some food in us."

"Foine?" Kate said.

"Mmm-hmm."

"Is that a word in your world?"

Nadine chuckled and hugged Kate tighter.

The front doors of the Town Hall stood open, spilling a rectangle of light into the evening's darkness. Kate and Nadine went up the steps, slipping away from one another to keep up the façade that they were "just friends". They took their seats near the middle of the room, on the aisle, and chatted with people nearby as the room filled up with stragglers.

Kate leaned forward to speak with someone from Amy's baseball team, and Nadine took the opportunity to glance around. The meeting room was extremely quaint in her opinion; it looked like someone's idea of a meeting hall from a century ago. Electric lanterns fashioned to look like gaslights ran the length of the walls to either side, filled with candle-shaped bulbs instead of true flames. Woodcarvings of people she assumed to be the island's first inhabitants hung between the sconces. She recognized Gabriel Sawyer, the man who had led the first expedition to the island and had a statue in the Memorial Park, but the rest were absolute strangers.

A man at the front of the room cleared his throat, and the buzz of conversation died down. Kate leaned back into her seat, facing forward like everyone else. Dominating the space was a stage that had hosted everything from school pageants to graduation. Two men in the familiar tan-and-black uniforms of the police department were seated at the far end. A fat, older man in a green suit was closer to the middle.

When the din of the crowd died away, the older policeman stood and walked to the podium. His uniform was crisp, his badge and bald head both reflecting the light in the hall. He gripped the edge of the podium, looked down at the papers lying in front of him and cleared his throat. "I, uh..." The microphone whined feedback, and he covered it with his hand. Nadine politely stifled a guffaw.

Offering only a slight grimace that spoke volumes about his irritation, he coughed into his hand and tried again. "I'm Sheriff Cal Rucker. And, ah, of course you all know Mayor Jameson Dugan," he said, gesturing at the man in the ugly suit. Dugan half-rose from his seat and offered a slight wave. *Like he's a Presidential candidate or something*, Nadine thought. She glanced at Kate and saw the sly grin that meant the woman had experienced the same thought. They smiled at one another, but said nothing out loud.

"Well, uh...I suppose we should start with new business," Rucker said. "If anyone has anything they want to discuss, grievances to air, I'd like to invite you to come up to the microphone in the aisle..." He waited, tightening and releasing his fingers on the edge of the podium for a few minutes as the room remained still. At last, he smiled and said, "Well, folks, as much as I'd like to call it a night right now, I'm sure there's *something* you'd all like to talk about."

There were a few chuckles, then an older woman near the front stood up. Rucker spotted her, and his smile widened. "Hello, Mildred."

Mildred Banks, a local gossip whom Nadine knew usually held court at the beauty parlor, walked to the microphone, angled it down, and said in a loud, clear voice, "I might as well speak up." She coughed and continued, "Is it true Fire Chief Bradley is going to retire at the end of the year?"

Rucker nodded. "Don has spoken to me about it briefly and, yes, he's planning to step down at the end of...of December, I think it was." He adjusted some papers and nodded. "We're already looking for a replacement for him and have a couple of options from mainland fire departments. If we can't find someone to take over by the time he leaves, Assistant Chief Wolfe will step in temporarily."

Mildred said, "Just find someone as good as Mr. Bradley. He helped rebuild my garage when it caught fire a few years back. Really nice fellow, really nice."

There was a smattering of applause as Mildred returned to her seat. Rucker said with a good-natured grin, "Yes, ma'am, old Don went above and beyond the call of duty. We shouldn't be surprised it finally took something out of him." He waited until Mildred had made it back to her seat before he scanned the room. "Anyone else? Grievances, questions...comments..."

A woman stood up on the far right side of the room. She tightened her blazer and sidled her way down the row of chairs toward the aisle. Kate muttered to Nadine, "Oh, God, not her." Her expression was filled with weary resignation. "You may get entertained after all."

Nadine glanced at Kate, then watched as the slender woman approached the microphone. She was wearing a crisply tailored business suit, and her hair was pulled back in a tight bun without a single strand out of place. A pair of small-framed eyeglasses hung precariously on the edge of her nose and seemed to threaten to fall with each step of her fine Italian shoes. She marched purposefully to the microphone, spinning on her heel like a general preparing to address her troops. Kate groaned and, from the dismayed look on Rucker's face, he was familiar with the woman as well.

He rested his chin on his left fist and gazed at her with patient acceptance. "Hello, Eleanor. What's the problem this week?"

Eleanor ("Eleanor Nelson," murmured Kate) ignored the tone of his voice and held her prepared statement clenched in her hand. She said, "Thank you, Sheriff Rucker. I have come before this meeting to request that a certain novel be taken off the shelves of our hallowed December Harbor Public Library. The book is entitled *Sparks of Love,* and it was written by a woman named Francesca Harland. This book depicts a...a homosexual relationship as normal."

Rucker sighed and straightened his back. "Now, Eleanor, someone else tried to remove that book from the library last month. The librarians read it, and they decided there is nothing explicit in the book, no graphic love scenes, or even strong language. It's a love story."

"It is a *lesbian* love story, Sheriff Rucker." Eleanor said "lesbian" with the same venom most people reserved for necrophilia and child pornography. She turned to address the crowd and said, "This book is listed in the card catalogue under the 'romance' title and can be checked out by any age group."

"That's not exactly—" Rucker began.

She interrupted him. "The children of this town do not need such prurient filth in their library. The children of this town..."

Nadine closed her eyes. She did not literally feel her temper snap; it was more of a sagging, like the weight of the day had finally broken a dam in her mind and her mouth was caught in the flow. She had read *Sparks of Love* and thought the novel was a gorgeous love story. It had made her cry. She owned her own copy and reread it as often as she could. Without even meaning to, she snorted and said aloud, "Oh, please."

Kate glanced at her, and Nadine saw a brief "what are you doing?" look on her face before she looked away. Sheriff Rucker seemed grateful for any distraction from Eleanor Nelson's rant; he turned and scanned the crowd. He seemed to have a general idea of where the voice had come from, but could not quite pinpoint Nadine's location.

"Did someone have something to add?" he asked.

A tiny voice in the back of Nadine's mind told her to stay quiet. To sit still, let it pass, make a quiet and anonymous complaint to the library if the book was removed from the shelves.

If she had not spent the entire day battling the unseasonable heat and a headache, she might have listened to the voice; if she had not had the painful confrontation with her father; if the whole situation with Kate had not been weighing on her mind all day...if and if and if. Goaded to recklessness, Nadine gripped the back of the folding chair in front of her and pushed herself to her feet. When everyone else in the room turned to look at Nadine, she saw Kate trying as hard as she could to melt into her own metal folding chair. Nadine shook her head and spoke directly to Eleanor. "Books don't make you gay, lady."

Rucker cleared his throat to get Nadine's attention and said, "I'm sorry, I don't recognize you. Your name would be...?"

"I'm Nadine Butler."

His eyes widened slightly. "The Pixie?" He smiled and slapped his palm on the podium. "Boy, you know, I listen to your show all the time."

"Thank you," Nadine replied perfunctorily. She turned to face Eleanor Nelson once more. "I've read *Sparks of Love* a couple of times, and it's a beautiful book. Keeping it out of the library is close-minded and... and stupid. You don't have a problem with Stephen King books being on the shelves. Dismemberments, graphically bloody murders — talk about a reason to censor those! But I don't campaign to hide those books, I just don't read them. Banning books is the height of ignorance. I mean, think of what we'd be missing if *Huckleberry Finn* had been banned because some old fogey thought it was racist. Some of the greatest books of all time have been banned at one time or another."

"I am sure," Eleanor huffed, "that you are not comparing this...this smut to Mark Twain?"

"It's not smut, you dense woman," Nadine snapped. Rucker recoiled a bit before hiding a smile behind his palm. "It's a beautifully written love story," she went on, angered by the woman's prejudice. "Maybe if you'd had some love in your own life, you'd recognize the difference," she added, which was admittedly a cheap shot.

Rucker coughed into his hand and had to turn around for a moment before he composed himself.

Nadine continued, "Reading books like this didn't make *me* gay. Books like that made me feel like I wasn't such a freak. It showed me there were other people going through the same thing I was. Taking this book out of the library would be the worst thing you could do. You'd be alienating teenagers, kids who are starting to feel different. They need books like this to let them know they aren't alone."

She looked around and realized she had taken over the whole meeting. People were staring at her, and she could feel her ears burning. Nadine smiled apologetically to Rucker. "Sorry." She smoothed the front of her trousers and took her seat again. She glanced at Kate and saw an expression of sheer terror on her face. Nadine shook her head and faced forward again, unwilling to face her lover's disapproval at her outburst.

"Nadine," Kate whispered forcefully.

"I had to say it," Nadine whispered back.

"Nadine, you just came out."

Nadine blinked. She shook her head slowly and whispered, "What? No. Just because I read a book doesn't mean..." The truth hit her like a back-handed slap. Stunned, every muscle in her face went slack. She realized every-one in the room was still staring at her — not because of her rant, but because of the one little fact she had dropped into the middle of it without even thinking. Even the sheriff looked dumbstruck.

Nadine covered her face with both hands and wished she had the power to turn invisible or travel back in time. "Oh, shit," she groaned through her fingers. "I just came out to the whole town."

Rucker managed to get the meeting back on track without too much trouble. As soon as she could escape without creating a further disruption, Nadine slipped from her seat and hurried to the door at the back of the room. She felt every eye on her and heard whispers as she passed down the aisle. She tucked her hands under her arms, ducked her head, and rushed out into the rapidly cooling night.

She stopped on the sidewalk and paced nervously between the cars parked at the curb. After several minutes, Nadine paused and looked down at the harbor. The water was barely visible past the police station, but she could see some sailboats coming in to dock for the night, the vessels bobbing on the waves. Behind her, the door of the hall swung open. She did not turn to see who had joined her, but she smelled Kate's perfume a moment later.

"Nadine..." Kate sounded unsure.

"What the hell did I just do?" Nadine whispered.

Kate walked around and faced her. The woman's eyes were still wide, her expression still shocked, her mouth apparently trying to form words against an uncooperative tongue. Finally, Kate turned toward the harbor. The sun offered a bit of shimmering light on the horizon, but the moon was already hanging low in the sky, flat and dull.

Nadine chewed her bottom lip and said, "How many people do you suppose were in there?"

Kate turned to face her again. "I don't think that matters, Dean."

Nadine was so struck by the nickname that it took her a moment to remember that Kate was the one who had actually started using it. Miranda had not picked the nickname up until about a year ago.

Kate continued speaking, "There were about thirty people in there, including Eleanor Nelson. It doesn't matter how many people are in there, by tomorrow it'll be all over the island."

A low mewling sound crawled out of the back of Nadine's throat.

"It's not a disaster," Kate said, giving her a faltering smile that was probably supposed to be reassuring. "You can still salvage it. Just say you were trying to prove a point."

"A point?"

Kate shrugged. "I don't know...like, 'this proves *anyone* could be gay! I might have been telling the truth, ha-ha-ha.' Something like that. I don't know, Nadine. I'm just saying that it's not the end of the world."

"I can't go back in there, Kate." Nadine gazed at the harbor and shook her head. "I'm...you know, I'm just going to go home."

"Okay," Kate said, a warning note in her voice. "But Dean, the article..."

It took Nadine a moment to realize what Kate was talking about. She frowned, then glanced at the notepad in Kate's hand. "The article," she whispered. "You're going to report on what happened?"

"I'd have to, Dean. You think I could get away with ignoring something like that?"

"You would...you'd do that to me?" Nadine could not believe what she was hearing.

Kate stepped forward and reached for Nadine's arm, but Nadine twisted away from her. Kate sighed. "I'm saying don't make me do it. If I leave it out, everyone in there will start to wonder what *I* have to hide."

"Out me to protect your own closet," Nadine scoffed. She could not believe this utter betrayal by someone who claimed to love her.

"Go back in there!" Kate cried. "Fix this while you still can! Before Eleanor Nelson can..."

"Stop!" Nadine interrupted. She was angry, torn to the very core, by the fact Kate would do this to her. "Eleanor Nelson could tell, what, twenty people? Maybe? You're sitting here admitting that you're going to put my speech in print. How many people will see *that*, Kate? You can blame Eleanor Nelson all you want — you're the one who's going to bury me."

A small plane crossed the sky overhead, the droning sound of its engine breaking the tension. She and Kate followed its flight path; Nadine, for one, was grateful for the distraction. The plane descended toward the small airport outside of town, but Nadine kept her gaze locked on the sky, struggling to compose herself. She watched as the sun sank behind the horizon and tiny pinpricks of starlight began to appear. Her nostrils flared as she took a deep breath and looked back at Kate.

"I'm going home," she repeated, turning around and starting to walk away.

Kate, apparently unable to just let her leave, called after her, "Can I come over later?"

"No," Nadine said without turning her head. She could feel Kate's gaze on her back, but she did not dare turn around. She did not know if she would have the strength to keep walking away if she did. At the corner, she finally glanced back. Kate had apparently returned to the meeting hall; the street was deserted.

She walked home slowly, letting the realization of what she had done sink in. After all these years, she had come out of the fiercely protected closet with a slip of her tongue! Unbelievable! Nadine glanced into the windows of restaurants she passed, paused to watch a flock of seabirds fly across the darkening sky, and saw an old man hosing off the sidewalk in front of his convenience store. She walked past her apartment building to Spring Street and stood on the corner.

People drove past; a few of them waved at her, and she always waved back. She could not shake the feeling that it was her last night as a free woman. If Kate was right, before long she would be the subject of stares and hushed conversation. She might as well enjoy her town while she still could.

Nadine directed her steps toward the harbor, unconsciously retracing the path she and Kate had walked after their first date. She stuck her hands into her jeans pockets and wandered for another half-hour, taking in the sights, smelling the breeze coming off the water. This was her town, where she had been born and probably where she would die, unless she was forced to leave. She had heard of it happening — towns where people had not actually run a person out or tarred and feathered them, but bigots made it a very unfriendly place to stay.

Before long, Nadine realized that the night had gotten colder, and she regretted not taking a coat to the meeting. When a cold gust blew right through her blouse, she finally turned to go home. Her legs ached, but the pain kept her mind from dwelling too much on thoughts of the future.

Returning to her building, she left the lights off as she went into her apartment, preferring to remain in the dark. She sat in front of the window and looked through the blinds at her little garden. The plants were mulched to protect them from the cold, but they had not been doing very well anyway. She had been thinking about trying a new fertilizer in spring to see if that revitalized them, but she had to wonder if it was her own self that needed the change. *Haven't I read somewhere that flowers respond to the mood of their tender? If so, those poor little plants never stood a chance.*

The past few years, Nadine had been feeling the weight of being in the closet. She hated it and not just because it caused her to commit to horrific work commitments just because she was "single". She lived in the public eye, so anything kept private should have been cherished, and yet keeping the secret continued to eat away at her. With so much of her life on display to the public via her radio show, it felt wrong that the best part — the person she loved — had to be hidden and kept secret like it was a shameful thing. Now, it was out there; her secret was in the open. People knew.

Then there was her actual relationship with Kate. Nadine sighed. It had been a decent enough relationship over the years, but now she was aching for something more...just something *more*. At least the idea of talking with Kate about their relationship did not seem so overwhelming now. If her outburst in the meeting had been like tearing off a band-aid, then talking things out with Kate would be like the sting of antiseptic —painful, but necessary.

Nadine closed the blinds and got undressed, sitting on the couch for a long time and ruminating over the possible consequences of her outing. She heard someone's footsteps tapping down the corridor and up the stairs and assumed it must be Kate coming home. Her thoughts were confirmed when she heard the door to the apartment above hers close. It was the oddest sensation, hearing Kate moving around in the apartment above her and not saying hello, not banging on the roof with a broom or sticking her head out the door to say, "Come on down. Hang out for a while."

She closed her eyes and imagined Kate's progress through the apartment. She was most likely walking through the living room now, dumping her jacket and notepad on the coffee table. Maybe a brief side trip into the kitchen before bed.

"Sleep well, Katie," Nadine whispered into the darkness. She felt like she was being attacked from all sides — her lust for Miranda, her anger at Kate, and the threat of being out before the whole damn town. She stretched out on the couch, pulled the quilt over her head, and closed her eyes.

Sleep was a long time coming.

Chapter Five

Kate went straight to bed as soon as she got home, but instead of sleeping, she merely lay on her back and stared at the ceiling. Lacing her fingers together and resting her hands on her stomach, she thought about the meeting. Everything in the meeting had been as boring as she had suspected it would be — traffic concerns, questions about the city's new garbage pick-up schedule, a lively debate about recycling bins.

And then there was Nadine coming out of the closet.

God, if it had been anyone but Nadine...the simple truth was that she would not hesitate to write the story if it had been anyone else revealing their previously well-hidden sexual orientation. Finally, Kate threw off the covers, got out of bed, and walked over to her laptop. She had once said she wouldn't do Nadine any favors, no special treatment in any of her columns. Besides that, her journalistic integrity required that she report the news as it happened, not cover up the truth or let her relationships curtail her responsibility to tell the public the facts of a story. This was not an issue of *if* she would write the story; it was an issue of *how* she was going to live with herself afterward. Nadine would never forgive her. She might never forgive herself. How could she out someone else when she herself was still firmly in the closet?

"I'm a reporter," she said. "I *report*." She held onto that thought, bit her bottom lip, and began to write.

RECYCLING BINS TO BE ALLOWED AT CURB

FIRE CHIEF RESIGNING

She covered the decisions and debates that had gone on, forcing herself to sound excited about garbage handling, before she got to the library debate. She typed a few words, mentioned Nadine Butler's "impassioned" plea to keep *Sparks of Love* on the shelf and then hesitated. It was the moment of truth. She had put it off as long as she could. Reluctantly, she began a new paragraph.

"The big surprise was when local celebrity Nadine Butler came out as a lesbian during her retort in favor of keeping the book on the shelves. No agreement was reached on *Sparks of Love*'s future in the December Harbor Library."

The required thousand words later, Kate was still writing. She filled up two pages, hoping to bury the word "lesbian" in as much pointless blather as possible. Finally, not allowing herself time for second thoughts or regrets, she sent the bloated column off in an email with a note that told her editor to revise it as he saw fit. She stared at the "Message Sent" page with guilt twisting in her gut.

"*Et tu*, Kate?" she murmured. No, that was hardly appropriate in her case, she decided. At least Brutus had waited for someone else to strike first before burying a knife in his friend.

She leaned forward and ran her fingers through her hair, scratching at her scalp with her fingernails, feeling weary to the bone. At last, she pushed her chair away from the desk, shut off the laptop, and walked back to bed.

Kate crawled under the covers and closed her eyes as a more appropriate quote came to mind: "To bed, to bed there's knocking at the gate! What's done cannot be undone. To bed, to bed, to bed..." She pressed her face into the pillow and fell into a troubled sleep.

The night city editor at the newspaper had not been present at the town meeting, but several people had already called to make sure he was aware of what had happened. A few of the emails in his inbox that evening were letters to the editor about this "stunning revelation" of Nadine Butler's confession. When Kate Price's email arrived with her Town Hall report, he found himself smiling, knowing the reporter would tear into the story like the headliner it was.

You wanted front page, Price, he thought. *Here's your ticket.*

He clicked the file open and felt his smile fade as he read through it. He sighed, opened a document, and rewrote the column, shaking his head at Kate's lapse. He sent an email back to Kate: "Nice try. I know the city beat is dull as dirt in a town like this, but next time actually go to the meeting. You missed the best stuff relying on word of mouth!" After he printed out his heavily edited version of Kate's story, he carried it down the hall to the copy desk for proofreading. Following that, he would contact the managing editor at home, informing him of Kate's scoop and the change to the front page. The layout of the whole damned paper would have to be shifted around, and it would likely take most of the night to get it done, but what the hell, for a story like this, he was willing to put in the work.

There was plenty of time to make the early edition, he thought in satisfaction.

Comfort the afflicted and afflict the comfortable. The public has a right to know.

The front page of the *Squire's Isle Register, Sunday Edition*, had a headline which screamed:

POPULAR RADIO DJ COMES OUT!
   By Kate Price, Staff Writer
   Local disc jockey Nadine Butler revealed last night she is a lesbian
   Last night's town hall meeting got an unexpected jolt of excitement when Nadine Butler, the KELF disc-jockey known as 'The Pixie', came out of the closet. The surprise announcement came during yet another diatribe by Mrs. Eleanor Nelson, whose most recent attempts to ban the book *Sparks of Love* from the shelves at the Squire's Isle Public Library inspired the popular local celebrity to break her silence.
   Ms. Butler could not be reached for comment.
   There was no mention of the recycling decision, and the Fire Chief's resignation was relegated to one sentence near the end of the column.

Due to a malfunctioning oven, a bout with insomnia, and the caprice of fate, Amy Wellis was the first person in town to read the news. She picked up the newspaper as soon as it thumped on the front stoop of Coffee Table Books and called "good morning" to the seventy-year-old "paperboy" as he continued down the street. Locking the door behind her, Amy unfolded the paper in search of coverage of her team's latest baseball game. She was sure that imbecile of a sports writer had gotten her name wrong, she just needed to confirm it before...

She froze. The startling headline was below the fold, but in big enough print to draw the eye. Her jaw dropped as she read over the article, then noticed the byline. "Kate...?" she whispered, shocked.

Amy remembered how, on their way to the ball field, she had broached the subject delicately. "Look, I'm not asking for me, just...trying to confirm a feeling. Is Nadine...?"

Kate had hesitated but finally admitted that yes, Nadine was gay. It seemed she had been in a relationship with Nadine for three years, and they were both very much in the closet. Amy was baffled.

How in the world could that conversation and this article be less than twenty-four hours apart?

"Kate, what did you do?" Amy asked aloud, wondering if she ought to call her friend and find out what the hell had happened.

Tamara Butler put down the plate and brushed past her husband. "You did want bacon today, didn't you, dear?" she asked him softly. He did not respond, but she had not really expected him to. Nathaniel Butler always wanted bacon for breakfast, no matter what the doctor said. Tamara had long since given up fighting him on it. As much as she hated the thought, a heart attack was the only thing that would convince him. No matter how many times she had pleaded with him to eat better, his argument had been the same: with the shape he was in, any heart attack he had would be mild. So what? She was beyond fighting him about it, although she did try to balance breakfast out with a health-conscious dinner whenever possible.

She hummed as she gathered the pans she had used to prepare breakfast and placed them in the sink. When she returned to the table, she saw Nathaniel had not moved except to fold the paper under his hands and turn his head toward the window.

"Honey-dear, your eggs are getting cold," she said, concerned.

Nathaniel pushed away from the table without a word, turned on his heel, and walked out of the kitchen. Tamara frowned and read the large-print headline that had caught her husband's attention. She sucked in her breath in a gasp, her chest clenching against a despairing pang.

"Oh, Nadine. Nadine, my dear, now everyone knows..." She balled her hand into a fist and pressed it against her cheek as she began to cry silently.

Miranda Powell did not want social niceties. She did not even really want the bare minimum of kindness. What she wanted was her one-night stand out of her condo as soon as possible.

While the young woman was in the shower, Miranda went around the apartment and gathered their strewn clothes. She separated her bra from the stranger's — what was her name? Sara? Kara? — and tossed the pile at the bathroom door. Pausing, she fingered the collar of her robe. "Find, uh, finding everything all right?" she called, feeling uncomfortable. The morning-after was always awkward, which is why she tried to keep her one-night stands to a minimum. Still, people did not stop drinking just because they eventually got a hangover, and what did *that* say about human nature?

"Yeah!" the cheery voice answered. "Can I use this toothbrush?"

"There's an unopened one in the drawer," Miranda replied, cringing. She silently thanked her dentist for always giving her a new toothbrush when she went to visit him. Pushing her limp, unwashed hair out of her face, she grimaced at how her hand got stuck in the strands. She tried to loosen some of the rat's nest her hair had become and regretted being too drunk on mead and on desire to have done something with it last night. The ringlets that had looked so wonderful yesterday had become tangles for her to try and unravel in the shower with cream rinse...if she ever made it.

There was a thump at the front door. Miranda checked her watch, impatient at the delay in her usual morning routine. *Damn it, you strange person, get out of my bathroom!*

She walked to the front door and, after glancing through the peephole to see the paperboy disappearing through the gate, unlocked the door. The newspaper was resting neatly on her welcome mat. She snatched it up before any of her neighbors could see her in her robe or, even worse, catch a glimpse of her disastrous hair. She shut the door just as Sara/Kara came out of the bathroom. The young woman was wearing nothing but an open robe, shamelessly flaunting her body...*in the house of a total stranger*, Miranda thought in disapproval.

Sara/Kara ran her hands through her still-wet hair, her manner almost mocking in Miranda's opinion, and asked, "Do you have any coffee?"

Miranda turned the paper over in her hands. "Uh, no...no. I, uh, actually have to get to work."

"On Sunday? What are you, like, a priest or something?" This was said without a hint of irony.

Miranda almost asked if the girl had misunderstood some of the "oh, my God's" she had yelled the night before in bed but shook her head instead. "Nope. Just busy." She walked toward the kitchen and paused. Along with the irritation she normally felt when someone overstayed their welcome, Miranda was ashamed. Just having this young girl in front of her was a reminder of how far she had sunk. *One-night stands with someone young enough to be my daughter*, she thought, angry at her own neediness. To add insult to injury, she finally had to ask the question she had been dreading. "Look, I don't want to sound rude, but...what's your name?"

"Jennifer," the girl said without a hint of embarrassment.

Miranda blinked. *Good God, I must have been really blitzed last night.* She nodded and said, "Okay, Jennifer, sorry...but could you get dressed and...well, just go?"

"Sure, no problem," the girl chirped with a smile, much to Miranda's relief. Jennifer turned and headed back toward the bathroom, presumably to gather her clothes.

"That was easy," Miranda said to herself. As she pulled the rubber band off her paper, she idly wondered how many one-night stands the young woman had taken part in. College student, away from school for the weekend...*Christ, she probably isn't even gay.* Jennifer could go back to school with a great story about how she had finally "experimented" with an older woman. *That explains some of her ineptitude, although there's something to be said for youthful enthusiasm.* Miranda chuckled to herself as she scanned the paper's headlines.

Jennifer came out of the bedroom just as Miranda was preparing to look at the second half of the front page. Without reading any further, Miranda pushed the paper aside and turned to face Jennifer. God, she looked young. *College-age*, she reminded herself. *No matter how young she looks, she's at least college-age.*

Having put on the uniform shirt she had been wearing yesterday at the Renaissance Faire, Jennifer stood in the living room, fiddling with the catches on her trousers. Miranda glanced at the clock and struggled to find something to say. Finally, the need to be polite drove her to ask, "Do you need a ride back to the park?"

Jennifer stared for a moment and then laughed. "Wow you really were drunk. I drove you home from the Faire last night. Remember?"

Miranda nodded, but only had a vague memory of the ride.

"I was planning to sightsee for a while before I headed back to the mainland. Maybe I'll see you around." Jennifer leaned across the breakfast counter and mashed her lips against Miranda's mouth in a clumsy good-bye kiss that Miranda endured with as good grace as she could muster.

At least the girl tastes minty fresh, she thought, resisting Jennifer's attempt to add tongue to the kiss.

"I had a great time," Jennifer said after she finally broke the embrace.

"Yeah," Miranda said, her voice flat, "me, too."

She waited until Jennifer had left before she pushed away from the counter. Not in the mood to read the paper and running late, Miranda started the coffee maker and headed into the bathroom to take her shower. With her hair to contend with, the coffee would be done by the time she finished.

There was not anything in the paper could not wait until later, she decided.

Kate threw on a T-shirt and boxer shorts as she cursed at the bare walls of her apartment. "Stupid whore, fucker, bitch-ass, Jezebel..." The insults were more for herself than her editor. She had known full well what would happen, and she had done it anyway. The editor had even called her to let her know the story had hit the front page. Kate had actually been proud — *proud!* — that she had finally made it. As soon as she remembered what the honor would cost, she became furious with herself. She threw open the door of her apartment and stormed downstairs, still cursing. Trying the door on Nadine's apartment, she found it locked.

She knocked just under the gold number four screwed to the door panel and called out, "Dean? Dean, it's me, it's Kate." She looked down and scanned the ground for signs of a newspaper. Did Nadine get the Sunday paper delivered? Had she already picked it up and read the article? She rested her forehead against the panel and closed her eyes. This was what it was like. She had finally gotten her dream of being on the front page, and it had cost her everything. She could not even enjoy the respect her colleagues would give her for getting the scoop and the headline.

Kate slapped her hand feebly against the door. "Nadine!"

A door opened behind her, and she turned, feeling as guilty as if she had been caught trying to break in. A woman, Kate had seen several times, tested to make sure her own apartment door was locked and slipped out of the foyer without glancing toward her. A heavy book bag hung from the woman's right hand, a cell phone firmly fixed between her left hand and her ear.

Kate turned back to the door and pressed her forehead against the cool, blue-painted wood. She closed her eyes and lightly slapped her palm against the doorframe. "Nadine...Nadine, open the door. Please, Nadine. I need to see you."

Poodle, the big brown mutt he had rescued from the animal shelter, stood in front of Hoagie's easy chair. The dog's club-like paws were spread, his muscles coiled; he seemed ready to spring in either direction, depending on where Hoagie went. Hoagie scratched the dog on his block-like head and shuffled his feet across the living room carpet. Poodle followed, wagging his tail and keeping his eye fixed on Hoagie's hands, probably hoping for a treat.

The gnawed- and peed-upon remains of the newspaper lay on the floor beside his easy chair. Poodle circled Hoagie and planted himself next to the paper, chuffing loudly and looking at Hoagie as if expecting a reward.

Hoagie gently pushed the dog's muzzle to one side as he dropped into his seat. "If you ate the sports section again, you're going back to the pound. And I'm tellin' them you got rabies." Poodle grunted and huffed, sending a stream of saliva onto the sleeve of Hoagie's robe. "Lovely. You big dumbass." He sighed and held the paper by its dry corners.

When it fell open, he spotted the word "lesbian" and locked onto it like a homing pigeon. "KELF...what the hell?" Seeing it was foolish to try and fold the paper to read it, he leaned forward and spread it out on the floor in front of him. Poodle, of course, rose from his haunches and moved to piddle on the laid-out paper as he had been trained. Hoagie pushed the dog away again and tried to read the truly yellow journalism. "Lesbian, popular radio disc jockey came...Nadine...? Nadine!" He rubbed his beard-stubbled chin and leaned back in his chair.

Nadine was a lesbo? Holy shit! He rubbed his stubble for a moment longer and pictured the Pixie with a certain famous actress, then chuckled to himself and bent down to read the rest of the article.

He was so engrossed that he did not notice the dog's shadow until the article was covered with another stream of urine. Hoagie groaned and shoved the dog away. Poodle whimpered and went into the kitchen.

After a shower and a twenty-minute battle with shampoo and cream rinse, Miranda came out of the bathroom with her blonde hair glistening and restored to its natural state. She combed it back out of her face and dressed in a pair of white cotton pajamas that were wonderfully soft against her skin. Finally, it felt like a brand-new day. Everything had been washed away — the Faire, the one night stand with...*God, what was her name? Jennifer? No, something...Kara?* Miranda shrugged. The name did not matter. It was over, she was clean, her hair was normal, and so was her life. She poured herself a cup of coffee and sat at the counter.

Picking up the abandoned newspaper, she scanned the articles, and her eyes were immediately drawn to the letters KELF. "Hey, front page," she said, delighted by the free publicity. The station's PR department must have been doing its job for once. She laid the paper out, folded it in half, and turned it around in her lap to read the below-the-fold article while she drank her coffee.

Miranda read halfway through the article, then the shock hit her like a sledgehammer and she felt the blood drain from her face. She spit the mouthful of coffee she had been about to swallow back into the cup as she groped for the telephone receiver. She did not have time to think about anything other than damage control; she did not have time to feel anything but numb shock. *Nadine? It can't be...*

But it was.

Eleanor Nelson felt peacock-proud on the bright winter morning. She wore her best Sunday suit, had her hair up in a lovely bun, and had even broken out her mother's favorite silver brooch as well as her "best" white hat adorned with fancy flowers. All but strutting into the Senior Ladies' Sunday School classroom, the pleated skirt of her dress flaring with each step, Eleanor let a knowing grin cross her face.

She had stayed up for hours after the meeting, detailing how she would drop the little bombshell she had been holding onto all night. "Well, ladies, I suppose we'll *all* have to be careful," she would say, cherishing her triumph at the other ladies' astonishment. "Some of *those* people are on the island...what, haven't you *heard*?"

Eleanor took her regular seat, balanced her handbag on her thighs, and was crushed when she discovered that her juicy bit of gossip had already made the rounds all over town.

One of the ladies saw Eleanor, waved a copy of the newspaper, and chirped, "Oh, El, can you *believe* it? Some of *those* people are on the island!"

Getting scooped by some nosy, blabbermouth journalist just ruined Eleanor's day.

Nadine was wide awake by the time when she heard the newspaper's delivery thump against her front door. She opened the door a crack, already crouching, and snatched up the paper as if she expected an attack. She had expended her tears and anger the night before; now she just felt numb. Nadine slammed the door, put the chain back on, and carried the newspaper to the couch. Dropping the paper on the coffee table, she stared at the exposed REGI of the paper's name for a long moment. Somewhere inside the innocuous roll of paper was the announcement she was gay, emblazoned there for the whole world to see. She would have felt less exposed if pictures of her in the nude had been printed on the front page. Her stomach churned.

She finally picked it up and searched through the pages for Kate's column. It was not in its accustomed place. Confused, Nadine closed the paper, and a headline on the front page caught her eye. *Lesbian. Nadine Butler. KELF.* The byline was Kate Price.

"Damn you, Kate," Nadine shouted. She tore several pages free and ripped them in half, throwing the ripped pieces on the floor. Her rage was not lessened a whit by the fact that the pieces of newsprint fluttered soundlessly to her feet instead of making a satisfactory bang, thud, or screech. She stared at the mess and sank back into the couch cushions, weary and trembling in every limb. She still felt sick to her stomach, and her eyes were burning with tears.

Nadine kicked aside the page that had landed on her left foot and went into the bathroom. Turning on the faucets, she stood by the tub to undress. When she was naked, she climbed into the tub despite the fact it was only half-full and sat down with a small splash. The water rose over her stomach. She sank lower until she felt the wetness slip like a gloved hand over her breasts. *The breasts Kate had licked and nibbled less than twelve hours ago*, she thought bitterly. *My lover. Hah!*

She reached up and stopped the faucet before the tub overflowed and lay back, letting her body go weightless. Her head and shoulders were the only thing above water. She contemplated sinking down completely to see how long she could hold her breath. To watch bubbles rise from her tear ducts. Crying air, she used to call it when she was a kid.

From the front of the apartment, Nadine heard Kate pounding on the front door and pleading to be let in. She thought about plugging her ears, but instead pulled her glasses off and laid them on the edge of the tub. Taking a deep breath, she lifted her feet from the opposite end of the tub and slowly sank under the water.

The sound of Kate's pleas faded into a hollow throbbing noise. The world transformed into a weepy blue haze. She tried to ignore everything — her thoughts, the chill of the water, and the unmistakable sound of Kate still calling from the front door. The world outside ceased to exist, and she was at peace for the first time since last night. She focused on the quicksilver bubbles rising up from either side of her nose.

Crying air.

Kate sat with her back against Nadine's apartment door, her hands clasped behind her neck and her head bowed. She was waiting, half-hoping, for the door behind her to open and send her sprawling. It was the least she deserved for what she had done. She had privately admitted that she could not blame anyone else for what had happened; the blame rested solely with her. While she did not think she stood a chance at salvaging their relationship, not now, Nadine deserved at least an apology. When she heard footsteps in the foyer, she assumed it was the student across the hall returning for something and did not bother looking. The footsteps paused directly in front of her, and a woman's voice said, "Oh."

Kate glanced up. A blonde woman was standing just inside the front door of the building, pulling off her sunglasses and looking down at her. Kate cleared her throat and asked, "Can I help you?"

"My name is Miranda Powell. I'm..."

"Nadine's boss," Kate said. She pushed herself to her feet, brushing off her rear end with one hand while offering the other to Miranda. "I'm Kate Price, the..."

"The reporter," Miranda said.

The way she said the word left no doubt in Kate's mind that the woman had seen the article. She blushed and looked away, ashamed that she was already notorious.

Miranda glanced at the door. "Is Nadine home?"

"If she is, she's not answering for me. Not that I blame her." Kate forced herself to smile at Miranda. "You're more than welcome to try. I have to go to work."

"You're going in to the paper?"

"Yeah. I have to. It's my job," Kate said. She looked up and met Miranda's gaze. She had put all her explanations and excuses into those three words, and she hoped Miranda was smart enough to pick up on it. "It's my job," Kate repeated. She finally stepped to one side. "Well, I...I don't know if she'll answer you, but I think you'd probably have a better shot if I'm not here. It was nice meeting you, Ms. Powell."

Kate stepped around Miranda and left the foyer. As the front door swung closed, Kate glanced back at the tall, beautiful blonde who had been Nadine's boss for the past five years. Her initial thought was, *why didn't Nadine ever mention how gorgeous she is?* This was quickly followed by the realization of why Nadine had never brought up her gorgeous boss. Nadine had a tendency to shut up when she was worried about Kate getting jealous of someone. The fact that she had never said anything was a clue to how Nadine felt about the woman.

Kate smiled ruefully and headed for her car. "Yeah," she whispered. "I bet you *will* have better luck than I did, Miranda Powell."

That woman is Nadine's girlfriend, flashed through Miranda's mind before she could silence it. She did not know what it was, but something about Kate's expression and the way she had been standing against the door made her realize the woman was more than a casual visitor. Kate Price — the writer of the wretched column — was gorgeous, even dressed as she was in sweats and without a trace of make-up. The woman possessed thin, high cheekbones that most women would kill for. Her luscious, dark hair was pulled back in a loose ponytail. Kate's hazel eyes, on the verge of tears, had flashed in the dim light of the foyer, and Miranda wondered how beautiful they would have been under normal circumstances.

Miranda hesitantly knocked on Nadine's apartment door and listened for sounds of movement within. "Nadine? It's Miranda Powell," she called. "Are you in there? We need to talk." She waited for a reply, then added on impulse, "Kate isn't here."

There was a pause and finally, she heard the click of a latch. The door swung open wide enough for Nadine to peek through. Miranda tried to give the woman a reassuring smile, not sure how well she was succeeding. The door closed, and Miranda heard the rasp of a security chain being disengaged. When the door opened again, the crack was just barely wide enough for Miranda to slip inside.

"Come in," Nadine urged. "Hurry."

Miranda slipped inside the gloomy apartment and heard the door slam shut behind her and the rattle of the chain. Nadine stepped into view. She was wrapped in a robe big enough to dwarf her and make her seem ten years younger, a little girl looking so lost, Miranda ached for her. Nadine's hair was still wet from a shower or bath, and she was trembling. The fact that she was not wearing her glasses added to the semblance of youth. Miranda had never seen her without them. It was as shocking as if she had answered the door completely naked.

Nadine went to the couch and began clearing debris from the cushions. Miranda ignored the destroyed morning edition of the newspaper on the floor.

"Sorry about the mess," Nadine said, sighing. She tucked a wet strand of hair behind her ear, started to sit down, and glanced at Miranda. "I take it you read the article."

"Yeah. I have to say I was...I was kind of shocked by it," Miranda replied. It felt odd being in Nadine's apartment like this, under these circumstances, especially seeing the normally effervescent Nadine Butler in her pajamas, cowering on the couch.

"*You* were?" Nadine scoffed. She took a seat and pressed her robe between her knees.

Miranda sat on the opposite side of the couch and was about to ask how it had happened when Nadine started speaking. She explained the entire thing, how she had let the wrong words slip and how she had been in a daze ever since. She concluded with, "I suppose you've been talking with Mr. Dugan..."

Miranda shrugged. That had been a memorable phone call. "He's not happy, but he can't exactly fire you just because you're a lesbian. It doesn't affect your work." Nadine nodded, looking ever-so-slightly relieved. Miranda went on, "You'll have to be on eggshells for a while, but..." She chewed her bottom lip. "It's a small town, Dean. It seems like the end of the world now, but in two weeks someone will find a bottle of Viagra in Sheriff Rucker's desk drawer and your sexual preference will be yesterday's news. I just wanted to stop by and make sure you knew that nothing was going to change at the station."

Nadine nodded again, appearing grateful. "Thanks. Thank you, Miranda." She looked like she was about to cry, and Miranda looked away, searching for a change of topic.

"So, this is your place..." Miranda murmured.

"Don't get jealous, I'm not interested in selling," Nadine said, giving her the tiniest smile.

Miranda said, returning the smile, "Well, I'm not going to force you if you don't want to leave."

Nadine's eyes suddenly widened and she blurted, "Oh, God! The...the Squire Days! I'm supposed to broadcast from..." There was a terrified expression on her face. "I can't. Miranda, please, tell me I don't..."

"It's okay," Miranda interrupted. "I figured you wouldn't be up to it, so I asked Ben to cover you."

Nadine exhaled and pushed her hair back, sleeking the damp mass with her palms.

Miranda lifted a hand to touch Nadine's cheek, but unsure whether the gesture was appropriate or would even be welcome, let the hand drop back into her lap. "I should probably go..."

"Right. Of course." Nadine stood up. "Th-thank you for coming by to make sure I was..."

"Sure, sure."

They went to the door, Miranda trailing slightly behind Nadine. Before Nadine disengaged the locks, she turned and suddenly wrapped her arms around Miranda. Unsure what the proper etiquette was for such situations, Miranda patted Nadine on the back and waited for the hug to end. This close, Nadine smelled like soap and water...*which isn't sexy at all, right?* Of course, she could not help noticing the press of body against body and the realization Nadine was almost definitely not wearing anything under that awful robe.

Miranda mentally kicked herself. *God, I've really been leaning on the "she wouldn't be receptive" excuse for ages. Now that I know she might be receptive, it's like I got the rug pulled out from under me.*

Nadine retreated before Miranda's thoughts could go any further, swiping at her eyes with both hands. "Ugh, look at me." She sniffled and regained her composure. "Thank you for coming by, Miranda. No matter what else happens, I'll...I'll remember that you were kind to me."

Miranda nodded and waited while the locks and chain were pulled back. She stepped into the foyer and turned back to say, "Don't worry, Nadine. I'm sure everything will work out fine. Just you wait."

Nadine nodded but was obviously unconvinced. "Thanks," she said. "Thanks for trying to make me feel better."

The door closed, and Miranda was left alone in the foyer. She was still shocked at seeing Nadine look so defeated. It was like being with her best friend after a break-up. She squared her shoulders, determined to do whatever she could to get the old Nadine back.

Miranda went into the office, a rarity on Sundays, but she knew she would have to field a million calls. Right after the article hit the streets, everyone she met and talked to seemed to be in a state of shock. Miranda got the impression that no one dared come out too strongly for either side. If they defended Nadine too strongly, suspicions would begin to rise that they themselves were gay, but if they demonized her, they were worried about being slapped with the labels of intolerant and homophobic.

A few people did raise their voices without caring what anyone else thought. Eleanor Nelson called in around noon — after church let out, Miranda assumed — and demanded the station take Nadine off the air immediately. The woman admitted to investigating whether they could legally kick Nadine off the island entirely. "I mean," she huffed during the call, "there *must* be some kind of provision in the island charter..."

Miranda called Sheriff Rucker at once to let him know Eleanor Nelson was causing a stink. He assured her that he had gotten quite a few calls from the woman himself and promised to do his best to use any "exile clause" he found to get rid of Eleanor herself.

The majority of her day was spent on the phone with Thomas Dugan, defending Nadine and her own choice to keep the station's most popular DJ on staff. Dugan told her that he owned the station and could fire them both if necessary. She reminded him that Nadine could sue him for wrongful termination and end up with a considerable settlement. That was enough to cause a quiver in the man's miserly heart. A lot of posturing and a lot of threats later, Dugan finally relented and "decided" to let Nadine stay on for the time being.

Miranda actually had to thank him before she hung up, then resisted the urge to take another shower. Speaking with Thomas Dugan felt dirtier than sleeping with a ditzy twenty-year-old whose name she could not even remember. *No, wait, the girl's name was Jessica.* She rubbed her throbbing forehead and decided the time had come to stop drinking at Squire Days.

Every customer who came into Butler Photography received the same speech.

Nathaniel Butler told everyone who would listen that he didn't know what had happened to his daughter, but he assured them that it was nothing he had done. If anything, he had tried to make sure she stayed on the right path, not that she'd listened, not that any kid ever did. If his wife had not been standing next to him, he most likely would have denied being related to her at all.

Tamara, on the other hand, kept her back to the main area of the store so the customers would not notice she was crying.

Kate sat at her desk at the *Register* and half-heartedly accepted congratulations from her co-workers. She felt sleazy, like the worst sort of bottom-feeding fraud. She would have felt less like a fool if she had plagiarized the article that was getting so much praise, but no. She could only blame herself for those words. She could only point the finger in her own face.

She remained at her desk as long as she could stand it before she headed home. She had not written a word, but that was all right. Her next damning article wasn't due until Wednesday. She had two whole days to think of someone else's life to destroy.

At eight p.m., Kate resumed her vigil outside Nadine's apartment door. She left at ten o'clock, dragging her exhausted body up the stairs and into bed. Despite her weariness, she could not fall asleep.

Oh, Nadine...

Nadine spent the night in the bathtub. Not taking a bath — she did not bother filling the tub with water — but just lying there on the cool porcelain surface, staring at the white tiled wall. She did not want to think. She did not want to make a decision or speak lest some other secret come out.

"Hello, how are you today," went the imaginary conversation, "I'm doing fine, like I was the day I stole ten dollars from my mom's purse when I was seven."

She was scared to move, scared to speak, scared to think.

Nadine remained in the empty tub, curled up her legs, and eventually fell into a troubled sleep.

Chapter Six

A crick in her neck woke Nadine on Monday morning. She sat up stiffly and rubbed the soreness in her neck away, searched for her glasses, and checked the clock on the wall. It was close to eight o'clock. Standing up and stretching, she groaned as her bones popped loudly. After undressing, she dumped her clothes on the closed toilet seat, pulled back the shower curtain, and turned on the water.

Nadine stood under the spray, letting the cold water assault her face and turn her body as numb as her mind. She opened and closed her mouth several times, ran her hands through her hair without bothering to shampoo it, and finally turned off the shower when her fingertips had turned to prunes. Leaving her dirty clothes in the bathroom, she walked dripping into the bedroom where she and Kate had so recently made love. Was it for the last time? She did not want to face such depressing thoughts now, when her outlook was already dim.

She pushed thoughts of Kate out of her mind and opened her closet. Miranda had rescued her from working Squire Days, but she still had to do her regular radio show. Nadine dressed in a pair of old jeans and a ragged Dash Warren concert T-shirt, then went to the living room and hazarded a peek through the blinds. There were no reporters in the courtyard — Kate had already said everything they needed, she supposed — and there were no pro-testers marching back and forth in the street. If she did not know better, she would have said it was a normal day. Nadine released the blinds and stepped back. *Okay. Maybe it isn't as bad as I thought. It's a tempest in a teapot, already blown over, yesterday's news.*

She sighed and went to the door. Maybe everything would be all right after all.

As she started to leave the apartment, Nadine became aware of an incon-gruous flash of white in the corner of her eye. The front of her door, once a solid, beautiful royal blue, was now marred by bold, angry-seeming strokes of white paint.

DIKE

Four letters stretching from one side of the door to the other, huddled tightly together to cram the misspelled word onto the available space. She stared at her vandalized door for a moment, her trembling hand on the door-knob, and felt something twist inside of her. It was indignation, it was frustra-tion, and most of all it was fury at the fact that someone had defaced her home. This was the first place she had lived by herself, the first place she paid for herself, and some ignorant, hate-mongering coward had violated it.

Had violated her.

She took a deep breath, held it until her composure was slightly restored, and finally stepped out into the foyer. Forcing herself to close the door quietly instead of slamming it shut, Nadine stepped away without looking at the hateful graffiti. She walked out of the foyer's back door and toward the complex's swimming pool.

The pool had been closed up for the winter behind a low black fence whose gate was latched with a heavy padlock. Rather than circling the entire perimeter of the fence, she stepped onto a brick ledge and jumped over. She rounded the lip of the pool and glanced down at the thin layer of half-frozen, scummy water at the bottom.

She remembered a day last summer — it had to have been ninety degrees — when she and Kate had taken advantage of the pool to cool off. Her memory provided a vision of crystal-clear water, bright sun, and playing Marco Polo, splashing each other with the sun beating down on their bare shoulders. There had been a lull in their play, no one else in the pool, and no one else in the courtyard, and Kate had kissed her. That day had been so perfect — the water, the sky, the heat on her face and the chill on her toes, and a slippery-wet Kate in her arms. Now the sky was gray, the wind was howling, and the pool was filled with black grime and piles of trash that had accumulated in the far corners. She shuddered at how quickly things could change and jumped over the other side of the fence.

The manager's office was a small brick building at the back of the complex. Nadine followed the concrete path and knocked lightly on the door. Through the half-circle of glass set at eye level, she could see the large, hennaed, teased-to-towering mass of Miss Wozniak's hair as it bobbed behind her desk.

The door swung open, revealing an elderly Jewish woman peering at her. Miss Wozniak, the landlady, was wearing her typical outfit, consisting of a red vest, red trousers, and a floral blouse with a flared collar. The woman lifted the glasses that hung on a chain around her neck, aimed the frames in Nadine's direction, and tutted in recognition before stepping aside and wandering back into the office.

"You want something?" Miss Wozniak asked over her shoulder. "People always want something if they come here before rent time. Never early, not with their rent checks."

Nadine cleared her throat and stepped into the peppermint-scented office. A pegboard covered with a second skin of notices and Post-its decorated the wall directly in front of the door. The desk held a computer, but the typewriter was front and center, obviously where the landlady pounded out all of her TO THE RESIDENTS notices. Nadine said, "Miss Wozniak, I was...wondering if, uh..."

"All day, the girl thinks she has." Miss Wozniak rounded the back of her desk and leaned forward. She cocked her hip and made a "get on with it" motion with one hand.

Nadine was not sure if Miss Wozniak had seen the newspaper or, if she had, what her reaction would be. She chose her words carefully when she finally spoke. "When Mr. Alonzo painted the doors last year...d-do you think he still has some of that paint left over?"

"You chip the door or something? Kick it in?"

"No," Nadine said. "It was...it was vandalized."

Miss Wozniak sighed, put a hand to her forehead, and uttered a string of words in what sounded like Yiddish. She turned around and waddled back to her desk. "Little *pupiks*. Ought to be strung up by their toes and hit with sticks. Like that piñata," she said, squinting at Nadine. "Are you Mexican? Gonna be offended about piñata?"

"No," Nadine said. "N-no, I'd...trust me, I'd be the first one in line with the stick."

Miss Wozniak nodded and clapped her hands together. "Okay. I'm going to fill out a work order for you..."

"No, that's..." Nadine cleared her throat. She stood up straight, kept her jaw tight and her voice steady. "If I could just get a can of paint from the custodian's shack, I'd rather do it myself."

The woman looked at Nadine over the top of her glasses. "You don't have to, dear. Custodial work is part of what you're paying for with your rent, you know."

Nadine nodded. "I know." The truth was, the thought of Mr. Alonzo seeing that word on her door... "I know. I don't mind doing it myself."

Miss Wozniak held up her hands in a gesture of surrender and said, "All right. Okay. You want to save me having to call Alonzo, fine by me." She opened the drawer and withdrew a key ring. "The paint cans are on the bottom shelf. Royal blue, but yeah, you know, you know."

Nadine had to step forward to retrieve the key. She glanced down and saw the Sunday paper on Miss Wozniak's blotter, the pages open to the crossword puzzle. The puzzle was in the back of the paper, but of course the woman had to have seen the front page headline. Dread rose within her, choking any comment she might have made.

Miss Wozniak followed her gaze and made a rude noise in the back of her throat. "Wouldn't line the bird's cage with that trash," she said as she thrust the keys into Nadine's hand. "Don't pay any attention to them people, none at all. Useless is what those people are, just useless." She closed Nadine's fingers around the keys, and her voice softened. "Go take care of your door, dear."

"Thank you," Nadine said quietly. "I'll bring the keys and the paint back when I'm done."

"Good, good." Miss Wozniak moved to sit down, and Nadine headed for the door. She was about to leave the office when the woman suddenly added, "My daughter is gay, you know."

Nadine turned, her eyes going wide. "W-what? You...you have a daughter, *Miss* Wozniak?"

Miss Wozniak smiled coyly but did not offer an explanation for her unlikely motherhood. "My daughter. Lovely girl. Gay." Miss Wozniak made air quotes with her fingers and said, "I think they say she's one of those 'lipstick lesbians'. Very attractive. I'm just saying." She shook her head.

"Does she...does your daughter live on the island?" Nadine asked before she could stop herself.

"Alaska. Just around the corner, dear! Think about it! I'm not saying you have to marry her, but I would never charge my own daughter rent, wink-wink." Miss Wozniak leaned back in her chair and flapped her hand. "Go! Paint your door!"

Nadine left the manager's office and closed the door behind her. Alone on the walkway, she actually surprised herself by laughing at what had just happened. Spray-painting hooligans aside, she would at least be able to look back fondly on Miss Wozniak trying to hook her up with her daughter.

She crossed the lawn to the tiny custodial shack and found the appropriate key on the ring. Inside, behind a sea of cobwebs and a stack of unused sheetrock scraps, she found a can of royal blue paint. On a second, higher shelf she found some paintbrushes that were not stiff as a board and stuck one into the back pocket of her jeans.

Nadine stopped at the office to drop off the key and had to accept Amanda Wozniak's telephone number — "Just in case!" — before the landlady let her leave. She was still chuckling when she walked back into the foyer and continued to her apartment, gazing at the scrap of paper with a telephone number scrawled across it.

When she glanced up, Nadine realized that her door had not gone unnoticed. Kate was standing there like a sentry, her hands clenched into fists. Nadine was about to back away and put off a confrontation, but she decided she would have to face Kate sooner or later. She put the paint can down and said, "Nice, huh?"

Kate's shoulders jumped slightly at the sound of her voice, but she did not turn around.

Nadine put down the paint can, crossed her arms over her chest, and said, "D-I-K-E. You'd think if someone had managed to go this far with their hate, they'd at least bother to learn the correct spelling." Kate still did not answer, so Nadine continued, "I only got one paintbrush from the shed, but you're welcome to lend a hand." She stepped next to Kate and finally looked at her. She was shocked to see tears flowing down Kate's cheeks; the woman's face was red with rage. "Kate...?" Nadine asked hesitantly.

Kate finally looked into her face. The woman's eyes were wide and haunted with some emotion that Nadine could not read, but which tightened her gut anyway. Kate shook her head and said, "I'm so, so sorry, Nadine. I'm...I'm sorry." She pushed Nadine aside and ran up the stairs to her apartment.

Nadine watched her go, unable to speak, and winced when she heard Kate's door slam shut.

Part of her wanted to run upstairs, grab Kate, and hold her, but another, bigger part of her was glad that Kate was suffering, too, after that damned article. Nadine sighed and knelt down to pop open the lid on the paint can. *Let her suffer alone for a while*, she decided. She dipped the brush into the paint can, took a last look at the word scrawled on her front door, and went to work eliminating it.

Miranda had not gotten any sleep Sunday night. She thought the calls would stop when she went home, but Thomas Dugan started calling her at home to yell some more. She had repeated herself so often, her mouth began automatically forming the shape of the answer before the question was asked. No, she hadn't known Nadine was gay. No, she didn't think it should have any bearing on her job. Yes, she knew what the public reaction would be. No, she didn't think she would reconsider.

The hardest part of the situation was dealing with the other DJs. Willa Lamb — a strong believer and churchgoer — found the whole thing scandalous, but promised not to say anything on the air against Nadine. Miranda thought it was important that the station present a united public front and thankfully, Willa agreed. She had not, however, agreed to show the same courtesy off the air and told Miranda she would be first in line to sign a petition asking Nadine to be removed.

Hoagie, the one Miranda was the most concerned about, seemed uncomfortable but willing to go along with a show of support. He hesitantly asked if he needed to act differently around Nadine, but Miranda assured him there would be no call for that. By the time seven o'clock Monday morning rolled around, she had already been up for two and a half hours fielding more calls. She changed into a fresh outfit and headed out to her car.

Work, Miranda thought, *where a thousand memos are probably awaiting a return call.* She sat behind the wheel of her car for a moment and took a deep breath, letting it out slowly and trying to calm her thumping heartbeat.

She would have to be an idiot not to realize the irony. Here she was, in the middle of a maelstrom of words like lesbian and scandal and homophobia when there had been nights when she had woken up screaming from nightmares about this exact situation. However, that had been about herself, her own sexuality exposed, leaving her vulnerable. The fact that the shit-storm was all coming down on Nadine Butler...poor, sweet Nadine, who had never hurt anyone in her life...it seemed so unfair.

Staring at the trellis that marked the end of her driveway, she made a decision. As long as she was in charge, no one was going to turn against Nadine.

If anyone on the island wanted to stop listening to KELF...well, Miranda had never forced them to tune in anyway. The station would survive losing a few homophobic listeners. There were always the tourists, a steady stream of new listeners who arrived fresh and unsullied every afternoon, eager to hear about local news and happenings. Most of the station's bigger advertisers catered to the tourist trade — KELF's strongest target demographic group — and she doubted they would be quick to pull their marketing campaigns. They might squawk, but business was business as long as the station's ratings did not drop. She made a mental note to have the PR department work on a reassuring message for their advertisers, reminding them of KELF's market-wide audience numbers.

She thought about the newspaper, too. If one article could cause such a problem, maybe another could be the solution. She knew some reporters in

Seattle who might be willing to do a human-interest piece on Nadine. Being fired for her sexual orientation would probably be enough to cause the gay interest groups to make some noise. There was no reason Nadine should have to fight this battle all by herself.

Her mind made up, Miranda checked her rear view mirror and finally backed out of the driveway. It felt like she was being spared her worst nightmare only because someone else — someone she truly cared about — was taking the bullet for her. The least she could do was catch some of the shrapnel.

Nadine's T-shirt and jeans were speckled with blue paint by the time the offensive four letters had been obliterated. She gave the door an extra coat of paint just to be sure the graffiti would not bleed through before sealing up the can. She hesitated, biting her lip, and finally trudged up the stairs, feeling like a kid being sent to bed without supper. She did not want to ask for a favor from Kate, but at the moment she had no other options.

Reaching the top of the stairs, she stared at the gold number five on the door and finally took the last step forward. She knocked lightly just under the peephole, then stepped back so Kate could see her.

After a short delay, the door swung open, and Kate was there, silhouetted against the interior of her darkened apartment. Nadine looked down and spoke to Kate's sneakers. "I was wondering if I could borrow your car because I'm not really looking forward to riding my bike across town with everyone...staring at me and...if you don't want me to, that's fine, I can..."

"Here," Kate said.

Nadine glanced up and saw the keys dangling from Kate's hand. She took them, looking into Kate's red-rimmed eyes. She wanted to say something, but the words remained stubbornly stuck in her throat.

Kate said, "Dean, you have to understand. I had to say *something*. It was news. I'm a reporter. If I'd ignored it, I would have lost my job. Do you realize the position I was in? You have to understand I was between a rock and a hard place."

Nadine chose her words carefully. "I know you'd never have done that to me willingly, but my worst nightmare has your byline underneath it. I can't think past that right now. I'm sorry, Kate."

Kate nodded and leaned against the door. "Have a good day, Nadine."

"You, too," Nadine murmured. She turned and practically flew down the stairs, eager to get outside before she allowed the tears to fall. Walking through the courtyard, past her mulched flowerbeds, she brought her hand up to wipe the wetness from her cheeks.

She found Kate's car in the parking lot that ran alongside the apartment building. She got in, took a moment to familiarize herself with the set-up, and started the engine. The radio came to life, tuned to KELF. Willa Lamb's voice came from the speakers. "...another call. You're on with Willa and Simon."

"Yeah, I just wanna say I think this Pixie thing is sick," a man's voice said. "I'll tell ya another thing, I'm turning the radio off when you guys leave, and I ain't turning it back on until Hoagie comes on. That's what I wanna say."

"That's wonderful," Willa said flatly, without a hint of emotion in her voice. "Could we play a song for you?"

"Yeah, could I hear—"

"No," Willa said. She disconnected the call and sighed. "How many different ways can we say it, Simon? Nadine Butler is not here right now. She cannot respond to any of your complaints, and I'm getting sick of talking about her. Can we *please* focus on something else? The weather? The ferry schedule? Anything. Please. Okay, next caller..."

Nadine punched the radio button angrily and silenced her co-worker's voice. *Great.* She wondered how she would get through a six-hour shift — a show that dealt mostly with called-in requests — without going completely bonkers. She started the engine and drove out of the parking lot, forcing her mind to focus on the road, the other drivers, everything that she could mostly ignore when she was on her bicycle.

As she turned toward the radio station's building, she was shocked to see a crowd of a dozen or so people milling around on the sidewalk. The few who were carrying signs were resting them against their legs, apparently waiting until she showed up to wave them. They seemed to be congregating around the bicycle rack, so she managed to slip her borrowed car past them without causing any alarm or uproar. As she drove by, she spotted Miranda standing at the front door. Their gazes locked. She continued past, and Miranda started down the sidewalk in pursuit, evading the crowd. Nadine pulled Kate's car into the parking garage next to the station, driving up the gentle slope to the second level before she climbed out.

Miranda caught up with her a few moments later and said, "Nadine. Are you sure you want to come in today? We'd certainly..."

"I'm not going to let them run me off, Miranda," Nadine interrupted. She had already lost one day hiding, and she was not about to make it a habit. "So I'll stick to the play list for once. I'm fine. Trust me."

"Okay," Miranda said. She looked over her shoulder, apparently to make sure she had not been followed. "Okay, come on. There's a back door you can use to get inside." She put her hand on Nadine's shoulder and shuffled her off toward the back of the station.

"Who are those people?" Nadine asked.

"'Concerned citizens' from the local churches," Miranda replied, her voice dripping scorn. "They showed up about half an hour ago, waiting for you to come to work."

"You...don't think they would have..."

"Hurt you?" Miranda said. "No. They seemed like they would've been happy to just yell and wave their signs in your face if you'd shown up."

"No, I mean, do you think they would have painted something on my door?"

Miranda stopped and turned Nadine to face her. "What are you talking about?"

"It's nothing. When I woke up this morning, there was...a word...painted on my door."

"I hate to guess."

Nadine winced and glanced away. She discovered she was ashamed to admit to Miranda what had happened. She went on regardless, "Dyke. Misspelled, of course."

"Yeah, well, ignorance is all-encompassing."

Nadine had to smile at the pithy comment and waited for Miranda to unlock the back door of the station. She frowned after a moment and asked, "Isn't this the emergency exit?"

Miranda pushed the door open and shrugged. "If this doesn't count as an emergency, what does?"

Nadine stepped into a short, dark hallway. The air was warm here, much warmer than outside. Miranda locked the door behind them; Nadine supposed this was in case any enterprising protester realized where they had gotten in.

"Getting you out will be the real problem," Miranda said. "If they were coordinated to be here right when your show was set to begin, they have to know when it ends. You may have to stay in the building until they give up and go home."

"Great," Nadine murmured, resigned to her fate. "A prisoner in my own workplace."

"Hey, you have a desk. At least you'll finally get to use it."

Nadine rolled her eyes, and they walked into the bullpen. Willa and Simon were already leaving the booth, their good-bye playing from speakers in the ceiling, and the first batch of songs had been set to play while Nadine got situated. They paused at the door with their coats draped over their arms, watching with guarded expressions as she walked down the row of cubicles and offered them a weak smile.

"Hey, guys," Nadine said. "Willa, thanks for not letting that caller—"

"The calls were interrupting my show," Willa broke in coldly. "I, for one, wouldn't care if they ran you out of town on the next ferry." She turned and walked to the stairs. Simon watched her go, looked at Miranda and Nadine, and merely shrugged. He waved good-bye as he headed to the ground floor behind his co-host.

Nadine closed her eyes, trying to hide the hurt that Willa's cutting remark had inflicted.

Miranda touched her shoulder and said, "Nadine, have you ever heard Simon speak when he was off the air?"

Nadine blinked and looked up. The question seemed apropos of nothing. "What? Sure, he...he's talked to me..." She frowned, her voice trailing off as she looked at the man's retreating back. "You know, I don't think I can remember a time when he did. You hired him. He must have spoken in the interview."

Miranda shook her head. "I read his résumé, and I hired him from a tape. You know, the more I think about it, the more I think I have never heard him speak in person."

Nadine suddenly realized what Miranda was doing. She smiled and put her hand on Miranda's arm. "Thank you."

"For what?"

"I didn't think about being a pariah for a whole five seconds. Thank you."

Miranda returned her smile and said, "It was entirely self-serving. I don't know what song Willa and Simon started, so you might be giving me dead air right now. Go. Get in the booth. Get to work."

Nadine offered a mock salute and headed for the booth. She knew Miranda was in her corner. For now, for the next couple of hours, she could pretend it was a normal day, the stresses from the weekend rising from her shoulders and leaving her spirits a little lighter as she opened the booth. From the small speakers over the door, she could hear playing *A Day in the Life* by the Beatles. Pausing before entering, she glanced around until she spotted Billy by the water cooler.

"Billy," she said, desperate for a bit of normalcy in her day, pleading in her head for him to be the same sweet Billy with the encyclopedic time-clock in his head. "How much longer on this song?"

He glanced toward the ceiling and said, "Total run-time, 5:33. Or infinite."

She frowned in puzzlement. "Infinite?"

"Auto-return mechanism on vinyl records," he explained. "But since this is a CD, I reckon you got about two minutes left, easy."

She felt a surge of warmth in her chest and smiled gratefully at him. "Thank you, Billy. It means a lot."

"What does?" he said. The tone of his voice told her he was truly clueless.

Nadine struggled for a way to explain the situation as concisely as possible and finally gave up, saying, "For treating me like...well, like me."

He looked at her like she had gone crazy. "Who else would I treat you like?"

It suddenly dawned on her that Billy was homeless or had been the last time she had bothered to check. "Billy, ah...did you read the Sunday paper?"

"I read the funny pages," Billy said as he went back to work. "Nothing else in that paper is worth paying attention to."

Point taken, Nadine thought. "Well," she said, "thank you, Billy."

"One minute left," he said as he resumed sweeping.

She nodded and opened the door to the booth, hesitating when she heard his voice behind her.

"You saw me for me first," he said.

"What was that?"

His hands wrapped tightly around his broom, his shoulders hunched as if he were trying to hide behind it. "You saw me. Not a homeless guy. You saw me. I see you." He finally glanced up and nodded at her.

Nadine smiled, but there were tears in her eyes. She was touched by his show of solidarity. "Thank you, Billy."

Moving into the booth and shutting the door, she wiped her eyes, and she lowered herself into the seat. She sniffled, cleared her throat, and picked up the headphones. There was a brief hesitation as she turned her gaze toward the harbor visible through the window. She knew, although she could not see them, that the picketers were still down there. They would be there when she left for home, and they would be there every damn day until they got to shake their fists in her face, but she had the whole day ahead of her. She was not going to spend it worrying about what might happen when her shift ended, not when she had Miranda and Billy supporting her.

Nadine finally put on the headphones and rested her finger on the microphone button. Closing her eyes, she took a deep breath and finally switched the mic on. She leaned in and said, "Hello, Squire's Isle. This is Nadine Butler, the KELF Pixie, and...well, let's be honest, you more than likely have heard a lot about me this weekend. I don't want to talk about that. What I want to talk about is music. Bob Dylan, the Bee Gees, the Beach Boys, and a lot more. Call in with your requests, and I'll do my best to get it on the air for you. This is KELF AM 1220."

She sagged back in her chair and sent the show to the first scheduled commercial. As the chair swung to one side, she saw Miranda standing in the window watching her. They smiled at one another, and Miranda gave her a thumbs-up. Nadine crossed her fingers. As soon as she had started speaking into the microphone, it was like coming home again. All her confidence, her self-esteem, had come rushing back into her. Now all she had to do was keep it up for the rest of the day.

"KELF, this is the Pixie," Nadine said into the mic.

"Could you play *Leaving on a Jet Plane* by John Denver?" asked the male caller.

"We've got the Peter, Paul and Mary version."

"Oh, okay, that's cool. As long as it's the song, it's all right."

"All right. What's your name?"

"Al."

"Can I call you Al?" she asked. There was no response. "Sorry, Paul Simon humor," she added quickly. "I'll get that on for you as soon as possible. Thanks for calling."

"This is the Pixie, thanks for calling. What can I play for you?"

"Like your paint job, dyke?"

"Ah, I'm assuming since you can use a telephone that you're not a monkey."

"Huh?"

"You misspelled it, you hooligan. Dyke has a 'y' in it."

"I...I guess you'd know..."

"Yeah, yeah. Hope you washed your hands real good when you vandalized my apartment, Mr. Nelson."

"What?"

"The station has Caller ID. Your mother Eleanor will be proud of you, I'm sure. I'm just sorry for Sheriff Rucker that he has to pay her a visit now on account of her law-breaking son. Hello? Mr. Nelson?" Nadine smiled grimly. "Guess there's nothing he wanted me to play, folks."

"Hi, you're on with the Pixie. What can I play for you?"

"Can you play *God Knows I'm Good* by David Bowie?" asked the female caller.

"Oh, I'm not sure we have that one," Nadine replied.

She scanned the stack of CDs, freezing when the caller went on, "You should listen to it sometime. God knows you're good, you can be cured by God if you pray..."

"Next caller," Nadine said, punching the phone line button to cut off the call.

"Hi, what can I play for you?"

"*American Woman* by The Who," the male caller said.

Nadine hoped there wasn't going to be a punch line at her expense. "All right, I'll get that on for you. What's your name?"

"Kevin."

"All right, Kevin. Keep listening and I'll get that on for you in the next half hour."

"You're on KELF with—"

"Homos burn in hell!" was shouted and followed immediately by a dial tone.

Nadine swallowed the bitterness that flooded her mouth and instead of a curse, muttered, "Well, at least let me finish my sentence..."

"Hi, you're on KELF with the Pixie."

"Hi. I just came over on the ferry, and I was wondering what the hell was going on. What's with these crazy calls you've been getting?"

"Hazards of the job, ma'am. What can I play for you?"

"Do you have *Whiter Shade of Pale*?"

"We do, we do indeed. I'd be happy to play it for you. What's your name?"

Nadine rubbed the back of her aching neck and leaned back in the chair. She had made it through the all-request portion of the show with only a handful of obscene or harassing phone calls. The phone numbers of those callers had been written down from the Caller ID and transferred to a memo that she planned to send to the Sheriff's Office at the end of the day. The list was not incredibly short, but it was nowhere near as depressing as she thought it could have been.

In fact, the turnout had been so good that she was debating whether or not to start a new contest. Nadine rolled her desk over to the drawer that held their vouchers for free dinners, pulled the drawer out, and rifled through, looking for something besides the stack of *Dinner for Two at Gail's Seafood Shack* coupons. Frustrated by finding only the gold-and-brown slips, she glanced at the commercial clock — she had a bit of time — and slipped the headphones off.

Leaving the booth, she hurried down the hall to Miranda's office, knocked on the open door, and waited until Miranda looked up from whatever she was writing. When she had Miranda's attention, she held up a handful of the Gail's coupons. "Hey, I wanted to try a contest, but I gave away about a thousand of these last week," Nadine said. "We have anything different? Joe Lack's Pizza, maybe?"

Miranda scratched the bridge of her nose and glanced away. "Um, no...no vouchers from there."

"Chin's, then."

Miranda bent back over her desk. "Mmm," she hummed noncommittally.

Nadine stepped into the office and picked up the stack of flyers on the edge of Miranda's desk, flipping through them. "Well, what about these from Spartan Café?"

"No," Miranda said. She reached out and gently took the vouchers from Nadine. Straightening the stack, she replaced them before she said, "Nadine...Chin's, Spartan, Joe Lack's, they've all pulled their sponsorship of your show."

Nadine blinked, shocked. "What?"

"They don't want you giving away their coupons." Miranda gave her a sympathetic look. "They called me at home this morning, and I had to pull their vouchers. I'm really sorry, Nadine."

"Sorry. People keep saying that to me," Nadine whispered. She looked down at her hands and shook her head, feeling resentful. "No, never mind. I'll give away the Gail's coupons. I'm going to get mighty sick of seafood, though, because I'm never eating at those other places again."

"Neither will I," Miranda said solemnly. "I truly wish I could fight this, Nadine, but..."

Nadine nodded. "You have to do what you have to do. I understand." From the speaker overhead, she heard the last commercial of the current block beginning and motioned over her shoulder. "I have about thirty seconds to get back to the booth."

"Yeah. I'll put in some calls, make some requests for other things for you to give away. It's not right, Nadine."

"I know. Thank you, Miranda."

She walked back to the booth, trying hard to keep her back straight and her shoulders square. It was incredibly difficult, but she managed to keep from slumping until she dropped into her chair. Putting on her headphones on, she leaned forward against the desk.

"Hey, loyal Kay-ELF listeners, this is your Pixie and I am going to send you to dinner," she said into the mic, allowing nothing of her disappointment to bleed into her voice. "Where, you ask? The best, freshest seafood on this coast or any coast, Clifton Gail's restaurant, conveniently next to the harbor. Just call with the correct answer to our trivia question and you could be on your way to one of the best meals of your life. Now...the question today..."

Chapter Seven

Hoagie parked his 4x4 in his regular spot in the employees' lot and climbed out of the cab. On most days, he wore jeans and a T-shirt to work. Nothing fancy, but he usually maintained a semblance of professionalism. Today, he was wearing a baseball cap with the edge of the brim worn down to fringe. He had not bothered to shave and had picked his muddiest pair of hunting pants to wear. His plaid shirt was ripped and stained and both sleeves were rolled up to show he wasn't all blubber. Miranda had called and warned him of the protesters outside the door, so his plan was to put the fear of Hoagie into them.

As he rounded the corner of the building, Hoagie pulled a cigar from the pocket of his shirt and lit it up. He blew a smoke ring and grabbed the shoulder of the first person he saw. The protestor was a thin man in a green sweater carrying a placard that read: *Homosexuality is a SIN!* The man stepped aside and nearly fell over when he saw Hoagie's size. He swallowed and tried to move away, saying, "Afternoon, sir."

Hoagie held onto the man's collar. "Howdy." He hooked his thumb toward the radio station and addressed the crowd with a thick drawl. "Y'all gonna stick it to that gay lady who works in there?"

The man cleared his throat. "Y-yessir. When she comes out after her show, the plan is..."

"All right, well, make sure you save some," Hoagie said, making a predatory grin around the cigar clenched in his teeth. "Me and my buddies are gonna want our fair share. I myself want her fingers."

The man's brows knit together. "Fingers...?"

Hoagie winked and moved his cigar to the other corner of his mouth. "Mm-hmm. Yeah. Love breaking fingers. Love the sound they make."

The protester's face went pale, and the placard began to tremble. "Oh! Oh, no, we're...w-w-w-we're not planning to be violent! Oh, no, sir. No, sir. Oh, heavens." He wiped the sweat from his brow and looked frantically, apparently searching for someone to back him up. "We're simply going to...s-shout at her."

"Good!" Hoagie slapped the man on the back and almost knocked him flat. "More for me and my friends."

"Friends?"

"Yep. Big ol' boys. We're gonna show her what's what. You can't just come onto Squire's Isle and do whatever you want." Hoagie smiled and waggled his cigar. "Yeah, it's gonna be a hoot and a half." Just saying the words, pretending to be this kind of person, made him sick to his stomach, but if it scared the protesters away and cleared the way for Nadine to leave, he was willing to do the distasteful job.

The man spun around and disappeared into the crowd. Hoagie crossed his arms over his chest and leaned against the wall. Within a few minutes, the good church-going folks began to disperse. Most of the people looked at him with fear as they dropped their signs and scurried for their automobiles. Some of them pretended they had gotten tired, put their signs down, and casually strolled away.

Hoagie maintained his intimidating presence, twirling his cigar, tapping his foot as if impatiently waiting for his friends to show up and cause a ruckus. When he was finally alone on the sidewalk, he crushed the cigar under his heel and stooped to pick up the remains. He dropped it into a squat trash bin that had a plaque on the side which read, KEEP THE STREETS OF DECEMBER HARBOR CLEAN OF LITTER! and headed inside the station.

The receptionist glanced up as he walked into the lobby. "Good afternoon, Mr. Hogan! I thought I saw your truck drive past a few minutes ago. What kept you?"

"Just keeping the streets clean," he replied, smiling as he continued to the stairs.

Nadine rested her elbows on the table and looked at the clock. It was nearly five. Hoagie was usually here already. She turned around in her chair and, sure enough, there he was, hunched over at his desk. She was a little anxious about his silent entry. Normally, he knocked on the glass, made faces at her, barged into the booth for the last five minutes of her show. The fact that he was at his desk...

She closed her eyes and clasped her hands in front of her. *Not Hoagie,* she prayed. *I think I can take everyone else turning on me, but not Miranda and not Hoagie, please.*

The current song faded out, and Nadine turned on the mic. "That was *Ruby Tuesday* by the Stones, and according to the clock, that will be the end of my show today. That old loveable lug, Joe Hogan is right outside the door, ready to hop in here as soon as I'm gone and...and please, guys. Give him a break and leave him alone about me. Just let the man play music." She sighed and continued, "That's a wrap for me. Thanks for everyone who called in to support me today and to everyone else...well, not much I can do for you. Hope you find something else to listen to on the way home from work."

Nadine switched off the mic and stood up. By the time she got to the door, Hoagie was waiting for her. "Miss Butler," he said.

She looked over his outfit and said, "Casual Monday, Mr. Hogan?"

"Hoagie," he said, giving her a smile. "I'm always Hoagie to you, Pixie." He nudged her with his elbow, almost sending her flying against the wall, and headed into the booth.

Miranda was on her way over and spotted Hoagie's apparent assault. She watched him disappear into the booth and snapped, "What the hell was that? Are you okay?"

"I'm fine," Nadine laughed. "That was just...Hoagie being Hoagie." Miranda still looked confused, so she shook her head and said, "Forget it, never mind. You ready to head out? Run the gauntlet?"

The door to the booth opened, and Hoagie stuck his head out. "Oh, by the way, ladies. The crowd downstairs won't be a problem."

Miranda blinked. "They just...left?"

"I politely asked if they would mind vacating the sidewalk." He smiled and shrugged. "What can I say; I'm a people person."

Nadine lifted herself onto her tiptoes and grabbed the lapel of his shirt. Pulling him close, she pressed her lips to his cheek, feeling the burn of stubble on her lips, but that did not matter. Even if she had stopped to think about it, Nadine was so grateful she still would have done it. When she released him, Hoagie staggered back a step and touched his now beet-red cheek.

"Well, hell, woman," he finally managed to get out. "If you'd just let the paper get a picture of you doing that, all your problems would be solved."

"Thank you, Hoagie," Nadine said.

He ducked his head like a bashful boy and went back into the booth.

Nadine wiped at her eyes before turning back to Miranda. "Well, I guess if the coast is clear, I don't need back-up," she said. "Thank you."

Miranda hugged Nadine. "Be safe. Let me know if you want a place to sleep tonight. I live in Sandpiper Condos. It's gated, so there's no way anyone is getting in."

Nadine pulled back but left her hands on Miranda's hips. "Thanks, but I let them keep me from my bike. I won't let them chase me from my home. Thank you for everything, Miranda."

"I aim to please. I..." the woman hesitated, then went on, "I've read *Sparks of Love*, too. I thought it was a great book."

Nadine shrugged and said, "See? Like I said at the meeting, reading a book doesn't make you gay. Just means you have taste." She looked at her watch and said, "I should...I should get out of here. Thank Hoagie again when he takes a break, will you?"

Miranda laughed. "Thank him? I may give him a raise."

Nadine moved her hand to Miranda's wrist and gave it an affectionate squeeze. "Okay. I'll see you tomorrow."

Miranda nodded and patted Nadine's shoulder. "I'll make sure the sidewalk is clear."

Nadine expressed her appreciation again, gathered her things, and headed for the stairs.

When Nadine was gone, Miranda sagged against the wall and pressed the heels of her hands against her eyes. She had been so close to saying it: "I have something to tell you. I know where you're coming from. I'm gay." One, two, or all three, it didn't matter. She could've said *one* of them. At least to let Nadine know she wasn't alone.

Telling Nadine, of course, was wrapped up in a lot of baggage; she had never said the words out loud. Her parents had died when she was in college, a year before she had had her first fling with another woman. It had been another two years before she realized how serious her flings were, how serious her feelings were. She had never had to come out to the rest of her estranged family.

Getting a woman home for the night was, for her, a matter of feeling the woman out and choosing the right signals to send. Her encounter with the Faire girl had been typical. Lingering glances, a slight raise of the eyebrows, a way of saying "You, too?" with body language.

But now that Nadine needed her, Miranda was not sure she could actually form the words. She was such a master of reading unspoken signs that when it came to the words...she was lost. *Dear God*, she thought as she watched Nadine leave. *It's been almost twenty years. Am I still this scared to admit it to myself?*

She squeezed the bridge of her nose and retreated to her office to avoid answering the question.

Nadine parked Kate's car in front of the *Register* offices and reluctantly went inside. There were only a handful of desks behind the front counter and none of them were occupied, so Nadine did not really feel a need to hide her face. The receptionist had not reacted to the sound of the bells over the door, so Nadine cleared her throat and gently rapped her knuckles on the desk.

In a heavily put-upon voice, the receptionist finally said, "How may I assist you?"

"I'm looking for Kathryn Price?" Nadine glanced toward Kate's desk out of habit, but it was as empty as its neighbors. Her computer screen was dark, and the area had the feeling of abandonment.

The receptionist confirmed her feelings by saying, "She didn't come in to work today."

"Oh," Nadine said, surprised. "Okay, thank you."

She turned and made it all the way to the door before the receptionist cried, "Hey! You're that DJ!"

Pushing the door open and rushing across the sidewalk to Kate's car, Nadine ducked behind the wheel, started the engine and pulled out in front of someone, waving an apology as she sped away from the curb. When she glanced in the rearview mirror, she saw the receptionist standing in the doorway of the *Register* offices, watching her with what appeared to be a mixture of shock and disbelief.

Nadine drove the rest of the way home hunched over the wheel, wary of pedestrians and other drivers. She had let her guard down. She was used to being recognized, but something in the woman's voice had told her this was not a fan. Nadine pulled into the parking lot without any further incidents and parked in the same spot she had left that morning. After locking the car door, she spent the entire walk up to the building debating what to do about her current notoriety. She could not ask everyone who came up to her if they were friend or foe. For the first time since becoming famous, she was considering the need for a disguise when she went out in public.

Stepping into the foyer, Nadine looked at the key ring in her hand. Her gaze shifted to her freshly painted door and then toward the stairs. She sighed and decided it was better to talk to Kate now rather than later. Going upstairs, she knocked on Kate's door and called, "Kate?"

There was no reply. Nadine shifted her weight from one foot to the other and glanced down at the ground floor. She flipped the keys into her palm, stepped closer to the door, and listened for sounds of movement. "Kate, it's me. It's Nadine. I have your keys."

A memory prodded her. There was an apartment key on the ring she was jingling. "Oh! That's why you didn't go to work." She mentally kicked herself and said loud enough for Kate to hear, "It's got your apartment key on it; if you leave, you won't be able to lock the door behind you. I get it."

Again, there was no reply. Nadine paced between the top of the stairs and Kate's apartment door, tapping her hands against her thighs. After a minute, she gave up and fished her cell phone out of her pocket. Dialing Kate's number, she leaned against the door as it rang and pressed her other ear against the panel. To her surprise, she could hear the quiet sound of *Sealed With a Kiss* playing from inside the apartment. She pressed her ear harder against the wood. It was definitely the ringtone Kate had chosen for her.

Nadine growled and snapped the cell phone shut. "Fine," she murmured as she singled out the apartment key. "Hide from me. I don't give a damn."

She slipped the key into the lock and raised her voice again. "Kate! If you're in there, I'm coming in." Turning the key, she pushed the door open and went inside. The apartment was darker than it had been that morning, now that the sun was on the opposite side of the sky. The curtains were drawn, and long shadows stretched across the cluttered living room. There was no music playing, no television. She peered toward the open bedroom door; the room appeared to be empty.

There was a small table next to the door meant for the mail. Nadine dropped the ring of keys there. "Kate! I'm leaving the keys right here."

She had the apartment door halfway closed before something hit her. She was not sure what caused the sense of uneasiness, but she opened the door wide and looked over the apartment again. Kate was not home or at work, she didn't have her car...*in a town as small as December Harbor, she* might *have walked someplace. But then why would her door be locked?*

Her gaze was drawn to the living room. The couch faced away from the door, creating a makeshift barrier between the entryway and the living room. Nadine glanced into the kitchen before she rounded the arm of the couch. What she saw made her gasp in shock.

Kate was curled on the couch in the fetal position, both hands tight against her stomach. Her face was deathly pale, her lips hanging slack. There was a beer bottle standing on the edge of the coffee table, but the real show was on the floor — an empty brown pill bottle and a wide pool of vomit.

Kate was not breathing.

Horrified, Nadine threw herself backward and almost fell over the coffee table. She drew in a sharp breath and let it out in a loud scream.

"KELF Radio, your place for the hits."

Nadine blinked and pulled the phone away from her ear. As she stared at it, not comprehending how it had gotten into her hand, a paramedic brushed past her and disappeared into Kate's apartment. Ignoring his passage, she put the phone back to her ear. "Wh-who is this?" she stammered.

"This is Susan, the KELF radio receptionist. How may I direct your call?"

Nadine did not remember pulling out her phone, did not remember dialing it, but she brushed away the wetness in her eyes and said, "Miranda Powell, please."

"One moment, please."

There was a click, and the line went to a live feed of Hoagie's show — the station's version of on-hold music. Chilled, Nadine drew her legs up to her chest and closed her eyes. She was seated on the landing outside Kate's apartment where she had been deposited by Deputy White, who had responded to the downstairs neighbor's call. Apparently, her scream had been enough to warrant three different calls to 911. Since then, everything had been a blur of tan and white police uniforms glimpsed in strobes of blue lights from outside the building.

A moment later, the tinny music cut off mid-lyric and was replaced by a crisp, professional voice. "Miranda Powell."

"Miranda," she whispered, "it's...it's Kate..."

"Who?"

"Kate!" Nadine nearly screamed.

"I'm sorry," Miranda said, "I don't think I know a...Nadine?"

"Kate's hurt." Nadine felt her tears starting again. The whooshing pulsebeat of blood in her ears kept drowning out Miranda's voice. She strained to hear the woman's response.

"Are you at home?" Miranda asked. Without waiting for an answer, she went on, "I'll be right there."

The call disconnected. Nadine pressed the cell phone against her forehead. She closed her eyes, tried to hold her breath, and failed after thirty seconds. When she exhaled, a fresh crop of frustrated tears flowed down her cheeks. She hated feeling so helpless, so afraid, not knowing if Kate was still alive or...

She was not sure how long she sat there crying with her head in her hands, but she did not come back to reality until she felt a gentle hand on her shoulder.

"Miss Butler?"

Nadine looked up at Sheriff Rucker's kind face and sniffled, wiping her cheeks with the backs of her hands.

"Can you stand up?" he asked. "They need to take the gurney out."

He helped her stand and move to one side as the paramedics took the gurney out of the apartment. Kate lay there, strapped in tight, so quiet, so still...one glimpse of the woman's cold, pale face and Nadine turned, pressing her face against Rucker's shirt until the clatter of the gurney faded.

The sheriff held her until they were alone on the landing, then patted her shoulder, saying, "Miss Butler, do you have someone who can give you a ride to the hospital?"

Nadine shook her head and tried to think. "I...n-no. Bike. I-I have a bike, I..."

"I'll take her."

Nadine spun around and saw Miranda halfway up the stairs. She released Rucker and lunged at the woman, letting out a relieved sob. Fortunately, Miranda seemed to have been prepared for such a reaction and braced one hand on the railing while she caught her with the other. She squeezed Nadine around the waist and offered a few whispered condolences before she turned her attention to Rucker.

"Sheriff, what happened?" Miranda asked.

"Kathryn Price seems to have attempted suicide, but it could've also been an accident. Our investigation is ongoing," he said.

Nadine kept her face pressed into front of Miranda's soft linen jacket. The warmth was comforting, the strong hands on her back keeping her grounded.

"Oh, God." Miranda lowered her voice and continued, "Is...is she...?"

"No," Rucker answered quickly. "She mixed the pills with alcohol and threw up most of it. They're going to pump her stomach at the hospital, make sure all of it is out. She's going to be fine."

"I'll take Nadine to the hospital," Miranda said. "Thank you."

Rucker nodded and headed downstairs, leaving them alone on the landing.

Miranda moved Nadine to one side and pressed her back against the wall. "Dean," she said gently. "I want you to take a deep breath and let it out."

She brushed her thumbs over Nadine's cheeks and waited until she did as she was told.

"Now, another."

Nadine complied faster this time and closed her eyes. The calm that came with the controlled breathing was a balm to her jangled nerves.

"Feel better? Are you okay?" Miranda asked.

Nadine gratefully covered Miranda's hands with her own. "Thank you, Miranda."

"Don't be silly. Come on; let's get you to the hospital."

The grumpy RN at the nurse's station did not want to give Kate's room number to non-family members. Miranda finally convinced the woman by telling her Kate had no family on the island or anywhere nearby.

"Don't you think," she concluded, "that Kate should have *someone*?"

The nurse finally relented and revealed that Kate had not been assigned a room yet. She was still in the emergency room getting her stomach pumped. The nurse pointed them to a waiting room where they could await word on their friend.

Miranda thanked her and walked Nadine to the appropriate waiting room. Guiding Nadine into a chair, she turned toward the door. Nadine lashed out and snagged the sleeve of Miranda's jacket.

"Don't, don't go," she pleaded.

Miranda gently freed herself from Nadine's clutching fingers. "I'm just going to find a coffee machine. I'll be right back."

Nadine nodded and moved her hands to her lap, apparently embarrassed by her panicky clinging. Miranda left her in one of the garish purple chairs and walked down the hall. She found a vending machine serving lukewarm coffee and bought two small cups. Carrying the cups back to the small, dim waiting room, she found Nadine staring blankly at the television mounted in the corner near the ceiling.

Aside from the chairs and television, the waiting room had one table for magazines and a little lamp that was doing its best to eliminate the gloom. The television was currently tuned to a documentary on the Discovery Channel and, since she could not see a remote anywhere, Miranda resigned herself to watching "Predators of the Kalahari".

Nadine apparently only became aware of her return when Miranda placed the coffee in her hand. She looked down at the coffee as if wondering how she had made it appear, then turned her head to focus on Miranda. "Thank you," she said quietly. She brought the coffee to her lips and took a sip.

Miranda placed her hand on Nadine's back and began moving it in slow circles that she hoped were comforting. Truth be told, she had never been in this situation. She glanced down into her murky coffee, looked at Nadine's tear-streaked face, and finally focused on the TV documentary that seemed to have entranced Nadine. After a moment, she had to ask, "Kate is your...your girlfriend. Isn't she?"

Nadine nodded.

"How long have you two...how long?"

"Three years."

Miranda blinked in surprise. "All those times I made you work overtime..."

Nadine smiled weakly and touched Miranda's hand. "It's okay," she whispered. "We were...I could always have said I was seeing someone and left it at that. We were just worried about people getting nosy. And I suppose...I could have always told *you* privately. I just...I don't know. I could never say the words out loud."

Miranda was stricken by the comparison to her own thoughts on the subject and said, "I...well." She paused for a long time and finally squeezed Nadine's hand. "I would have understood."

"I know."

Nadine and Miranda sat quietly until Nadine broke the silence.

"Why would she do that?" The question was softly spoken, but Nadine's voice was raw. "Why would...I mean...if anyone has the right to..." She shook her head as if refusing to finish the thought.

Miranda bit her bottom lip. She had only met Kate briefly and did not want Nadine to think she was being judgmental. "Kate wrote the article that...the article. Right?" When Nadine nodded, she went on, "This is just me talking, but I doubt she meant for it to be presented the way it was."

Nadine shrugged. "She said her editor rewrote the entire thing. But the bare bones were there, I mean...she had to have known what she was doing."

"Even so, Dean, Kate loves you. She could be seeing everything that's happening to you as her fault. You're in agony and if she was blaming herself for it..."

Nadine was quiet for a moment. The documentary's narration, delivered in an English accent, filled the room as she apparently mulled over what Miranda had said. "I guess so," she finally whispered. "God, I've been so full of myself and what was happening to me..."

"You had a right," Miranda said. "But Kate...Kate was caught in the middle, too. I assume she's in the closet?"

"Yeah."

Miranda thought back to what she had originally felt. "Then this is probably her worst nightmare, too. She's probably been deathly afraid of someone finding out. It's like the dream where you go to school naked. Everyone knows your deepest darkest secret. And it's worse for her, because she's not only inflicted it, she's done it to someone she loves. And she had to watch it all happen right in front of her."

"I wouldn't even talk to her."

Miranda nodded and looked at the TV. Nadine put her coffee cup down and leaned against Miranda's shoulder. They sat together in the dim waiting room, were startled when the lights came up in response to the sun going down outside, watched the documentary on the small TV, and drank stale, cold coffee.

At the next commercial break, Miranda's bladder began complaining, the result of all her coffee drinking. She said, "Dean, I need to..." Looking down, she saw Nadine had fallen asleep. Rather than wake her after the poor thing had endured such a brutal day, Miranda crossed her legs and settled in for a long wait. Fortunately, she thought, the documentary was about desert animals rather than marine life.

A few minutes later, however, the option of letting Nadine sleep was taken from her. A petite woman in a doctor's lab coat stepped into the doorway. "Miss Butler?" she asked in a quiet voice.

Miranda reached up and stroked Nadine's cheek. "Dean...wake up, dear."

Nadine stirred and stared at Miranda for a moment before she realized they were not alone. She murmured something incomprehensible and sat up, straightening her glasses. "Yes, I'm Nadine Butler."

"I'm Kate's doctor, Rachel Tom. We pumped Miss Price's stomach as a precaution; the medics reported that she made a common mistake and attempted to wash the pills down with alcohol, which caused her to regurgitate most of her stomach's contents. Nevertheless, she's lucky you found her when you did. She was conscious when she came in and told us she hadn't been out long when you found her. She's resting at the moment, but once we've moved her to a room you can see her briefly if you'd like."

"Thank you, Dr. Tom," Miranda said.

"Thank you," Nadine echoed.

The doctor left, and Nadine sat up straighter in her chair. "Was I drooling?" she asked, wiping her chin.

"No," Miranda replied. She smiled an apology. "If you'll excuse me, I've had way too many coffees..."

"Oh, God. Go, go," Nadine said, flapping her hands.

Miranda hurried out into the corridor and found the closest ladies restroom. After washing her hands, she leaned on the sink, gazing at her reflection in the glass. She had nearly had a heart attack when she answered the phone and heard Nadine sobbing on the other end. She had hated herself, but when she arrived at Nadine's apartment to find someone else on a gurney, she had actually been relieved. All Nadine had said on the phone was "Kate's hurt." She had not had any idea what she would find when she had come running to the rescue. Fortunately, everything seemed to have worked out fine.

She could not believe her cowardice. When she had been given another chance to come out to Nadine, she had chickened out again. "What will it take?" Miranda asked her reflection. "She didn't have a choice. She was forced to come out, and all she needs is a friend. Someone to..."

The door opened, and a nurse came into the bathroom. Embarrassed to have been almost caught talking to herself, Miranda covered her mouth and faked a cough, smiled at the pretty young nurse, and left the bathroom. She found Nadine still alone in the waiting room, huddled in her chair, looking as forlorn as a little girl waiting outside a day-care center, alone and desperately waiting for someone to take her home. Miranda slid into the seat next to her and took Nadine's hand. "You can lean on me again," she said.

Nadine did so without hesitation. Miranda closed her eyes, enjoying the moment and feeling a little guilty about it due to the circumstances. After a moment, Nadine said, "Cheetahs can purr, but they can't roar."

Miranda's eyes popped open. "Egotistical housecats," she said.

Nadine chuckled. After a long moment, she turned her head slightly and said, "I'm glad you're not...scared of me."

"What?" Miranda said. "Why would I be scared of you?"

"Not me. That I might...you know...turn you. Or something. Like being gay can be contagious."

"There's little chance of *that* happening," Miranda said. She could have added "I've known I was gay for years" or "I'm already infected." Anything. But she kept her mouth shut. Even if she could overcome her fear of coming out, now was not the time. They watched the Discovery Channel documentary for a while, then Nadine dozed and Miranda stroked her hair.

Finally, around ten o'clock, Dr. Tom returned and told them that Kate was ready to see them. Nadine stood and stretched, turning to face Miranda. "Do you want to come in with me?"

"Unless you need me to be there...I think it's something you should do on your own, I think," Miranda said. This was something Nadine needed to do without Miranda standing there holding her hand.

Nadine nodded. "I'll be back in a minute," she said, following Dr. Tom down the hall to the room they had placed Kate in.

Left alone in the waiting room, Miranda leaned back and stared at the television. She picked up her coffee cup, sneered at the bitter contents, and waited for Nadine to return.

Kate was lying on her back, the hospital sheet pulled to her waist and her hands resting on her stomach. Nadine thanked the doctor and waited for the door to close before she walked to the foot of the bed. The curtains were open, and the moonlight was casting a pale shadow against the glass. Kate's eyes were sunken, the dark bags underneath them accentuated by the light over the bed; her lips were pale and bruised, and her face was haggard. There was the shadow of a charcoal stain on the side of her mouth. Nadine felt an ache just under her ribcage at the sight of her lover's suffering and nervously touched her arm. "Kate...?"

Kate's eyes opened slowly. She scanned the room in apparent bewilderment. When her wandering gaze found Nadine, she said, "Dean."

"Hey," Nadine said. "Your insurance must be better than mine. Private room and all."

Kate smiled and shrugged. She lifted her chin and managed to say, "Sorry." Her voice, a voice Nadine had adored since hearing her sing in the shower, was scratchy and thin. She swallowed and a grimace of pain exploded across her face. Kate managed to relax her features and moved her hand across the mattress. Nadine met it halfway, touching their fingertips together. Kate continued, "Sorry...'bout the...article..."

"It's your job," Nadine shrugged. All her anger at Kate had evaporated on seeing her in such a vulnerable condition.

"Shitty...excuse."

"Yes. Well," Nadine said. She blinked back her tears and decided not to beat around the bush. "You scared the hell out of me, Kate. I mean...what if I hadn't come in? I almost didn't come in and...oh, God. If I had gone back downstairs and been mad at you all night...do you know what that would have done to me?"

Kate was weeping now, quiet tears that rolled down her cheeks.

Nadine brushed a tear away, letting her hand linger against Kate's chilled skin. "Do you want me to call Amy? Let her know that you're..."

"No," Kate said quickly. "I don't want...anyone to...know."

"My..." Nadine hesitated, then went on, "My boss knows. I called her to drive me to the hospital. She's been sitting with me ever since."

"Good...boss," Kate said, smiling wanly.

Nadine smiled back. "Yeah. The best." She glanced at the medical monitors, hearing the steady beep that was the heartbeat she had listened to on so many quiet nights. The past weekend meant nothing now, not when Kate was in such pain. Looking Kate in the eye, she asked, "Is there anything I can do for you, sweetheart?"

Kate shook her head and said, "I think I want...to sleep. My stomach feels like...I did ten thousand sit-ups."

Nadine brushed her fingers against Kate's arm and nodded. "Okay. Anything else?"

"Ask the...nurse for more ice chips?"

"Okay." Nadine stroked Kate's cheek one more time and then bent over the bed and lightly brushed Kate's mouth with her own. Moving her hand from Kate's cheek to her hair, she tucked several dark strands back behind Kate's ears. She kissed the tears away from Kate's eyes, tasting bitter salt. "I do love you, Kate," she murmured. *Funny how a near-tragedy could make you give up grudges and be far more forgiving than you would be otherwise.*

"I love you, too, Dean."

Nadine kissed Kate a last time before she stood up and said, "I'll come back and see you when you wake up in the morning, okay?"

Kate nodded.

Nadine slipped out of the room. Dr. Tom was at the nurse's station writing in a chart when she approached.

"Doctor," Nadine said. The woman glanced up and she continued, "Kate wanted...um, ice chips."

"Okay, I'll get a nurse to bring her some."

"Do you know when she can be released?"

"We'd like to keep her here for another twenty-four hours, just to keep an eye out for possible complications. We'll schedule a psych evaluation at that time to ensure she's no longer a danger to herself."

"She's not," Nadine assured the woman.

Dr. Tom nodded. "Still, we'd like to be certain before we release her."

"I understand."

"Will you and your friend be staying overnight? We could arrange to have a cot brought into your friend's room."

"No, no," Nadine said. "We...I'm sure we'll go home at some point. Thank you, Dr. Tom."

The doctor nodded and returned to her charting. Nadine found her way back to the waiting room. "Hey," she said to Miranda, who turned and rose from her seat.

"Hey," Miranda said. "How is she?"

"They're going to keep her for observation."

Miranda nodded. "You want me to drop you at your place or...?"

"Yes, please." Nadine rubbed her face and said, "I don't think I could stand staying here all night. The antiseptic smell, knowing Kate's...no," she said firmly. "I can't stay here."

Miranda curled an arm around Nadine's shoulders and softly said, "Come on."

She allowed herself to be guided through the quiet corridors of the sleeping hospital and downstairs to step out into the cold night air. Unprepared for the sudden chill, Nadine hugged herself. She stepped behind Miranda as they walked to her car. Miranda undid the belt on her trenchcoat and slipped it off her shoulders. She stepped closer to Nadine and wrapped the coat around her shoulders. Putting her arm around Nadine in a tight embrace, she escorted her across the parking lot. Nadine trembled against Miranda's body as she unlocked the car door.

Nadine got into the car, scooting over to the passenger side so Miranda could climb in behind the wheel. Miranda slammed the door, switched on the ignition, and cranked up the heater. Nadine sat quietly while warmth blasted against her feet, waiting to defrost from the trek across the parking lot.

Miranda cleared her throat and said, "Almost didn't make it."

"When did it get so *cold*?" Nadine asked. "It was *sweltering* yesterday!"

"I think a cold front blew in halfway through that cheetah special."

Nadine cupped her hands over her mouth and blew into them, trying to thaw her frozen fingers. She felt as if the last few hours had been a dream and she was only now coming out of it, awakening to real life.

Without preamble, Miranda said, "I talked to one of the managers over at Joe Lack's Pizza after you left today. I gave them some marketing statistics from the most recent Arbitron survey to think about. They're going to reconsider the promotion deal, and I'm confident they'll continue to sponsor your show. I'm going to give the other sponsors a call tomorrow and see if I can loosen them up."

Nadine closed her eyes, touched by the generosity and the selfless sacrifices Miranda was making. She was going out of her way to help Nadine at a time when it seemed everyone was against her. All she could manage to say was a weak, "Thank you."

"Eh, Lack is a pushover."

"No, not for...not just for that. Thank you for everything you've done for me the past two days. You've been so, so great during all of this when it's not even your fight. It means a lot to me."

"I have a stake in it, too, you know."

Nadine nodded. "Yes, of course. I haven't said how sorry I am that this is affecting your radio station. It's not fair that you should suffer..."

"I have a stake in it because I'm gay, too, Nadine."

Nadine stared, flabbergasted.

Finally, Miranda's face split into an awkward smile; she held her hands out to either side of her face and said, "Surprise!"

Nadine retracted her earlier thought. Maybe she hadn't woken up quite yet after all.

Chapter Eight

The harbor lights were just visible over the rooftops, creating a pale yellow haze around the buildings near the hospital. The car windows were starting to grow opaque from the heater and their combined breath. Not a word had been spoken since Miranda's sudden revelation and the atmosphere in the car was beginning to feel a bit claustrophobic.

Nadine was staring at the rapidly whitening windshield. She was in shock, completely speechless for the first time she could remember. Out of the corner of her eye, she saw that Miranda was focused on a loose thread from her coat sleeve. Nadine chewed her bottom lip, unsure of what to say.

Miranda sighed, breaking the silence, and said, "Well?"

Nadine turned to face the other woman. Her glasses were starting to fog up so she took them off, wiping the lenses with her shirtsleeve. "You're gay?" she asked.

Miranda nodded.

Nadine put her glasses on and pressed back against the seat. She looked at the misty halo of light through the windshield and finally decided on a follow-up question. "How long?"

Miranda seemed to give the question due consideration. "Since I was about...around twenty, I guess."

"That long?"

"Hey!" Miranda slapped Nadine's arm in mock offense.

"Sorry," Nadine said.

They looked at each other, and Nadine felt a smile tugging at the corners of her lips. She covered her mouth and shook her head. "I shouldn't laugh. I'm sorry, it's just...the idea of you being gay. All this time. I mean, we've worked together for five years. I thought I would have...you know...assumed. Or at least suspected. Have you been in a relationship?"

Miranda shook her head. "Nothing that lasted more than a night...not since I came to the island. I was always kind of concerned about...well, this." She made a vague gesture. "What the reaction would be if I ever got caught."

Nadine nodded and said, "I wouldn't wish this on anybody." She shivered violently and grunted low in her throat. It was really freezing, and Nadine was starting to wish they had had this conversation inside the hospital. "Look, I'd really like to keep talking, but could we do it someplace warmer?"

"God, yes," Miranda said. She flicked on the headlights, backed the car of the parking space, and headed for the street. "Where do you want to go? My place or yours?"

Nadine gave her a raised eyebrow.

Miranda blushed and cleared her throat, clearly embarrassed. "I didn't mean that the way it came out...I just meant that my place has..."

Nadine interrupted, letting the woman off the hook. "We can go to your place. My apartment has crappy heating anyway."

As they drove through the near empty streets, Nadine stared out of the window, watching the few people who were braving the low temperature. She noticed Leah Nettles was on the air; the DJ's sultry voice came through the radio speakers as soon as a Rod Stewart song finished.

"Hey, everyone out there tonight," Leah said. "Whether you're warm in bed or out in this cold, cold night, I hope you have someone with you to help keep you warm."

Nadine glanced at Miranda guiltily, was surprised by what seemed to be an identically guilty expression on the woman's face, and had to look away. She was not used to seeing her boss so vulnerable, so open, and emotional. It was quite surreal.

Their route took them past Nadine's apartment building. Nadine turned in her seat as they drove by.

Miranda looked in the rearview mirror. "What is it?" She slowed down. "Do I need to turn around?"

"No," Nadine said, relaxing into her seat. "I was just making sure nothing looked...out of place." *Like a big slur on my door,* she thought, *as if that would even be visible from the street.*

"Did you see anything? Should we stop?"

Nadine shook her head. "If something *was* wrong, I would want to stay and fix it and..." She waved her hands as if erasing the thought from the air. "No, just keep driving."

"My place isn't much further," Miranda assured her.

They passed the high school. Miranda turned the car toward the gated entrance to Sandpiper Condos. The car rolled to a stop just in front of the closed gates. She clicked on the interior light and waved to a bored-looking guard hunkered in his little wooden shack. He returned the wave as he pressed a button and the gates began to part down the middle. Miranda turned off the light and drove slowly through the gap.

Nadine noticed the condos hugged the stone wall that surrounded the community, all the properties connected by a single oval road. In the center was a small park that contained benches, a basketball court, and a stand of mailboxes. Miranda pulled in at a tidy yellow house that, save for a knee-high white fence around the yard, was identical to its neighbors.

They walked to the front door together, Nadine huddled against Miranda's side as the woman found her key. Miranda pushed the door open, and they both rushed inside. Nadine sighed. It was still cold, since the house had obviously been abandoned all day, but the temperature here was far more comfortable than it had been out in the wind. Miranda closed the door and turned on the living room light. She gestured at the kitchen area and asked, "Can I get you something to drink? Orange juice, soda..."

Nadine said, "Water is fine..."

Miranda headed down a corridor, and Nadine stepped into the living room. The space was nothing like what she expected; it was a quaint living room that looked so clean and unlived-in that it seemed to be lifted directly out of a TV soundstage. A sofa and chair faced the television, and a small unlit fireplace was against the back wall next to a window. There was an untidy stack of books on the tiled hearth.

Nadine walked to the fireplace and knelt down to scan the book titles. She laughed when she found a well-worn paperback copy of *Sparks of Love.* She pulled it out of the stack and thumbed through the dog-eared pages. The spine was cracked, the binding a bit loose, and there was the ring of a coffee stain on the back cover; the book was obviously well-loved and well-read.

"Ah, you found my library," Miranda remarked, returning to the room.

Nadine stood up with the novel in her hand. "A book called *Sparks of Love* sitting in the fireplace. Appropriate."

"Well, I never used the thing," Miranda said. "The fireplace, I mean." She handed Nadine a plastic cup with *Gail's Seafood Shack* printed on the side. "Pretty soon, the books just...migrated there."

Nadine thumbed through the book a second time. "I guess you don't have to worry about it being removed from this library's shelves."

"Yeah," Miranda laughed and took the worn-out novel out of Nadine's hands, returning it to the stack. "It seemed so innocent when I bought it back when. I guess now, though, seeing this is going to be like seeing a rainbow sewn onto somebody's jacket."

"Did you buy it on the island?"

"Online, through a second-hand book seller, so it wouldn't show up on my Amazon history." Miranda shrugged. "I guess not so innocent after all, huh?"

"I guess," Nadine replied. She took a sip of water and turned the cup to look at the logo on the side. She tapped the cursive name of the restaurant with her fingernail and said, "Are you supposed to take these?"

Miranda, who had a glass of something brown that smelled alcoholic, shrugged and said, "It's probably not encouraged."

Nadine smiled. "I only ask because I don't want to offend my one and only sponsor." She walked to the couch and took a seat. Miranda sat on the opposite end and pulled her feet underneath her. Nadine scratched her fingernail along the curved rim of the cup and said, her smile fading, "I don't remember if I've said it yet, but...thank you for being there for me today. I was a total...I was destroyed when I found Kate. I can't believe..." She caught herself and looked toward the window.

Miranda reached out and took Nadine's right hand. "What?"

"Mm, no. It's awful."

"I won't tell anyone." Miranda's smile softened. "Trust me; I'm good at keeping secrets."

Nadine let out a bitterness-tinged laugh and gazed at the water in her cup. "I was just thinking on the way here that...it's amazing I didn't try to kill myself."

"You didn't hole yourself up in your apartment, either," Miranda said.

"What do you call what I did on Sunday?" Nadine asked sadly.

Miranda shrugged. "You were taking a breather. You let me in."

"Yeah. I did." Nadine turned her palm up and, just like that, they were holding hands.

"It only lasted a day. When you had to get up, you brushed yourself off, came to work, cleaned up your front door, whereas Kate just shut down."

"If I'd been there for Kate..." Nadine glanced at their joined hands. "If it hadn't been for you, I don't know. I might've been in that hospital room next to Kate."

Miranda shifted uncomfortably. "I wouldn't give myself that much credit."

"Oh, I definitely would," Nadine argued. She faced Miranda and went on, "You've been wonderful throughout this entire ordeal. If it weren't for you, I'd probably still be in my bathtub staring at the wall and Kate..." She glanced away again, feeling embarrassed. "So really, you saved two lives."

Miranda took another drink before putting her glass on the coffee table and saying, "I think I've had enough." She added when Nadine flinched, "Enough alcohol, I mean. Please, continue with the effusive praise."

Nadine let out a relieved chuckle and put her plastic cup down. "Actually, I think I'm done, too."

"Well, should I drive you home? Or...I mean, it's awfully late. You could go ahead and crash on the couch if you wanted."

Nadine thought for a moment, then shook her head. "I probably shouldn't. That guard saw you pull in here with an island-renowned lesbian. I think it would be best if he saw you take me home, too."

Miranda hesitated. "I want to. I mean, I want to take you home if that's what you want. But I'm not going to do it just so Paul the guard doesn't think I'm gay." She leaned back against the arm of the couch. Without looking at Nadine, she said, "Do you regret it?"

"What?"

"Coming out. The way you did it, I mean. Do you wish you could take it back?"

"Of course," Nadine breathed. "I mean, my God...Kate wouldn't be hurt, those picketers wouldn't be blocking the front door of the ratio station...but if you're asking would I go back in the closet? No. Absolutely not. It feels..." She chewed her lip and glanced around the room, trying to pick the right words to describe how she was feeling. "Like I was holding my breath and I finally got to exhale. I definitely wouldn't go back, no. But I would try to find a better way to do it."

Miranda nodded. "I can understand that."

The stifled yawn in the middle of Miranda's sentence prompted Nadine to look at the clock. She gasped and looked at her own watch for confirmation. "Oh, God, is it really that late?"

"We were at the hospital for ages," Miranda said. She stood up. "If you're sufficiently thawed..."

"I am." Nadine remembered the smell of alcohol in Miranda's drink and went on, "Oh! Should you be driving?"

"I only had a few sips," Miranda said. "I practically need a carafe before I get drunk."

"Okay. But could I use your bathroom before we..."

"Sure, sure." Miranda pointed. "It's down that hall, second door on the right."

Nadine went down the darkened corridor, located the second door by feel, and groped around until she found a light switch. The sudden flood of illumination made her blink, then she blinked a second time in confusion. She was in a slightly messy, thoroughly modern kitchen, not a bathroom. Stepping back into the corridor, she called, "Um, Miranda..."

"First door," Miranda replied, sounding chagrined. "I meant the first."

"Okay," Nadine said, struggling to keep from giggling. "I was about to say that was the most unique bidet I've ever seen."

She shut the bathroom door on Miranda's laughter and took care of business. When she finished, she took a moment to admire the décor. It was obvious to her that a lot of thought and hard work had gone into the decorating scheme.

The walls were streaked with white, blue, and very light blue in a treatment that emulated a waterfall. The floor was covered in white and grey tiles. A small gray rug that looked like a stepping stone lay in front of the tub, which had a green and white shower curtain hanging from the rod. Nadine felt like she was standing in a pool of water as she washed her hands at the sink.

A picture framed in seashells caught her attention. It was nestled between the hand lotion and soap dish underneath the mirror. She carefully pulled it free without disturbing the surrounding toiletries. Miranda Powell had never seemed old to her, but the version of the woman in the picture was a positively radiant teenager. Miranda was wearing a knit ski cap and goggles. Both arms were wrapped protectively around a smaller brunette girl. They were smiling into the camera, the sun burning with a fierce yellow glare in the background and washing out some of their color.

Nadine ran her finger over the curve of Miranda's cheek in the photograph and wondered who the other girl was, if they were lovers or just good friends. She returned the picture to where she had found it and quickly finished drying her hands before she stepped out of the bathroom.

When they arrived at the apartment building, Miranda offered to walk an uneasy Nadine home. Nadine agreed, went into the building first, and breathed an audible sigh of relief when she saw the vandalism on her front door had not been repeated. She found her keys and said, "Safe for another day. Hopefully there was just the one artist and I scared him away."

"Let's hope." Miranda looked up to the second floor and saw a single strip of yellow crime tape running across Kate's apartment door. It made her feel sick to her stomach, the kind of sight she had gotten fed up with in New York. This was a small town. In her opinion, small town apartments should not have crime-scene tape across their door, damn it.

"It looks so lonely," Nadine whispered.

Miranda had not realized Nadine was staring in the same direction. The woman's jaw was set tight, but her eyes were swimming with unshed tears. Miranda put her hand on Nadine's shoulder, squeezing lightly. "She was lucky you came home when you did."

"I was so angry with her. I thought she was avoiding me like I had done to her. If I had just gone downstairs to stew, I..." Nadine looked at Miranda as if surprised to see her there and shook her head. "But I...I'm babbling."

"No, you're *talking*," Miranda said, smiling. "And I'm listening."

Nadine hesitated but began speaking again. "If you hadn't come to see me Sunday, I would probably have not come to work today. I probably would have stayed in, like Kate, and wallowed. And I'm...I'm not sure what I would have done."

"I don't think you would have tried to kill yourself."

"The thought crossed my mind."

Miranda was caught off-guard by this admission, and she could not hide the fear that crossed her face.

Nadine must have seen the expression because she said, "Don't worry. After seeing Kate like that and...you don't have to worry." She turned and put her hands on Miranda's shoulders. Leaning forward, she kissed the corner of Miranda's mouth, her lips lingering for a moment before she stepped back and moved her hands away. "Thank you," Nadine went on, "for being there tonight and for...everything. Thank you, Miranda."

"Y-you're...you're welcome. Nadine." She was too stunned to say anything else. Her tongue felt like it was simply hanging loose in her mouth, disconnected and useless.

"I'll see you tomorrow. Do we have a staff meeting?"

"Hm? No. No, the, uh, third Tuesday of the month."

Nadine frowned. "Tomorrow *is* the third Tuesday."

Miranda blinked. She was surprised a little kiss could fluster her that way. "Uh. Yeah. Then, yeah, staff meeting at ten-thirty."

"Okay." Nadine smiled. "Good night, Miranda. Thank you so much, again."

"It was my pleasure," Miranda managed to say. She left the apartment and waited for Nadine to close the door before she stepped out of the foyer. Walking across the courtyard to her car, she shoved her hands deep into the pockets of her coat. The wind was whipping her hair like a dervish, her cheeks were raw, and her lips were chapped, but the only thing on her mind was that little bit of moisture at the corner of her mouth and the thought that kept circling in a never-ending loop: *She kissed me. Nadine kissed me...*

Nadine stood at the window and watched Miranda walk away. She wanted to run after the woman, to ask her to stay and curl up with her on the couch. She desperately wanted to be held in Miranda's arms, but she was not sure she trusted her emotions. Where had these feelings come from? This was Miranda Powell, her boss — the same person she had an occasional lunch with, the same person who had yelled at her when she accidentally said a curse word on-air last year.

What she felt could not be a real attraction, Nadine decided. It was just the knowledge that Miranda was gay that was making her feel this way. It was the fact that with so much hatred beating down on her from all quarters, Miranda was still her friend, still being nice to her. *That's all it is.* Nadine stepped away from the window as Miranda's car pulled out of the parking lot. She went to the couch and turned on a lamp before flinging herself onto the cushions. Her head was throbbing with pain, but the thought of popping any kind of pills, even an aspirin, terrified her after seeing Kate at the hospital.

She took off her shoes and glasses and leaned back on the sofa. Her lifeguard was gone, she was in the deep end on her own. It was fine. She would make it until morning without Miranda holding her hand, she hoped. Nadine closed her eyes and heard Miranda's voice in her head.

"I'm gay, too. Surprise!"

God, talk about understatements. Miranda gay? Nadine knew she would never, not in a million years, have considered the possibility. But would she have guessed, if she had been in Miranda's house before the revelation? The picture in the bathroom, the *Sparks of Love* book...then there was the fact that she was apparently as terminally single as Nadine herself. It seemed so obvious in hindsight, but after a little thought, Nadine figured she would have chalked it all up to wishful thinking and gone alone on her merry way.

She checked her watch, groaned, and forced herself to get off the couch. As she stood up, the headache returned in full force. After stumbling down the hallway to the bathroom, Nadine undressed in front of the sink and sat on the edge of the tub as she ran the faucet. She looked at the freezing porcelain and saw, very clearly, a ghostly image of herself from the day before — so alone, so despondent, seeing the razor as a distinct possibility; how the deep cut, following the blue line of the vein that ran up her inner arm to her elbow, would hurt a little, then all the pain and fear would go away.

Nadine pictured an emotionally devastated Kate in her own apartment, staring at a bottle of pills and deciding that was the answer to her problems. No one had gone to Kate's door, no one had offered a hug and a friendly shoulder. The one person to whom she had reached out had slammed the door in her face.

Nadine stuck her hand under the water and let the flow pummel her fingers. She felt the possibility of what might have happened weighing on her. If not for Miranda, where would she be right now? Sitting on the edge of the tub or in a bed at the hospital? Or worse? When the water was warm enough, she stood up and stepped into the water. She sank into the tub, closed her eyes, and let the water gather her in its warmth.

Once she returned to her own apartment, Miranda left the overhead lights off and stopped by the mirror in her entry hall. "I'm gay," she told her reflection. She was out, at least to one person. One of her best friends, she had to admit, and someone she worked with on a daily basis. It was out there, the fact that she was gay, and she was somewhat amazed that she did not look or feel any different.

"Like I'd been holding my breath," Nadine had said.

Miranda stopped waiting to feel the change and instead focused on her features, noticing the little laugh lines next to her mouth and eyes, definite signs that she was getting older. She leaned forward and tried to determine if her blonde hair was beginning to turn grey. *Not yet*, she thought, but it was not easy to check. Miranda did not want to be vain about it, so she refused to turn on any more lights, refused to continue the hunt.

She went into the bathroom and undressed, retrieving a towel from the shelf under the sink. Turning on the faucet, she sat on the edge of the tub, watching the level of water rise. She was thinking about what Nadine had said about knowing how Kate must have felt. The thought of Nadine in danger made her blood run cold. She was almost superstitious enough to think that just imagining it could make it come true, so she scrubbed the thought from her mind and focused on the sound of the water splashing. When the tub was almost full, the cell phone in her pants pocket went off.

Cursing the god of bad timing, Miranda spun the knob to turn the water off and dashed over to the pile of clothes. Searching the pockets of her pants, she managed to find her phone while it was still ringing. She flipped it open without looking at the screen, positive that it was Nadine. Something had happened after all, some mark of vandalism not readily apparent from outside or...*oh, God, what if someone was inside waiting for her?* "Hello? It's me, what's wrong?" Miranda said hastily.

There was a short pause on the other end of the line before a man's voice asked, "Miss Powell?"

Her eyes went wide, and she shot to her feet. "Mr. Dugan. What are you doing calling me at this hour...sir?"

"I've only just gotten off the phone myself, Miss Powell. I've been speaking to Joe Lack about...harassment?"

Miranda closed her eyes and rubbed her suddenly aching temples. Leaning against the sink, she caught a glimpse of her startled reflection when she opened her eyes again. *Oh, shit. I'm talking to Mr. Dugan naked. I hope he's wearing something. Oh, shit, why did I think of that?* She stepped into her pants and bent down to pull them up. "Um...I'm not sure what you're...talking about, sir," she said as she wriggled, getting the pants up over her hips and buttoning them. She did not bother with the zipper.

"Mr. Lack requested that his sponsorship be pulled from this Pixie show after the...the announcement in yesterday's paper. He said you spent most of today arguing with him on the phone, trying to get him to change his mind. He finally said yes just to shut you up, but as soon as you left him alone, he called me. I assured him that Ms. Butler will *not* be advertising Joe Lack's Pizza any time in the near future."

"You can't do that," Miranda argued. She grabbed her blouse and managed to get both arms into it by shifting the phone from one hand to the other.

Doing up two of the buttons to give a semblance of being dressed worked; she immediately felt more professional. "Nadine has done nothing wrong."

"If Joe Lack wanted to pull his sponsorship because Miss Butler refused to play his request, we would honor that. If Joe Lack wanted to pull his sponsorship because Miss Butler said something offensive about him or his restaurant, we would honor that as well. Hell, if she mispronounced Saskatchewan and Mr. Lack didn't like it, he could pull his sponsorship. He doesn't *need* a reason. It's his money. We're going to honor his decision, and all of the other pulled sponsorships, to keep their business with our other shows."

Miranda sank onto the closed toilet lid and covered her eyes with her free hand. "Who else?"

"I don't have a full list, but I've spoken with the managers of several places today. Let me check." There was a ruffling of papers, and Dugan cleared his throat. "Yolk Folks, Duck Soup Restaurant, Joe Lack's Pizza as I said, the Spartan Café, Chin's Chinese Buffet, Gail's Seafood Shack..."

"No!" Miranda said, unable to stop the outburst. "No, you can't do that. Gail's is..."

"Withdrawing their sponsorship of Nadine Butler's radio show. I spoke to the owner."

"You talked to Clifton?" Miranda asked. Gail's had been a strong advertiser since the restaurant had opened. They were also one of the biggest sponsors of Nadine's show. She knew Clifton and thought he was an honorable guy. It was hard to believe he would cave under the pressure of what had to be a vocal minority.

"No, his father, Markus. Clifton is just the manager. Markus Gail, I shouldn't have to tell you, was appalled to hear Miss Butler promoting their restaurant today. He called to be sure I would make amends as soon as possible."

Miranda was on the verge of tears. "Mr. Dugan, please. If all of these places pull their sponsorship, there'll be nothing for her to play between songs."

"Nothing for her to play, period."

"Exactly! It's..." Miranda suddenly felt a wash of cold over her body as the triumphant tone of his voice registered. She tightened her grip on her cell phone and heard the casing crack slightly under the white-knuckled pressure. "You cannot...you can't do that."

"KELF is still *my* station, Miss Powell, no matter how much influence I let you wield. Nadine Butler has a six-hour show in the middle of the day. If I cannot advertise during that time, I cannot very well justify her paycheck or the raise you recently debated me about. Tomorrow is your monthly staff meeting, right? I expect you to inform Miss Butler that she is no longer employed at the station. Tomorrow will be her last show."

"You prick." She could not stop herself and, once the words were out, refused to apologize. She could not blame Dugan for wanting to protect his business, but he did not have to sound so goddamn smug about it.

"I do not believe in belaboring the point. To allow her another week on the air would only cause bitterness on everyone's parts. And believe me, that week would hardly be quality airtime on her part. It's best to just get her out as soon as possible."

"She's a human being."

"She's my employee. As are you. So I expect the two of you to follow my direction. Do we have an understanding, Miss Powell?"

She leaned forward, fighting nausea.

"Do we have an understanding, Miss Powell?" he repeated.

"Yes," she snapped. "Okay. Nadine...Nadine is gone tomorrow."

She hung up on him and dropped the phone in front of the tub. Covering her flushed face with both hands, she sobbed and let the tears fall.

The next morning, her headache reduced to a dull throb, Nadine rode her bike to the hospital on her way to work. She found Dr. Tom and confirmed that she was allowed to see Kate before making her way up to the second-floor room. The hospital was considerably cheerier in the morning hours; a window at the end of the corridor flooded the ward with natural light to help counteract the ubiquitous fluorescent illumination. Even the tiny waiting room did not seem as cavernous as it had the night before.

Nadine knocked on the door to Kate's room and entered after a whispered, "Come in." She poked her head in and registered the presence of a nurse, whose back was to her. Walking into the room and moving past the nurse, Nadine smiled when she saw Kate.

Sunlight did wonders for her, as well. Gone was the ghostly pallor that had worried Nadine. Some color had returned to Kate's cheeks, her hair had been washed and combed — although it was a bit limper than Nadine was used to — and she actually managed a return smile.

"Good morning, you," Kate said, her voice still somewhat raspy.

"Good morning." Nadine stepped aside to allow the nurse to leave the room. She moved closer to the bed and said the only thing that came to mind. "How are you feeling?"

"Like something Death brought with him in a suitcase."

Nadine had to grin. "I love it when you quote classic rock to me."

Kate held out her hand. Nadine took it as she sat down next to the bed in a hideous orange plastic chair that made her back twinge. "Are you really okay?" she asked.

"I hate that question," Kate said. She groaned and nodded toward the door. "I met the psychiatrist first thing this morning. She caught me washing my hair in the bathroom sink and treated it like I was being reborn."

"I guess it was a sign you were planning to be around for a while."

"I guess," Kate murmured. "They didn't put a seventy-two-hour hold on me or move me to the psych ward, so I guess it's a good sign like you said."

Nadine shifted in her seat and scooted forward. "Kate, I have to apologize. I am...so sorry about this weekend."

Kate frowned. "Sorry?"

"I shut you out. You wanted to talk, and I just...I turned my back on you. I'm sorry I wasn't there for you, Kate."

Kate looked horrified. "No. Nadine...no. Nothing about this is your fault. Please don't think that. It's all because of that stupid article. If I'd never written it..." She bit her lip and ran her thumb along Nadine's knuckles. "If I had died with you thinking that, I would...it would have..." She clenched her jaw and went on, "I would've come back to haunt you until you wised up!"

Nadine laughed and covered her mouth with her free hand. "You would not."

"Trust me," Kate said. "When I was about to go into the light, I saw two doors. Afterlife. Haunting. I would've picked haunting."

"Well, I was going to worry about you today, but if you were just going to *haunt* me..." Nadine smiled and shook her head. It felt wonderful to smile, to laugh with Kate again, to hear Kate joke, to see the light in her eyes. It was enough to banish the fear Nadine had felt ever since walking into Kate's apartment and finding her unconscious on the couch, so terrifyingly small and pale and still. "I know I just got here, but...work. Staff meeting. I just wanted to come by and see you before I went in."

"It means a lot. I've been thinking about you all night."

Nadine stood up and bent over the bed, brushing her lips over Kate's. "Mm, you'll have to tell me about it when you're feeling better..."

"No, not that way," Kate tightened her hand on Nadine's and went on, "Could you...wait? Just for a few minutes? There's something we need to talk about."

"I'm on the bike, and..." Nadine realized the station was not more than a couple of blocks away. She checked her watch and nodded. "Yeah, I think I can stay. What is it?"

Kate looked down at their interlocked hands. "I didn't want to do it like this, but...you shouldn't have to wait. Your boss. Minerva?"

"Miranda," Nadine said.

"Whatever," Kate said, giving her a sly grin. "You said she brought you here last night. Sat with you. Held your hand?"

"Yeah. Kate, you don't have to worry about..."

"Shh, Dean, let me finish, dear, please. You should go for her."

Nadine nearly jerked her hand away in shock. "What? Miranda isn't...isn't gay."

"Please," Kate said. "Investigative reporter here, Dean."

"You met her for five minutes!"

"I saw enough to know she wasn't a boss checking on her employee. She was here for you, Nadine. For no reason other than she cared for you."

Nadine shifted uncomfortably. It was not her place to out Miranda. And now, as much as she hated to admit it, she knew she had to be careful what she said around Kate. "Even if she was..."

"Okay, we can play the hypothetical game. If she was gay." Kate sighed and continued, "Honey, I'm...I do love you. And I love what we have." She sounded contrite. "But I know that you've been drifting away from me lately. In a way, it was my fault you were at that meeting in the first place."

Nadine's hackles rose. She snapped, "Stop blaming yourself!"

"I'm not, I'm not," Kate soothed. "You were just desperate for a real connection. A date, I guess. I've been lying here thinking and I can't remember the last time we were together on a date, just enjoying each other's company. That's what the weekend was supposed to be, that's why you came with me to the meeting. Maybe we could've had what you wanted, but I think it's too late for us now."

Nadine bowed her head to hide the tears welling in her eyes. "Are you breaking up with me?"

"I guess," Kate whispered. "Not because I'm angry with you or tired of you or...it's because I love you, Nadine. You deserve to be in a relationship that's actually going somewhere. A relationship where you can say 'I am in love with this person' and it's not just about sex. Can you honestly say that about us?"

Nadine was both ashamed and relieved to hear those words from Kate; she had been thinking the exact same thing over the past few weeks, but hearing the words come from Kate....it was one thing to know it with her own heart, but quite another to know Kate was feeling the same thing. "I can't," she admitted, feeling her heart break. "I can't say that. I'm so sorry, Kate."

"Don't be sorry," Kate whispered. "Kiss me."

Nadine kissed her again, long and soft and sweet, the kind of kiss they had not shared in a long time.

Kate touched Nadine's cheek and slipped her hand around the back of her head, holding her in place. When they parted, Kate said, "I love you, Nadine. Enough to let you go."

"You're such a cliché," Nadine laughed. Her tears finally slipped free and fogged up her glasses. Hugging Kate gently, she continued, "I love you, Kate."

"Go to work," Kate said. "I'm crying, and I can't waste the moisture."

Nadine chuckled straightened up, wiping her wet eyes with the pads of her fingers. "I'll come back after work. Unless...do you want me to?"

"Yes, please. I want to see you." Smiling, Kate released Nadine's hand. "Go on," she said, making a shooing gesture. "I don't want to make you late."

"Okay, okay. I know where I'm not wanted. Get some rest, Kate."

"I will."

"See you in a few hours."

Nadine waved once more before she left the room and headed for the stairs in a near-daze. She and Kate were actually broken up. Apart, separated, no more, et cetera. Beyond that, she was shocked by Kate's mention of Miranda. She was elated, shocked, surprised, stunned...her emotions were at war, but she did not care. Outside in the cool air, she looked up at the cloudy sky and said aloud, "I'm free. I'm free, Miranda came out last night...I have Kate's blessing..."

Speaking the words did not make them any easier to believe. Nadine repeated the mantra inside her head as she unlocked her bike and climbed onto the seat. *Free. Miranda's out. Kate's blessing.*

For the first time in a long time, and especially since Saturday, Nadine felt liberated. After all this time...Kate was going to be all right, and they had finally — finally! — come to an understanding about their relationship. She was ready to cry, she was so relieved. They may have parted, but the break-up had been so easy, so amicable and friendly that maybe some sort of friendship could be salvaged. They had always been friends first, lovers second...maybe now they could be best friends without the "benefits".

Nadine rode her bike into the wind, the breeze cold on her face as she pedaled down the street.

Life was looking better.

Chapter Nine

Nadine, flushed from her conversation with Kate and out of breath from pushing her bike to its limits, rounded the corner at speed, feeling like the leader of the Tour de France. Protesters lined the sidewalk across from KELF, held at bay by a blue-painted sawhorse and Deputy Randall White's patrol car parked at the curb. The sight of the protesters dimmed her mood slightly, but she was still riding on the wave of good feelings her visit with Kate had given her.

She rode past the deputy's position, and the voice of the crowd rose into an incoherent shout. Nadine waved to White as she went past and parked her bike next to the rack. The deputy climbed from his car and started across the street. One of the protesters with a particularly booming voice shouted, "What you're doing is unnatural!"

White turned and walked backwards as he shouted back, "At least she's having sex!"

The protester, a whippet-thin college kid, shrank back from the ex-soldier's gaze. White faced forward again and stepped onto the curb, giving Nadine a surprisingly sheepish smile.

"Sorry about that, Miss Butler. That was crude of me," White said.

"Oh, hell, no," she said. "If I had the guts, I would've said the same thing. Or...well, maybe something less crude."

He smiled and tilted his head toward the crowd. "I'll be out here as long as I can, make sure they behave themselves. No matter what, though, I'm going to be here when you get off at five to keep the peace."

"Thank you. It means a lot."

"Just doing my job, ma'am. Have a good show."

She thanked him again, and they separated, her to the front door of the station and him back to his patrol car. As soon as she stepped into the heat of the KELF lobby, the sweat on the sides of her face began to evaporate. She swept a hand through her wind-tangled hair and smiled at Sue. "Morning, Sue."

Sue was immediately on her feet, her hands fluttering around her collar. "Oh, Nadine, was that *you* on the phone yesterday? I am so sorry, I had *no* idea. Can you ever, ever forgive me for..."

Nadine moved quickly around the desk and hugged Sue. "It's all right. I'm fine. Everything worked out fine."

"Are you sure?"

"Absolutely. No hard feelings."

Sue exhaled, looking relieved. "Okay. Thank you, Nadine. I'm so sorry."

Nadine assured the woman again that everything was fine and went upstairs to the office. The round table they used for their meetings had been set up to one side of the cubicle maze and Hoagie was already in his seat, his head down, his eyes closed, apparently asleep. Nadine dumped her coat at her desk and headed toward Miranda's office at the back of the room.

She stopped at the door and took a moment to admire her boss. Miranda was wearing a red suit, an outfit she had worn before, but something about it seemed different; she seemed softer yet more *real* than she had ever been before. Nadine wondered what she felt was a typical reaction to being in someone's home late at night, taking comfort from their presence. Knowing Miranda was gay could also be a part of it.

Miranda finally looked up and caught her lurking. She smiled faintly and went back to her work. "Hello, Nadine."

Nadine had to fight to not flinch at the coldness in that voice. Was something wrong? She cleared her throat and said, "Hi. I went to see Kate this morning."

When Miranda looked up, her gaze had softened a bit. "How is she?"

"Doing better. The psychiatrist didn't see any reason to hold her, so they may release her later tonight."

Miranda breathed a sigh and straightened her back. "That's wonderful. Are you going back to the hospital later?"

"I planned to go after work."

"Tell her I said hello. We only met once, but..."

"I'll tell her. She'll be glad to know you're thinking of her."

Miranda nodded and said, "Okay. I'll start the meeting in a minute." She took her seat and rested her head on her hand. She began massaging her temples as if they ached.

Nadine could not hold back any longer. She glanced at the table where Hoagie was still sleeping and stepped into Miranda's office. Rounding the desk, she lowered her voice to a whisper. "Miranda, is everything all right? Are you uncomfortable because of what you told—"

"No," Miranda said, equally softly. She reached out and took Nadine's hand. "I don't regret telling you. But...we have to talk privately. I've asked Willa to take the first few minutes of your show, so we'll speak after the meeting, okay?"

"Okay...something we can't talk about at the staff meeting?"

"No," Miranda said again. "I'm sorry, Nadine. We should go out there."

Nadine stepped back and let Miranda stand up. They walked out of the office together while Nadine tried to ignore the niggling voice at the back of her mind and tried to brush off the familiar chill warning her that things were about to go wrong.

As they walked toward the table, Leah Nettles arrived in the bullpen. She was dressed in a ragged white T-shirt and jeans, her black hair hanging limply around her face. She was the youngest DJ at the station, but her outfits usually cut off an extra ten years from her apparent age, lending her a distinct jailbait impression. Nadine politely waved hello and paused when Leah waved her over.

"Nadine, come here a minute," Leah called.

Nadine glanced at Miranda, who gazed coolly back at her, and crossed to meet Leah halfway across the bullpen. "Hi, Leah," she said. "What's up?"

"Not much," Leah said. "I just wanted to let you know I've got your back. Hundred percent."

"Thanks, Leah. That means a—"

"And also, I don't know if you're seeing anybody, but if you want a date some Friday or Saturday, give me a call." She slipped a piece of paper into Nadine's hand.

Nadine blinked in astonishment. "You're gay?" She was wondering if being a five or six on the Kinsey scale was some kind of prerequisite for working at the station when Leah laughed.

"No, I'm not gay!" the woman said. "I am curious, though. So if you'd like to hang out, get a little wild, give me a call." She winked and brushed past Nadine, squeezing her ass cheek in passing.

Nadine squeaked and jumped at the unexpected touch. She spun around and saw Leah giving her a wide feral smile, tongue sticking between her teeth lewdly as she trotted toward the meeting table. Nadine followed her, surreptitiously dropping Leah's phone number in the garbage. She had been there and done the experimental fling thing. Maybe it was fun in her twenties, but not now. Leah would have to find her own guinea pig.

She continued her walk across the room. At the table, she took a seat next to Hoagie and nudged him gently. He sat up immediately, blinking sleepily at her and rubbing both eyes with the heels of his hands. "What? I'm up, I'm up." He sniffled. "We ready?"

"We are," Miranda said. She glanced at Leah and said, "Are you okay with the early start time, Leah? We didn't wake you or anything?"

"Like I sleep," Leah scoffed. "I'm fine, boss lady."

Miranda nodded and began straightening her notes. "Okay, first order of business is...oh." The door to the broadcasting booth opened, and Willa slipped out to join them. Nadine knew that she and Simon alternated which of them attended the monthly meetings, and it looked like this time he had won the coin toss.

The meeting got underway with discussions about contests, station identifications, and one or two complaints (not related to Nadine) that had come in. They discussed an upcoming event and decided that they would be broadcasting live from the concert. Hoagie raised his hand as volunteer to do that duty, but Nadine had the sinking feeling that, despite the controversy and Miranda's new knowledge, she would still end up going in his place.

After a quick resolution regarding who would fill in for Ben that weekend — Leah volunteered — the meeting broke up. Hoagie headed for his desk, where he promptly dropped into his chair, put his head down, and resumed his nap. Leah spoke briefly with Miranda, turned with a swish of her hips and rubbed the top of Hoagie's head as she headed out of the building. She was gone as quickly as she had appeared, leaving with only a waft of perfume to show she had been there at all.

Nadine stood up just as Willa was heading back to the booth and they ended up face-to-face. Nadine forced a smile and said, "Willa...thank you for covering the first part of my show. I know you don't agree with me or..."

"I don't agree with what you are," Willa said curtly, "but I've always thought of you as a friend. So...here." She reached into her pocket and slapped a pamphlet into Nadine's hand. "Read that when you're ready to change your life for the better. Despite this little bump in the road, I have always liked you, Nadine."

Nadine waited until Willa returned to the booth before she looked down at the pamphlet. *Reparative therapy: a way to a happier, healthier, holier you*, she read.

The cover showed a man and woman huddling together in front of a horse, looking blissfully happy and undeniably heterosexual. "I guess I'll go straight," Nadine muttered. "I've always wanted a horse like that." She resisted the urge to rip the offensive pamphlet in half and instead stuck it into her back pocket. Going to Miranda's office, she paused in the doorway to push down the anger she was feeling at Willa, then stepped inside the office. "You wanted to speak to me about something?"

Miranda had just poured a small white pill into her hand from a prescription bottle. "Yes, please close the door," she said. She put the pill into her mouth, following it with a swig of water. Nadine twitched. She wondered how long it would be before she could see someone pop a pill without worrying.

Closing the door, Nadine took one of the seats opposite Miranda's desk. The foreboding chill had returned, making her arms prickle with goosebumps. She crossed her legs and tried to remain casual. "What's wrong? Miranda, if I did anything last night that..."

"Stop blaming yourself," Miranda said. Nadine was struck dumb by the déjà vu of the moment; it was exactly the same thing she had told Kate in the hospital room. Miranda continued, "Last night after I dropped you off, I got a call from Mr. Dugan."

Nadine braced herself for the worst. If a call from Dugan was making Miranda this uncomfortable, it had to be bad news. "This won't be good. Will it?"

"No," Miranda said softly. She had yet to meet Nadine's eyes. "He called to say that Joe Lack was indeed pulling his sponsorship. There was a...a miscommunication, I suppose." She rubbed the bridge of her nose and went on, "But he's not alone. Also pulling out are Chin's, Yolk Folks, Duck Soup Restaurant, and...Dean, I'm so sorry. Gail's pulled out, too."

"Gail's?" Nadine breathed. It was like being told her oldest friend had turned their back on her.

"It's something to do with his father. I don't know. I don't...it doesn't matter. Dugan is furious. He says that if we can't advertise during your show, we might as well...not run it at all. Dean, he wants..."

The chill had transformed into a block of ice, hanging just behind her ribs and freezing everything it touched. "I'm being fired. Aren't I?"

"No," Miranda said firmly. "He said you were last night, but I managed to talk him down. It's a...a temporary leave of absence."

"Please," Nadine scoffed. "You and I both know that if I walk out that door, I'm not coming back in there. Not to work, not ever again. And we both know I'm being fired because I'm gay."

When Miranda finally looked up, Nadine was shocked to see she was crying. "Yeah. Basically, yes, you are."

"That's wrong, Miranda. That is..." She could handle losing Gail's support, but now she felt like she was losing Miranda's as well.

"You don't think I know that, Nadine? I haven't slept the past two nights because I've been fighting this tooth and nail, but I can't fight forever, and I can't sacrifice my own job, Dean. You have to know I fought as hard as I could for you."

"I know you did," Nadine said softly. She got to her feet. "Thank you for fighting a little for me, Miranda. It means a hell of a lot."

"Don't do this to me, Dean."

"My name is Nadine." She did not care if it sounded petty. In the past three days, two people who supposedly care for her had sold her out for the sake of keeping their jobs. She was sick of it.

"Dean," Miranda said firmly. She stood up and went on, "Sit your ass back down."

Nadine reluctantly took her seat. Miranda sat down and leaned forward across the desk. "You are my friend," she said. "If I hadn't proven that before, I did last night. As long as I have this job, you're going to have an advocate. I won't let you go without fighting, but you have got to back off. Just for now. Give Dugan a little win so he'll be more willing to give in a little in a week or so."

Nadine closed her eyes. "I'm tired of waiting for another week or so. I'm just so tired, Miranda. I may have come out accidentally, but...hell. Maybe I *wanted* out. Maybe I finally got sick of it and forced myself to do it subconsciously. I don't know. Freud would have a field day with it, I'm sure."

The music that had been filling the room as white noise suddenly cut off, and Willa Lamb's voice took its place. "That was *Life on Mars* by David Bowie and no, you're not hearing things. I'm still Willa Lamb and I'm just filling in for Nadine Butler for a couple of minutes. She'll be here with you soon with music by Bob Dylan, Manfred Mann, and War. One of us will be here to take your calls after these commercials."

Nadine frowned at the wall-mounted speaker. "What did she just say? You just said..."

"It's your last show," Miranda said, "before the suspension kicks in. It was Dugan's idea, actually, since you were coming in anyway for the staff meeting. He said that it was the least he could do for your listeners."

"So he admits I have listeners but not that people want to hear me. Great."

Miranda opened her mouth, perhaps to apologize again, and closed it before she could say anything.

Nadine stood up again. "Well, I guess I better get in there for my swan song."

She left before Miranda could call her back. As she walked toward the booth, Nadine gazed out over the bullpen one final time. There was Hoagie, still asleep at his desk. Billy was washing off the white marker board that listed current long-running contests and upcoming concerts. She saw her jacket draped over her own chair, something so familiar and everyday that it almost made her cry to think it might be the last time she would see it that way.

Pushing down her emotions, she opened the door to the booth. Willa already had her things gathered and stood up as soon as Nadine stepped inside and said again, "Thank you for filling in for me, Willa."

Willa nodded and stopped at the door. She turned and said in a sickly, falsely-sweet voice, "You will think about that program, won't you, dear?"

"Yeah. I'll think on it a lot," Nadine said. Willa started to walk out; Nadine waited until she was almost to the stairs before she continued. "I think it's funny, though."

Willa turned, her eyebrow lifted in mute inquiry.

Nadine went on, "Gays and lesbians are shunned, and we're treated like we have some kind of disease. Like everyone's afraid it's some disease you can catch. But it seems to me that straight people are the only ones who are trying to do the converting. Toaster oven jokes aside, we don't try to turn anyone gay, but you guys won't stop until all us heathens are straight." She smiled sweetly. "It just seems bizarre to me."

Willa huffed and disappeared down the stairs.

Billy turned from the white board and smiled. "Good one, Miss Butler."

"Thanks, Billy."

"Need any song times?"

Nadine glanced at the microphone, at the currently dark on-air sign and said, "No, Billy. Not today."

"All right, Miss Butler. You just let me know if you change your mind."

"I will."

She went into the booth and shut the door. Glancing at the knob, she bemoaned the lack of a lock. After scanning the room, she spotted the chair Simon used for the morning show. Nadine grabbed it and unfolded the seat, made sure it was sturdy, and jammed it under the knob so no one could get into the booth. Her heart was pounding in her chest as she rounded the table and took her seat.

The headphones fit her well, disturbing her glasses a little but not enough to be distracting. She rested her finger on the on-air button and closed her eyes. They had backed her into the corner — Willa, the protesters, Thomas Dugan...now it was time to show them that the Pixie could fight back.

If it was going to be her last show on the air, she was going to make it count.

Nadine hit the on-air button and began to speak.

Miranda splashed her face with cold water in the tiny private bathroom next to her office. Tears had been threatening all day and, until the confrontation with Nadine, she had been able to hold them at bay by negotiating over the phone with Thomas Dugan in a last ditch effort to change his mind. But being forced to be the messenger, telling Nadine she would have to be off the air for an indefinite amount of time, had finally broken down her defenses.

She splashed a little more water on her face to be presentable and went back into the main office. Nadine was justifiably pissed at her and, for the first time since coming to Squire's Isle, she felt like the bad guy. She had left her Manhattan job when it became more about office politics than actually running a good radio station. As much as she hated to admit it, maybe it was time she packed up and moved on to a new place.

Miranda returned to her desk just in time to hear the tail end of the commercial for the charter flight services before Nadine's voice returned.

"Honey?" Tamara Butler called to her husband as she entered the back room of the photography studio. "Do you have the packet for Erin Williams?"

Nathaniel looked up from the table and cleared his throat. "Yeah, right here." He walked to the counter and began rifling through the bags of developed film. She walked past him and switched on the radio that was tucked underneath the film developer. "What are you doing?" he asked without glancing around.

"Hush, I want to listen to Nadine a little," Tamara said.

He growled low in his throat and finally found a packet marked Williams. As he carried it into the other room, Tamara angled the radio antennae toward the ceiling, adjusting the reception until Nadine's voice came through the speaker.

"Good morning, everyone. My name is Nadine Butler and, if I sound a little subdued today, it's for good reason. You see, I'm going on a temporary leave of absence from my job. And we all know what that means: I got canned." There was a flushing toilet noise, and Nadine went on, "Thank you to Hoagie; hope he doesn't mind me borrowing his sound effects."

Tamara brought a quaking hand to her cheek and said, "Oh, no. Oh, my poor Nadine..." Her eyes filled with tears as she listened to her daughter's defiant voice coming through the speakers.

Hoagie hated waking up with someone touching him, especially if he did not remember going to bed with anyone. He cracked an eyelid, finding Billy hovering over him. "What do you...oh," Hoagie said. "You need to clean here or..."

"No, Mr. Hogan," Billy was the only person who never called him Hoagie. "I think something's about to happen with Miss Butler."

"Is she all right?" Hoagie asked, immediately awake. He stood and looked around the room, half-expecting to see the protesters had gotten into the building.

Billy looked uncertain, but finally he nodded. "I think so. Physically, least-ways. But I don't know if she's all right in the head."

Hoagie started toward the booth just as Miranda flung open the door to her office and began running in the same direction.

Deputy White's car pulled away from the curb just after Nadine began broad-casting. A call had come in, and Sheriff Rucker was tied up at the office. He figured that nothing would happen so long as Butler was safe and sound inside the radio station, so he radioed Dispatch that he was answering the call. Rucker agreed and told him to be sure to return before she went off the air in case the protesters hung around.

As he drove by the knot of protesters, he saw someone near the back of the crowd holding a portable radio. A chorus of loud boos went up. White was not quite alarmed, but in his book it paid to take precautions. He picked up his radio mic, steering the patrol car around the corner one-handed. "Sheriff, the protesters are making a bit of a ruckus. Where's Adam?"

"Still up dealing with those drunk tourists in Sholeh," Rucker replied. "They look like they're going to cause any trouble?"

White peered into the rear view mirror. "More sign-waving most likely. But you may want to have Adam swing by when he gets a chance, remind them we're watching."

"I may do it myself when I get caught up with this paperwork. Thanks for the heads-up, Randy."

White hooked his mic back up and concentrated on driving, leaving the street in front of KELF unprotected.

At Coffee Table Books, KELF was played loudly on the radio during Nadine Butler's program. There was a special on pink frosted "I Support the Pixie" cookies. Amy Wellis was pulling another sheet of the cookies out of the oven when someone in the main room began shushing people loudly. She walked out to see about the commotion just in time to hear Nadine announce that it was her final show.

A chorus of boos went up from the patrons of Coffee Table Books, and Amy smiled. She rang the service bell on the counter and said, "Pixie support-ers, listen up. I've got a way to let her know we're here for her..."

Kate grimaced as she was angled into the wheelchair by the nurse. Her stom-ach still felt like it had been doubling as a speed bag while she was uncon-scious, and she held herself like a pregnant woman as she sagged down into the seat. The nurse put a hand on her shoulder and assured her that the doctor would be there in a moment with the discharge papers. Kate nodded, and when the nurse had left, wheeled herself back to the bed.

She leaned over the railing and found the television controller, then punched a few buttons until she found the combination that turned on the radio. She tuned it until the static cleared and heard her girlfriend — no, ex-girlfriend — speaking loud and clear.

Her smile was short-lived, however, as she listened to what Nadine had to say. By the time Dr. Tom arrived, Kate was staring in disbelief. The doctor looked at Kate, listened to Nadine, and then gasped as well. Kate looked up at her, finally noticing she was not alone, and smiled proudly.

"That's my ex-girlfriend for ya," she said, chuckling.

"Good morning, everyone. My name is Nadine Butler and, if I sound a little subdued today, it's for good reason. You see, I'm going on a temporary leave of absence from my job," Nadine said into the mic, "and we all know what that means. I got canned." She punched a button to add the recorded sound of a toilet being flushed to her broadcast. "Thank you to Hoagie; hope he doesn't mind me borrowing his sound effects. Officially, I'm being fired because advertisers have been pulling out. But since they're pulling out because of the announcement in last Sunday's paper, I'm finding it hard not to feel discriminated against.

"So in the time since I was given this information — about four or five minutes ago — I've been thinking about what my final show should be. Would I do what I normally do? That'd be great, except I really can't. I don't have any sponsors, so I can't give away any tickets or any free dinners. I am going to play music, though. It's my job, it's what I love to do, and I'm not going to stop just because of some homophobic idiots. But between songs, we're going to be doing things a little different.

"Last night, I had a talk with someone. I won't tell you who; it's not my place. But this person revealed to me they were gay. That they'd been hiding it for years."

Looking through the window, Nadine saw Miranda leaving her office as if it was on fire. She went on, "And I got to thinking about it. How many other people on this island are gay? I know there have got to be a few. I've slept with some of them." She played a rim shot, another Hoagie sound effect.

"I only ask because I like to know whose bullet I'm taking. So call in. If you're gay, if you're willing to fight this fight with me, call in. Announce yourself. Let people know that I am not the only one here.

"I'm not angling to put anyone in my shoes. I would not wish what I've been through on anyone. But the feeling of liberation that comes from being out, from not hiding myself anymore? I wouldn't trade it for anything. I would not go back into the closet if I was given the chance. Life doesn't end with coming out. It can be hellish, yes. It can hurt you. It can cause strife, of course. I'm a good example of that. I've had a derogatory word painted on my apartment door. I nearly lost someone I love to suicide. Coming out is by no means an easy thing. But it is so much harder to do it alone.

"The phone lines are open, 232-5353. I'm Nadine Butler. I am a lesbian. And this is *Smiling Faces Sometimes* by the Undisputed Truth. Pay attention to the lyrics, folks. I'll be back after the music. You don't have to be on the air, but I'd sure like to hear from you. Please, give me a call."

Nadine pulled the headphones off and glanced at the window again. Miranda, Hoagie, and Billy were crowded together there, gawking at her through the glass, just as she had expected. She picked up a Sharpie and wrote on the back of the play list. Standing and walking to the window, she placed the paper against the glass so they could read what she had written. *I'M NOT SORRY & I'M NOT GOING OFF-AIR.*

Miranda pointed at Nadine and twirled her finger around her ear.

Nadine shook her head.

Miranda mouthed, "What were you thinking?"

Nadine shook her head again and shrugged. She walked back to the console and put down the play list. The phone lines were all flashing crazily. She hit the button to answer Line One.

"Good morning," Nadine said. "You're on the air with KELF and the Pixie."

"Hi, Nadine. This is Amy Wellis. We met at Squire Days on Saturday...remember?"

"I remember. Hi, Amy. Is it all right if I record this for...?"

"Yes, please, air it. Um...I work at Coffee Table Books. I inherited it from my father, and I've been serving locals and tourists for about five years now. And if this changes anyone's perception of me or my store, well...there's nothing I can do about it. I'm a lesbian."

"Thank you, Amy."

"Thank *you*, Nadine. I want all of your listeners to know that I'm having a special on 'I Support the Pixie' cookies. They were just going to be a fun gimmick, but I want everyone to come in and show their support of the greatest DJ in Washington State. If I could afford advertising, you'd have at least one sponsor."

Nadine laughed. "Thank you. It's the thought that counts, but money is nice, too. I'll talk to you later, Amy." She switched to Line Two and checked the counter on the song. She had *Quinn the Eskimo* coming up next; long enough to take at least one more call.

"This is the Pixie, Nadine Butler. Who am I talking to?"

"Reverend James McCoy from First Baptist Church. I run a reparative therapy class. I was listening to your show and if being a lesbian has led to such strife, perhaps you..."

She choked back the angry response that came to mind and struggled to keep her tone civil. "Reverend, if I may interrupt? It's not the fact that I'm a lesbian that's hurting me. Unless you're telling me that a straight relationship would be simple — no fights, no disagreements, and no heartache. If that's what I'll get from your reparative therapy, then sign me up. I've tried being straight, trust me. You want someone to lie to herself, I'm better than you religious guys at that. But I am gay and sitting in a cold folding chair talking to a group of people isn't going to change that. Thank you for your call."

She hung up before he could retaliate, and she glanced at the counter. There was not time to take another call, so she pulled Willa's pamphlet out of her back pocket. The happy, shiny straight people and their stupid horse smiled up at her from the paper as she unfolded it and began to read.

When Manfred Mann finished singing, she angled the microphone back toward her and hit the button to turn it on. "Hello, everyone," she said. "I'm sitting here reading a pamphlet I was handed this morning, and it is *very* informative. Let me tell you some things I'm learning about myself: I am mentally disturbed. I am a 'struggler'. Apparently, I feel alienated by other women and strive to gain their acceptance by any means possible, including — and I quote — 'compulsive sexual gratification'. Wow, that's very good to know.

"On top of being gay — the stigma attached to it and the reaction of my friends and coworkers — why don't I add the fear of being told it's just because I'm mentally damaged? There's another reason to stay in the closet for a while. The guilt, the pain of going through one of these reparative therapies...I've heard of them. Of course I have. When I was denying who I was, I thought a *lot* about going to one.

"The problem is this: when I was living as a straight woman, going out with men, I couldn't change myself no matter how hard I tried. I couldn't change my thoughts, my desires. I've known people who went through this conversion therapy. They tried to change their sexuality by force. One of them, it actually seems to have worked. He's married, has a kid, seems to be happy, and I'm happy for him. The others...one of them is an alcoholic. One of them is severely depressed, still in therapy and trying to undo the damage done to her psyche. I hope she makes it."

Nadine cleared her throat and blinked away tears. "The answer can't be found sitting in a circle munching on stale cookies. You have to find the answer inside yourself, and if you try to jam your foot into a shoe that doesn't fit, you're just going to destroy your toes." She shook her head at her mangled metaphor. "Maybe that doesn't make sense, I don't know. You'd have just as much trouble trying to reform a lefty. You can train him, you can tie one hand behind his back, but he's still going to cut himself when he tries to shave."

She cleared her throat and glanced at the clock. "Okay. Okay, um...I'll probably have more to say on that later. Right now, I'm going to play *Why Can't We Be Friends?* Stick with the Pixie."

Nadine shut off the mic and, a moment later, her cell phone rang. She fished it out, looked at the Caller ID and frowned. Spinning around in her chair, she saw Miranda in the bullpen, cell phone against her ear. She was holding a piece of paper against the glass.

PICK UP, read the paper.

Nadine answered her phone and was the first to speak. "I'm not going off the air."

"Nadine," Miranda sighed. "What the hell are you doing? This isn't right."

"It's the best course of action."

"According to whom?"

"To me!" Nadine said. She was suddenly furious. She had taken this lying down for long enough, and it was time she took a stand. Not only for herself, but for Kate, for every person who had ever hidden an essential part of who they were because of shame and fear. She stood and walked closer to the glass. "I have been letting people steamroll over me ever since I came out. But I'm not going to take it any more! I'm making a stand. I have one last show; let me use it the way I must. Please, Miranda."

Before Miranda could answer, Sue appeared at the top of the stairs. Nadine frowned and pointed.

Miranda turned, pulling the phone away from her ear. The plump secretary's voice came through Nadine's cell phone, tinny and distant.

"Miss Powell!" Sue was leaning against the wall and frantically gesturing toward the stairs. "Mi-Miss Powell! You have to do something!" she cried.

"What is it? What's going on?" Miranda said.

"As soon as Miss Butler started talking, the protesters crossed the street! They started banging on the glass, and I managed to get the doors locked when I saw they meant to come in. But then they started leaning against the doors a-and I think they're going to try and break in!"

"No," Miranda said. She shook her head and said, "Deputy White is out there. I saw him myself when I came in..."

Sue interrupted. "No, ma'am, he's not! He left as soon as Nadine went on the air. I think he got a call, but...there's no one out there to stop those crazy people! What on earth do they want?"

"Me," Nadine said, knowing no one could hear her. Fear constricted her chest until it was hard to breathe.

Miranda turned and put the phone back to her ear, locking gazes with Nadine through the glass.

Nadine was terrified. Her lower lip trembled as she spoke into the phone, "They're going to come in and yank me out."

Miranda jumped suddenly and turned back to the stairs.

"What happened?" Nadine asked.

"I think I just heard something crack," Miranda reported. "Like glass."

Nadine swallowed hard. She locked eyes with Miranda and said without a hint of irony, "They're coming to take me away. Don't let them. Please, Miranda, don't let them get in here."

Chapter Ten

When Willa left the radio station after her show ended, she walked directly across the street and joined the crowd of protestors. Her Sunday school class was gathered near the curb. One of them carrying a portable radio started a chorus of boos when Nadine came on the air. Willa embraced one of her friends and turned to Eleanor, who asked, "Did you give her the pamphlet, Willa?"

"I did," Willa said, sneering at the memory of Nadine's less-than-enthusiastic reception. "But she insulted it *and* us. Of course, I wouldn't have expected anything less from one of *them*."

"Peace, sister," another woman said. She laid a comforting hand on Willa's shoulder. "Love the sinner, hate the sin."

"The bright side is they're firing her after today," Willa said, eager to impart this bit of excellent news. "This is her last broadcast."

Eleanor nodded proudly, as if she had had a direct hand in Nadine's firing. "Oh, yes, Ms. Butler brought that up right away." She eyed the radio as if it was venomous. "Right before she started rallying the troops."

"What?" Willa snapped. She moved closer so she could hear the broadcast for herself. When Nadine began mocking the reparative therapy process, Willa spat, "That won't stand. That won't stand at all. Someone give me a phone! I'm going to..."

Eleanor interrupted. "No, we're not going to call in to her show, make spectacles of ourselves for her and her little homosexual friends. We're going to shut her up right now." She raised her voice and addressed the crowd. "Who's with me? Who will silence this unnatural woman who wants to corrupt our children and destroy our way of life?"

The crowd fell silent and watchful. A few people shifted nervously to the back of the crowd, seemingly uncertain of their loyalty to the cause. Willa watched them out of the corner of her eye, but her attention was quickly diverted back to Eleanor, who was still speaking.

"Who will be a soldier for God? Who will join me in silencing the disgusting pervert who is still spewing her filth?" Eleanor's eyes gleamed with the fervor of a true fanatic.

Willa shivered, transfixed by the woman's transformation. Eleanor seemed to gather substance to herself, to grow in stature and loom larger, to crackle with a mesmerizing electricity she had never owned before. The Lord was there, shining measureless in Eleanor; Willa could sense it.

"The law won't help us. We have to help ourselves! Who will stop Satan's work today? Who will make a stand for righteousness? Who will end the abomination?" Eleanor's voice cracked, becoming a shrill shout. "Who will join me?"

There came a moment when time seemed to have stopped, as if the world was holding its breath. A couple of people on the fringes of the crowd were beginning to slip away, slinking down the street like beaten dogs. Cowards! Willa felt ashamed for them that they did not have the fortitude to carry through with their holy mission. Fury beat at her insistently. Why was Nadine such a popular DJ? She was no better than Willa. No better at all! Nadine was just an abomination in the eyes of the Lord. A filthy abomination! Anger hummed through Willa and settled hot in her belly.

Tension shattered as voices rose around her in a cry of wordless rage.

A man screamed, "Stop her! Stop her now!"

When everyone surged across the street, led by Eleanor, Willa obeyed instinct and followed the pack.

Hoagie said to Miranda, "We won't let them get her. Trust us." He headed for the stairs and saw Billy anxiously wringing his mop handle with both hands. Hoagie paused and motioned downstairs with his head. "Come on, Billy. You wanna lend a hand?"

Billy nodded and said, "Anything for Miss Butler, Mr. Hogan."

Hoagie slapped the man on his back. Together, they ran toward the stairs. As they passed Sue, Hoagie hooked his arm in her elbow and said, "I'm going to assume you want to leave, right?"

She looked nervously between Hoagie and Miranda. "Um...y-yes?"

"Not a problem," Hoagie said. "I totally understand. When we get downstairs, Billy and I are gonna make sure you get out okay."

Sue exhaled and said, "Thank you, sir." She looked grateful.

Billy took the time to pull his mop free from the bucket as he hurried to follow Hoagie downstairs. He brandished it like a sword, flinging droplets of soapy water against the walls. Hoagie could hear the glass-fronted doors rattling as the people outside tried to fight the locks. He thought the locks would hold, but it was only a matter of time before one of the protestors shattered the glass.

Hoagie ushered Sue toward the reception desk. "Call Sheriff Rucker and get him down here *now*! Billy, give me your mop."

Billy tossed the mop across the room. Hoagie snatched it out of the air. He spun around and moved toward the door, rapping the wooden end against the tile floor. Each crack sounded like a shotgun blast. The people at the front of the crowd saw him coming and began backing away from the doors. Hoagie swung the wet end of the mop at the doors and shouted, "All right! Back off and shut up!" When the din died down a little, he continued, "You are not getting into this station! You are not going to damage this building any further, and you are most definitely not going to harm Miss Nadine Butler. We've called the sheriff, and he's going to be down here in just a few minutes. Have I made myself crystal clear?"

At the word "sheriff", several members of the mob began to back off. One or two remained against the glass, and Hoagie lunged forward at them. They retreated at last and moved closer to the curb. He waved the mop once more for good measure. Sue moved up behind him and ducked the swinging head of the mop.

"The sheriff is on his way," she said, watching the crowd with wide eyes.

"Good," Hoagie said. "I look forward to having a nice little chat with him." He stepped forward and twisted the lock open. "Stand back! We're just letting this lady out so she can go home. Stay away from the doors." The crowd stepped into the street, and Hoagie found himself wishing for a convenient garbage truck to come by and solve the problem for him. He opened the door wide enough for Sue, and she stepped gratefully outside.

"Tell Miss Butler that I'm pulling for her, but I...I just..." Sue stammered.

"She'll understand," Hoagie assured the woman. "Go on, get somewhere safe."

Sue ducked out and dashed toward the parking lot. Hoagie shut the door before anyone could get any bright ideas. He stepped back, keeping the mop by his side. Looking at Billy, he said, "Well, looks like we're going to have us a good old-fashioned standoff."

"S'okay," Billy replied, shrugging. "I didn't have no plans today anyway."

Hoagie laughed and patted the man on the back, though he could not help feeling a little remorseful. He was happy to help Nadine and all, but he had really been looking forward to napping at his desk.

Miranda was alone in the bullpen. While Nadine watched her, she pulled a chair from a nearby desk and sat down next to the window. She leaned forward, resting a hand on her knee, the other clutching her cell phone to her ear. "Nadine, I wish you had talked to me about this," she said.

"Yeah, right," Nadine scoffed into her own phone. "Like you would have let me get anywhere near this booth if I had told you what I'd planned?"

Miranda sagged back in the chair and kept her gaze locked on her feet.

Nadine sighed. She did not feel the need to apologize, but after all Miranda had done, she deserved at least an explanation. "I'm not saying this is the most brilliant idea I've ever had. But I had to do *something*, Miranda. Can you at least see that?"

"I can," Miranda said, sitting up slightly. "I think it's either the bravest or the craziest thing I've ever seen. And I promise you, Nadine, as long as you're in there, I'll be out here for you."

Nadine pressed her palm against the cool glass and closed her eyes, grateful to know Miranda was still in her corner.

"Nadine..." Miranda's voice was insistent.

"I'm not crying," Nadine replied.

"No, Nadine...dead air."

Nadine's eyes snapped open, and she turned around, automatically checking the clock. The song had ended, and the station had been broadcasting silence for the past fifteen seconds.

Closing her cell phone, Nadine slid her chair back into place. She slapped the headphones on, missing one ear entirely as she jabbed the on-air button with her thumb. "Whoa, hey, sorry about that folks. We're having a bit of excitement here at the station...seems a couple of uninvited guests are trying to get in the front doors. But don't you worry. I've got some great friends here watching my back, and we're not going down easy. Right now, I'm going to answer a few more of your calls. You're on the air with the Pixie. What's your name?"

"James." It was a teenager's voice, Nadine thought, not many years since it cracked at puberty. "I-I-I...my name is James," he repeated.

"Hi, James, thank you very much for calling."

"Am I on the air right now?"

"You are. Would you prefer not to be?"

"No, it's okay. I just...I wanted to ask if you were really happier. Being out, I mean."

"I am," Nadine said. She was not surprised to learn that she meant it. Her life had been one disaster after another since she came out, but at the core of it all was relief and yes, she had to admit a kind of happiness. "With everything else I'm going through right now, it's a...a relief to not have to worry about hiding it anymore." There was silence on the other end of the line, and she went on, "James, are you still there?"

"Yeah."

"Take your time. You don't have to do or say..."

"I'm gay."

Nadine closed her eyes. She knew how hard those words must have been for him. She knew what they had to have cost him. "Have you told anyone else, James? Anyone at all...?"

"No," he said. He was sobbing quietly into the phone.

"James, listen to me. Find someone to talk to. Not me, I don't know you. Find someone you trust, a counselor, a teacher...anyone who you think will listen without judging and will help you figure this out. You've made a big step, but you've got a hard road, okay? You need to talk to someone."

"Okay."

"Promise me, James."

He sniffled and said, "I promise. Thank you, Nadine."

"Thank you for calling, James." She switched off the call and thought about what to say for a moment. She felt vindicated; if that one phone call was all she got, if James was the only person she reached today, then it was all worth it. Finally, she said, "James, if you're still listening, I wish you the best. I hope you find someone to support you because it's hell going through this alone. I've had someone wonderful holding my hand since this all started. I don't think I'm exaggerating when I say I owe my life to her." She turned in her seat to face Miranda. The woman had her head down and was wiping at her cheeks. Nadine smiled and turned back to face the mic. "If she's listening, I want to say...thank you to her. From the bottom of my heart. Thank you."

After clearing her throat, she went on, "Okay, uh...we're going to continue with our theme with a little mellow music. I'm going to dedicate *Bridge Over Troubled Water* by Simon and Garfunkel to my guardian angel. Stay tuned and keep listening to KELF."

Nadine switched the song on and stood up. By the time she reached the door of the booth, Miranda was already there. Without thinking about defense or keeping the lines firmly drawn, Nadine yanked the chair out from under the knob and pulled the door open. She fell into Miranda's arms and hugged the woman tightly, feeling Miranda's wet cheeks against her hair.

Holding Miranda, she felt something almost like love stirring inside of her. It was not just seeing Miranda's house, it was not just the fact that she was gay. Kate was right, there was more than a simple attraction there. She cupped the back of Miranda's head and whispered, "Thank you so much, Miranda." She kissed Miranda's cheek and let her lips linger for a moment. Miranda pulled back and rested her forehead against Nadine's, looking into her eyes. Nadine was frightened to see that there was something like love reflected there as well. "Oh, God, what have we gotten into?" she asked.

Miranda smiled and kissed Nadine's lips. "I don't know. But until we find out, I'm here for you."

Nadine squeezed Miranda's hand.

Sheriff Rucker's patrol car cut through the crowd of protestors, the lights flashing and the siren bleating every few seconds to make sure everyone in the mob knew he was there. He parked at the curb outside the station doors and stepped out onto the pavement. The crowd had not quite dispersed, but they were under considerably more control than he had heard they were a few minutes ago.

At the sight of the tan uniform and badge, Hoagie unlocked the door again. He held the door open and said to Billy, "No one gets in here but me or the sheriff."

"You got it, Mr. Hogan. Ain't no one gonna hurt Miss Butler on my watch."

Hoagie gave the man an approving grin and stepped outside. Rucker was already standing in front of the door and examining the buckled frame. Hoagie smiled. "Glad you could make it, Sheriff. Don't know how long we could've kept them back with just a mop."

"Better than paperwork, son," Rucker said. "How many people were trying to knock this down?" he asked.

"A few of 'em," Hoagie said. He scanned the crowd, but could not definitely point at any one person as the culprit. "Can't name anyone specific, though."

"Problem with mobs," Rucker said, shrugging. He scratched his cheek and added, "I already got them all on disorderly conduct, public nuisance, blocking a public roadway...I might as well add vandalism to the charges." He looked at the ruined door. "I think I could even make a case for attempted assault. This circus got a ringleader?"

Hoagie spotted Willa at the back of the crowd. They regarded each other silently for a moment. Hoagie kept his voice flat and emotionless as he said, "I didn't see anyone being more troublesome than anybody else."

Before Hoagie could speak, a new voice cried out, "Some madwoman has taken over my station!"

Hoagie turned to see. Thomas Dugan hauling his six-foot-four frame out of his car. The station owner pushed aside protesters that got in his way and planted his considerable bulk in front of the shorter, thinner police officer. "Sheriff," he said as he smoothed down the front of his expensive-looking tailored suit, "I want to know what you plan to do about this."

Rucker did not seem intimidated by the looming man. He placed his hands on his hips and calmly said, "Well, until I have a little more information, Mr. Dugan, I'm not sure what I can do. I had my deputy down here watching things, but he was called away. Mr. Hogan here was just about to explain exactly what was going on when you interrupted."

Speaking rapid-fire, Hoagie explained the situation as best he was able without growing too angry. He recapped the morning meeting and the leave of absence Nadine had apparently been slapped with.

Dugan made a scoffing sound and interrupted, "She should have just been fired, saved everyone all this trouble. No last show, just a severance check — a generous severance package, I should mention, Sheriff — to avoid all of this ballyhoo."

"Ballyhoo?" Hoagie asked incredulously.

Dugan sighed and slowly said, as if speaking to a mentally deficient person, "It means a ruckus."

Hoagie frowned. "I know what it means, you patronizing twit. It's just a stupid-sounding word."

Rucker held up his hands and said, "Gentlemen, please. Now, I know you're not going to like hearing this, Mr. Dugan, but at the moment I don't think there's anything we can do."

"What?"

"According to Mr. Hogan here, Miss Butler was allowed one final show. Did you agree to that with the station manager?"

Dugan huffed and crossed his arms over his chest. "Well, yes, we spoke briefly about..."

"Okay," Rucker interrupted. "Mr. Hogan, how long is she usually on the air?"

"Eleven till five," Hoagie said, with a grin. He knew exactly where this was going, and he intended to enjoy every micro-second.

Rucker glanced at his watch and shook his head. "Well, there you go, Mr. Dugan. So far all she's guilty of is doing her job. The job you paid her to do, that you gave her permission to do one last time."

Dugan gestured at the building. "I did *not* give her permission to do this! I have a serious complaint with the...the...the content of this program!"

"File a complaint with the station manager, and it will be addressed in a timely manner," Rucker said. "It's the way you handle all other complaints, so I don't see why this should be any different."

"If I could add, Sheriff?" Hoagie asked. Rucker nodded, and Hoagie turned to the owner. "In your own words, Mr. Dugan, you don't know a darned thing about being on the radio. Said it when you hired me. You told me that you'd always be a hands-off boss. Said you'd be happy to let us follow our inspirations to make our shows the very best. It's how I became Hoagie and how Nadine became the Pixie."

"You cannot possibly think I meant..."

Rucker stepped between them. "Okay, Mr. Hogan's assertion aside...it sounds like there's really nothing you can do, Mr. Dugan. If you'd like, I could make sure she doesn't attempt to re-enter the premises tomorrow morning."

"Tomorrow," Dugan scoffed. He put his hands on his hips and glared at the building. "Damn it. Fine. It's not worth it. Let her get her kicks, so long as she's gone tomorrow." He aimed a finger at Rucker and growled, "But I'll remember this, Rucker. Remember whose name is on your paychecks!"

Rucker frowned. "The Mayor's name...that would be your *brother's* name, wouldn't it? You want to drag His Honor into this, you go right ahead."

Dugan huffed a few more times before admitting Rucker had called his bluff. "Fine!" He spun around on his heel, storming back to his car.

"Thanks, Sheriff," Hoagie said with a sight of relief.

Rucker's expression was stoically neutral, giving nothing away. "Everything I said to Dugan was the truth, Mr. Hogan. Up to a point. Dugan owns this station. He could have made an official complaint, fired her outright, charged her with trespassing, unlawful broadcast. There's a whole number of things he could've done rather than stand here and yell at me, and I would have had to stand aside." A tiny smile touched the corners of his mouth. "Of course, if he's not smart enough to think of it himself, I am under no obligation to bring them up."

Hoagie laughed. "You're a good man, Sheriff. I almost wish I'd voted for ya. No offense."

"None taken. I never listen to your show."

Hoagie laughed more heartily and slapped the sheriff on the back. "You're all right, bud."

The sheriff staggered at the blow and nearly fell on his face.

"This is Nadine Butler and, if you're just joining us, we're having a special show today," Nadine said into the mic. "Since I came out as a lesbian on Saturday, I have been met with hate, prejudice, and anger. I'm trying to turn some of that around today by drawing together supporters. I've lost my advertisers, so this will be my last show on the air. But I'm not going to go quietly, and I am not going to play nice.

"If anyone out there is gay, in the closet and wants to come out, please call me. Come out here, on my show. The number is 232-KELF. Give me a call." She glanced across the board at Miranda. After their hug, Miranda had asked to come into the booth. Nadine barely hesitated. They replaced the chair under the door as an added precaution against anyone trying to pull her broadcast. Miranda promised to remain until the end of the day.

Now there was no doubt; they were in this together.

Nadine smiled and said, "Right now, we're going to clear off some of the call board so you can get in. If you try to call and get a busy signal, keep trying. I'm answering these as fast as I can. Just call back and we'll get to you."

She hit a button to send the feed to music and spoke to the caller on Line One. "Hi, you're on KELF with the Pixie."

"Hi, Nadine. Ah...Miss Butler. Sorry. I feel like I know you. But, um, my name is Clifton Gail, the manager at Gail's Seafood Shack? I just wanted to let you know my father is the one who pulled sponsorship, not me."

"I understand his decision, Mr. Gail. It may be inconvenient for me, of course, but..."

"No, I'm not done," he interrupted. "Sorry. I'm not mad at you. Far from it. The reason I didn't pull the restaurant's sponsorship is because I didn't see what had changed. I don't think you should be persecuted this way. My father had no right to make that decision; he left the responsibility for the business to me years ago. And as a business decision, I'm letting you know that your show will always be sponsored by Gail's Seafood Shack. Come hell or high water, as long as I'm in charge. You've always been my favorite DJ."

Nadine laughed in delight and said, "Thank you, Mr. Gail."

"Cliff."

"Thank you, Cliff."

She answered a few more calls, then turned on the mic. "Hey, everyone out there in the world. Thank you all for your calls, and we're clearing the board just as fast as we can. Stick in there! We're going right back to the music right now with Mr. Bob Dylan and *All Around the Watchtower*. Stay tuned to the Pixie and keep those calls coming in, please!" She leaned back in her chair and grinned at Miranda. "Gail's Seafood Shack."

Miranda made a sour face. "You'd think they sold seesaws the way they keep going back and forth."

Nadine laughed and covered her mouth. "Yeah, you'd think, but I don't care. It's a step in the right direction. I know one sponsor won't change anything, but..."

"It sure feels good to know you're not alone."

"It does," Nadine said, looking pointedly into Miranda's eyes. She realized Miranda was still holding her free hand and debated what to do. She finally cleared her throat, squeezed Miranda's fingers, and pulled away in order to set up the next song. That task done, she leaned back in her chair. "Thank you again. For being here for me."

"You don't have to keep saying it."

Nadine shrugged. "I keep being amazed by it. That you're here, that you're...that you're gay."

Miranda smiled but made no reply.

"Let's do something together," Nadine blurted. She looked down, feeling kind of shy, and went on, "When this is all over, I mean. Before I go riding off into the sunset, let's...let's get dinner. Go to the mainland and see a show or something."

Miranda glanced at the console, a faint flush on her cheeks. "What...what about Kate?"

"Kate broke up with me this morning," Nadine said, flinching at how blunt that statement sounded. "Well...no. That's a little harsh. We both decided it was best to end the relationship. We'd been in a lull for a very long time. My coming out was just the last nail in a very large coffin."

"Still," Miranda said, "I'm so sorry. Three years...that must suck, which I know is the understatement of the year." She grimaced and shook her head. "In that case, Dean, yes. I'd love to do something with you this weekend." Her eyes shifted to the clock. "The song is almost over."

Nadine scrambled with the mic. "Damn it!"

"How did you ever manage this without me?" Miranda asked.

"It's easier without you here distracting me," Nadine said playfully. She would not have guessed it at the beginning of the day, but she was actually having fun, so long as she avoided thinking too hard on what was waiting for her outside.

Miranda held up her hands. "Hey, I can leave."

She started to stand. Nadine grabbed the hem of Miranda's blouse and growled, "You sit your ass down, missy."

Miranda smiled and took her seat again. Putting her feet up on the console, she asked, "Can I make a request?"

"Troublemakers don't get to make requests."

"Boo," Miranda said.

Nadine went on, "There's Pepsi in the fridge if you get thirsty. Now I still have a job to do — for the next couple of hours, anyway — so I have to get back to work."

She pressed down a button as soon as the song set ended. "Hey, there. You're still on KELF, I'm still the Pixie, and I am still taking a stand. We've got some Elton John coming up — oh, how appropriate, it's *I'm Still Standing* — some Kansas, Sonny and Cher, and lots more. So stick with me the rest of the day, you're sure to be entertained. I'm still taking your calls at 232-KELF. Let me know what's on your mind and let me know what you want to hear. I'm Nadine Butler, and you are my last hope."

Since it seemed to keep the protesters on the opposite side of the street, Hoagie remained outside. He leaned against the wall next to the main doors, his arms crossed over his chest, Billy's mop clasped in one hand. He was so busy staring down the picketers that he almost failed to turn around when he heard Billy rapping on the glass. Hoagie finally realized the man was trying to get his attention. "What's up?" he asked.

"Trouble, Mr. Hogan, I think," Billy said.

He pointed down the street, and Hoagie finally saw the crowd moving his way. They were walking on the station-side of the street and seemed to be twice the size of the original mob. Hoagie tightened his grip on the mop and pushed away from the building, whistling through his teeth to get the sheriff's attention.

Rucker, who had returned to his car, glanced up and followed Hoagie's gaze to the end of the street. He was out of his car by the time the group had reached KELF's front doors.

The new crowd was not carrying signs. They were led by a brunette woman wearing an orange sweater and blue jeans. The sweater was partially covered by an apron emblazoned with a logo: a steaming coffee cup sitting on top of an open book. She was holding a large tray covered with blue and white napkins.

Rucker held up a hand and said, "That's far enough, ma'am."

"No one's getting into the station today," Hoagie added. "Sorry."

The woman smiled at him. "I recognize your voice. You're Hoagie, aren't you? You have such a great voice for radio."

Flustered by her friendliness, Hoagie spluttered a moment and finally replied, "People, ah, people usually say I have a *face* for radio..." He glanced at Rucker for help.

Rucker did not look amused. He said, "If you kind folks are here to join the picketers, I suggest you do so in a..."

"Oh, no," the woman protested. "No, you don't understand. My name is Amy Wellis and I run Coffee Table Books. Right around the corner there...see?" She indicated the printed artwork on her apron. "That's the logo of my store. Anyway, I called Nadine's show and came out. You know, as a lesbian." She had been speaking at a near breathless rate, but the confession caused her to stop. Her gaze trailed from Hoagie down to the sidewalk, and she softly repeated, "I came out."

Hoagie felt positively distraught at the idea that this gorgeous woman was gay. "Congrats," he mumbled.

"Thank you," Amy said. She seemed distracted for a moment longer, then shook her head. "Anyway. The cookies. I thought Nadine could use a little pick-me-up, a show of support from her friends and neighbors. It's gotta be a change from..." She jerked her head toward the people on the opposite side of the street.

"Who are all these people following you? The children of Hamelin?" Rucker asked.

"Children of...oh, that's clever," Amy laughed. "Yes, I'm the Pied Piper of Squire's Isle." She waved at the throng of supporters behind her. "When I told people in my store what I wanted to do, they loaded up right behind me to come along. They want Nadine to know she's definitely not alone in this fight."

Reaching out, Hoagie took the tray from her and lifted up a corner flap. I SUPPORT THE PIXIE was emblazoned in frosting on each pink cookie. He picked one and gestured to find out if it was all right to eat it. Amy nodded, and he bit off a piece. After chewing thoughtfully, he raised his eyebrows in appreciation. "That ain't half bad. Want one, Sheriff?"

"Don't mind if I do," Rucker said. He took a cookie, shrugged, and said, "I don't see what harm a single care package could do." He took the tray from Hoagie and walked to the front door. Billy opened it for him and Rucker handed him the tray. "Take this up to Miss Butler," the sheriff said. "Tell her they're from Amy Wellis and the Pixie's loyal supporters at Coffee Table Books."

"Will do, sir!" Billy replied. He glanced at the tray, looked at the crowd, and moved a step closer to Rucker. "Sheriff, sir, you think Miss Wellis would mind if I ate one of the cookies myself?"

"Well, no," Rucker said. He lowered his voice to the same conspiratorial whisper and added, "But even if she did, I'm sure Nadine would be happy to give you one. There's plenty to go around, and you're earning it by protecting this door. I'd say take two."

Billy smiled and took a cookie from the tray, then hurried toward the stairs with the tray carefully held with both hands. Rucker watched him go before returning to Hoagie's side. Amy and her crowd had moved back a little; the lively buzz of conversation could be heard. Hoagie shook his head. "I'm all for this broadcast thing, the whole *viva la revolución* thing Nadine's got going on..." He paused.

"But?" Rucker prodded.

"But it's hard enough for a guy to find a date on this island," Hoagie groaned. "If Nadine outs all the eligible bachelorettes, I'm gonna have to move to Spokane."

Miranda stood up and removed the chair being used as a makeshift lock in time to open the door and intercept Billy before he could knock.

"Miss Powell!" Billy cried. Miranda took the tray, and he closed his eyes, obviously concentrating. After a moment, he said, "Sheriff Rucker says these are from Ms. Amy Wellis and the Pixie's loyal supporters at Coffee Table Books. I took two of the cookies for myself. I hope you don't mind, Miss Butler."

"I'd insist on it, Billy," Nadine said. "Thank you."

"Yes, ma'am," he panted. "I gotta get back. Guarding the door and all that."

Nadine rose so he could see her. "Thank you so much for keeping us safe, Billy."

He nodded. "I'd be out there on the street, weren't for you, Miss Butler."

"Please, Billy. Call me Nadine. I'm begging you."

"Okay. Nadine." He nodded at her. "I'm here for you even if you wanna sleep with...like, animals." His words were sincere, but he grimaced.

"I don't want to sleep with animals," Nadine assured him, laughing.

"That's good, Miss Nadine. I better get back!" He saluted both women, then turned around and headed back toward the stairs.

Miranda carried the tray over. Nadine wondered aloud, "Why do people always go straight from gay to bestiality or pederasty?"

"Lot of sickos out there," Miranda commented, shrugging. She put the chair back under the door and whisked the napkins off the tray, revealing a pile of pink frosted cookies. "Aw, how sweet." Miranda chose a cookie. "You have fans."

Nadine smiled. "You laugh, but yesterday I was starting to wonder if anyone..." She picked at the icing on one of the cookies and shook her head. "It's really nice."

"Yeah, it..." Miranda hesitated.

Nadine glanced at the controls; nothing seemed amiss. "What's wrong?"

"Do you hear that?"

"The booth is more-or-less soundproof," Nadine said.

Miranda walked to the small window that overlooked the harbor. Nadine followed her, pressing her ear close to the glass. Very faintly, she could hear a chant rising from the street. "Three...Free. Free the..." Her face broke out in a smile, and she said, "Free the Pixie."

"Free the Pixie," Miranda confirmed, grinning.

Nadine blushed with pleasure. "My loyal supporters from Coffee Table Books."

"Loyal indeed," Miranda said.

"They like me. They really like me," Nadine chuckled. It had been a joke, but tears were welling in her eyes. She bit her lip and brushed her hand under her glasses to wipe away the wetness.

"They're..."

Whatever Miranda was about to say was cut off by Nadine's kiss. Her hands grasped Nadine's upper arms, and she hesitated. When Nadine's tongue flickered against her mouth, Miranda groaned and yielded; more than that, she took control, pressing Nadine against the wall and returning the kiss with a heated passion that struck sparks in Nadine. Miranda was a fantastic kisser, using her lips and tongue firmly, not forcefully, but just right to stoke Nadine's desire even higher, until she was whimpering. Nadine slid her fingers under the hem of Miranda's shirt and found amazingly soft, warm skin over firm flesh. A muscle in Miranda's back flexed when she moved, fitting her body tightly against Nadine's.

Nadine pulled her hands out of Miranda's shirt, earning a moan of protest. She fisted Miranda's hair, holding the woman in place while the kiss continued. Miranda pushed Nadine's shirt up, her hands clutching Nadine's waist. Nadine groaned into Miranda's mouth and hooked a leg around Miranda's hip. Miranda growled low in her throat and broke the kiss to nip at Nadine's neck. At the same time, she dragged Nadine's shirt up high in the back and tugged at the clasp of Nadine's bra.

Nadine felt what the woman was doing and went rigid, easing Miranda away. It was hard to think clearly through the haze of lust, but a warning bell began ringing loudly enough inside her head, telling her to stop immediately. "Wait, wait, wait," she gasped.

Miranda abandoned Nadine's neck, moving her lips to Nadine's cheek. "What?" she whispered. "Put on *American Pie* or *Paradise by the Dashboard Light* or something...something really...long." She tugged the clasp of Nadine's bra again, undoing the hooks.

Nadine closed her eyes and breathed, "Yes...God, but no...no, Miranda..."

Miranda backed off immediately. She was flushed, her eyes glazed and her blouse rumpled where their bodies had been pressed together.

Nadine licked her lips, tasting the sweetness of the cookie Miranda had eaten. That sent a jolt of pure desire through her which she ruthlessly and reluctantly forced under control. She reached behind her back to refasten her bra as she explained. "Miranda, I'm not rejecting you, it's just...my relationship with Kate was entirely about sex. We slept together the first night we were a couple, and I think that set the tone for the three years that came after. You can call me an idiot, but..."

"You're not an idiot," Miranda said, combing her fingers through the tangled mess of her hair. "I've been there. God, have I been there! But I know exactly what you're talking about. If we jumped into bed together right now, it would probably cause problems down the road..."

"We wouldn't be jumping into bed," Nadine said, touching her mouth, which felt swollen and tender. She could hardly believe what had just happened. Clearing her throat, she went on, "It would probably be on the floor here or in your office. On top of your desk would..."

"You are really, *really* not helping, Nadine," Miranda gritted.

Nadine snapped her teeth together on a retort and smiled instead. "Sorry." She brushed past Miranda, feeling a bit of static tingling on her skin that she told herself was just from the carpet, and dropped back into her seat. "The song is almost over."

"Yeah," Miranda said.

"What was your request? You...you said you had a request."

"*The Sun Ain't Gonna Shine Anymore.*"

"The Walker Brothers?"

"Yeah."

"Okay, I'll try and get that on for you. Thanks for calling and keep listening to KELF," Nadine joked to ease the tension in the booth.

Miranda sat down and threw a napkin at Nadine, hitting her in the head with it. Nadine chuckled and put her hand on Miranda's thigh. She let the touch linger, her fingers just a little below the hem of Miranda's skirt, before she withdrew it. She smiled nervously and turned her attention back on the dials and buttons of the console, forcing her mind back to the mundane task at hand.

Chapter Eleven

"Hello again, thank you for joining us on KELF, I am the Pixie," Nadine said, continuing her show. "I can see the ferry pulling into the dock right now, so I want to say hello to any tourists who may have their radios tuned to 1220. Since you're just joining us, let me fill you in on what's going on. We're in the middle of a very special broadcast. You see, a few days ago, I came out of the closet as a gay woman. Since then, well...a lot has happened, too much to go into. But the main point is I was fired from this radio station. Advertisers were pulling out, and it wasn't financially feasible to keep me on.

"So I was given this one final show to say good-bye, and I'm doing it the best way I know how — I'm giving every other gay person on this island an outlet, so to speak." She grinned at Miranda, who wrinkled her nose in response. Nadine went on, "I'm giving them a forum where they can come out without feeling persecuted or judged. You don't have to give your name, and you don't have to be on the air if you don't want to. I totally understand not being ready.

"But if you are ready...if you want to come out on the show, please give me a call at 232-KELF. That's 232-5353. I'm looking forward to hearing from you. And to any tourists on the ferry; welcome to our little island. I may be a lame duck, but I'm still taking your requests. Give me a call. Right now, we've got *The Boxer* by Paul Simon and Art Garfunkel. I'm cut and I'm down, but the fighter still remains. This is the Pixie on KELF AM 1220."

Miranda had been nibbling on a cookie; she broke it in half and tossed the uneaten portion back onto the plate. She had taken off her jacket, leaving her clad in a sleeveless white blouse and skirt. Nadine leaned back and admired the view. *As great as Miranda's legs are*, she mused, *her arms are quite something themselves.* Nadine noticed Miranda's lips closing around the frosting-scrawled word PIXIE, and she had to smile. She did not say anything about the symbolism of Miranda's snack, however.

"Getting your fill?" she asked.

"Of you or of the cookies?" Miranda groaned. She put her hand on her stomach and glanced at the clock. "Wow. Time really does fly in here, huh?"

"Yeah," Nadine said sadly. The arrival of the ferry meant she had three hours and twenty minutes left on the air. It did not feel like enough time, not enough time at all. "I can't believe this is it."

Miranda's eyes were filled with compassion. "Have you always wanted to be a DJ?"

"Always," Nadine said. "My parents own Butler Photography, across the street. Maybe you know it?"

Miranda blinked and glanced toward the wall, in the direction of the photography shop. "I pass that building every day. I can't believe I never put that together."

Nadine shrugged. "When I was a little girl, I used to help my parents at the shop. One day, we got a package that was supposed to go to KELF. It was a slow day, so I decided to walk it over. The receptionist was taken by me and invited me to come over any time I wanted. Before long, the DJs found out about this little squirt that was stalking their place of business and started inviting me upstairs. I was just...I was floored by the whole process of broadcasting. It was magic. I mean, they were talking to the whole island at once! So I sat in the booth during the show, I ran out and bought them snacks when they were hungry...when I was fifteen, I got Billy's job. Cleaning up trash, hanging around in case anything needed to be done. I went to school, got a degree in broadcasting, and came back to the Elf."

"Who gave you the Pixie nickname?"

"Christopher Hamm. Hamm Bone, they called him. He used to introduce me by saying that he needed some cheering up, and he'd sprinkle some fairy dust. My intro was some musical chimes that he'd play to cover the sound of the door opening. 'Here's my little pixie now!' he'd say." She smiled at the cherished memory and twisted her seat back and forth. "He's the one who suggested I become a disc jockey. I was content behind the scenes, but he loved my voice. He gave me the push I needed to get through school."

"What about your parents?"

Nadine glanced at the song counter. She tried to control the emotion in her voice when she finally answered. "Butler Photography is the family business. With me breaking tradition, it'll probably close down when he and Mama retire. Either that or it'll go into the hands of someone else. Whichever happens, it doesn't matter. I let my dad down and he's hated me ever since for it." She bit her bottom lip and finally smiled wryly. "What the hell, right? People have given up a lot worse for their dreams."

Miranda took Nadine's hand off the console and held it, offering silent support.

"It's why you sticking up for me meant so much," Nadine explained. "I'm not exactly used to it."

"Well, get used to it," Miranda said. "I'm here for the long haul."

Nadine's heart thumped at the affection in the other woman's expression. She avoided Miranda's gaze and glanced at the phone bank where every line was blinking for attention. "I should answer these. God, I never expected to get so many calls..." She answered Line One. "This is Nadine and you're on with the Pixie. What's your name?"

"I'm Jake."

"Hi, Jake. You want to hear a song?"

"No, I'm calling about the other thing. The gay thing?"

"Uh-huh," she said warily.

"Well, I'm a straight guy, but...you know, if sleeping with women makes *you* bad at *your* job, maybe that's the reason *I'm* bad at *my* job."

She frowned and raised her eyebrow at Miranda. She was not sure if she should be amused or offended. "Are you...are you bad at your job, Jake?"

"Yeah, I kind of am."

Nadine and Miranda both chuckled. After composing herself, Nadine asked, "Jake, do you think I'm bad at my job?"

"No, I think you're great! But I've only been listening for, like, five minutes. I came over on the ferry."

"Well, let me win you over. What do you wanna hear? We're a classic rock station, by the way."

"Something by the Beach Boys, maybe?"

"*Something* is by the Beatles, Jake."

"Hah, laugh riot. Let me hear some *Good Vibrations*."

"You've got it, Jake. And guess what? You are my tourist of the day." Nadine hit a button and a pre-recorded sound effect of the ferry horn played. She went on, "Since Gail's Seafood coupons are all I'm allowed to hand out, it'll have to do. Just make sure you pick it up early so you have time to eat before you head back to the mainland. Sound good, Jake?"

"Sounds awesome! Stay strong, Pixie."

"You too, Straight Man. What's your last name, so we don't accidentally give your coupon to someone else?"

"Paulson."

"Okay, Jake. Come on by the station sometime before five, and we'll feed you."

"Awesome. Thanks!"

She disconnected the call and asked Miranda, "We do have coupons for Gail's, right?"

Miranda nodded and stood up. "I'll go grab one out of my desk and give it to Hoagie or Billy. I'll be right back."

As Miranda walked to the door, Nadine turned in her seat and watched the woman walk past her. She focused on the way Miranda moved — the sway of her hips, the way her legs seemed to go on forever under the business-like skirt, the perfect curve of her ass...she glanced up to see Miranda smiling over her shoulder.

"Pervert," Miranda snickered before she slipped out of the room.

Nadine blushed and answered another call. "Hello, you're on with the Pixie..."

Miranda walked the coupon down to Hoagie, gave him Jake Paulson's name, and told him what the caller won. To her relief, the protesters had returned to the other side of the street, where they were being watched by Sheriff Rucker. When she returned to the booth, she sat down and leaned back in her chair.

"So do you do that a lot?" she asked.

Nadine held up a finger and spoke into the microphone. "Okay, I'll try to get that on for you. Thanks for listening to KELF and thank you for your support." She disconnected the call and turned to Miranda. "Do what?"

"You know," Miranda said. She gestured over her shoulder. "Check me out."

Nadine blushed and shifted uncomfortably in her seat. "The truth? Yeah. Kind of a lot. Mostly when you wear skirts or those pants that end just below the knee...God, what are those called?"

"Capri," Miranda said. "You really like my legs?" She bent her knees and examined her calves, running her hand over the firm muscles. She liked taking care of herself, and Nadine's open admiration was nice.

Nadine exhaled and said, "Yeah. So, um...stop touching them or we'll have to play *American Pie*. Twice. And *Stairway to Heaven*, too."

Miranda grinned and stopped touching herself, straightening up in the chair.

Nadine fanned herself, smiling. "So, okay. While we're sharing secrets...tit for tat. Have you ever looked at me?"

Miranda hesitated, so used to her secrets that it felt odd to bluntly admit them this way. She finally nodded. "Yeah. Occasionally, I've watched your show from the window with a...well, a less than managerial interest."

"Like when? Give me an example."

It was Miranda's turn to blush. "Are we really going to do this?"

"Oh, yeah," Nadine said. "The song's got three more minutes, and the phone lines aren't too crazy at the moment." She leaned forward, her lips curving in a wicked smile. "So tell me, Miss Powell...exactly when have you ever checked me out?"

Miranda considered the question for a moment. "Well, one day springs to mind. Last summer, you came to work wearing this sexy little dress. Thin shoulder straps, very light material. Your legs were...so, so tan..."

"I'd been at the beach, I think," Nadine said.

"I can believe it. You were practically charbroiled, but it looked good on you! Don't get me wrong." Miranda shrugged. "Anyway, because of the thin straps and how low it was cut in the front, you were wearing a T-shirt underneath the dress, and I spent that entire day wondering how great the dress would have looked on you without the T-shirt."

Nadine arched an eyebrow. "Undressing me with your eyes, were you?"

"Just down to the T-shirt!" Miranda quickly added.

"Well. Still," Nadine glanced toward the phone lines, "it's..." Her voice cut off, and she straightened slightly in her chair.

Miranda straightened up, too, and glanced at the console. "Dean? What's wrong?"

"Nothing," Nadine murmured. She punched a button and the ON AIR light came to life. "That was *Uncle Albert/Admiral Halsey* by Paul and Linda McCartney. Uh, we're...we're going right back to some music now so I can answer more of your calls. I'll be right back with you here on KELF."

Nadine's gaze remained locked on the flashing lights of calls waiting to be answered. After a moment, she said, "Miranda...please don't take this the wrong way, but would you mind leaving for a few minutes?"

Concerned, Miranda glanced at the Caller ID. "What is it?"

"I'll be okay, I just...I need to answer this call alone."

"Okay," Miranda said. She leaned in and kissed Nadine's cheek, letting her lips linger a bit longer than necessary. "I'll go downstairs and check on Hoagie. Are you sure you'll be all right?"

When Nadine nodded, Miranda had no choice. She left the booth, troubled by Nadine's insistence and knowing the woman was far from all right as she claimed.

The door shutting closed behind her made Miranda flinch, but she walked across the bullpen anyway. She went directly downstairs and found Billy standing just inside the front doors of the station, a sentry against any unauthorized entrance and a gatekeeper for those who belonged. She put a hand on his shoulder as she passed, thanking him silently for his work, and stepped out into the sunshine. It felt like years since she had been outside and decades since Nadine's broadcast began.

Hoagie was seated on the sidewalk outside, keeping his eyes on the milling crowd. Sheriff Rucker was parked across the street, a barrier between the mob and the station. To Hoagie's left, a brunette woman she knew as Amy from Coffee Table Books had set up a table with drinks, cookies, and donuts, assisted by another person.

Miranda stopped next to Hoagie and asked, "Everything still calm out here?"

"Hey, Miss Powell," he replied, glancing at her. "And yeah, everything's A-okay. That Jake kid stopped by to pick up his coupon already."

"Good. Glad to hear it."

"How is Nadine holding up?"

"She's doing well, so far," Miranda said. She looked up at the small window that gave the broadcasting booth its outside view of the harbor. What was going on in there? Who had called? She struggled with the urge to run back up the stairs and fight the battle for Nadine, protect the woman from whatever had made the blood drain out of her face that way. She shook her head and scanned the street. "No problems I should know about?"

"Nothing the sheriff and I can't handle. Those Coffee Table chicks offered to protect Nadine when she came out. Make sure no one tries anything."

"Her own personal Secret Service." Miranda chuckled at the image of the cookie maker and her patrons surrounding Nadine like bodyguards as she walked to her bike. "Okay, I better get back in there," she said, patting Hoagie's broad shoulder. "Thanks for being here, Hoagie."

"No problem. Happy to help."

Miranda walked back upstairs. Through the window, she saw Nadine with her head down on the desk. Alarmed, Miranda ran across the bullpen and burst into the broadcast booth, going over to Nadine. She felt her heart wrench with each of the woman's quiet sobs. Putting her hand in the middle of Nadine's back, she swore that whoever had been on the other end of the line, whatever they had said, they were dead meat.

Nadine waited until Miranda was gone before she looked back at the Caller ID. The display cut off the full name, but it was hard to ignore what *Butler Photo-*

gra meant. She cleared her throat and hit the button to answer the call, choking out, "Hi."

"Nadine," came the reply.

What she heard was so unexpected, she jerked and nearly pushed her chair over. Gripping the edge of the table with shaking hands, she focused on the solid yellow light burning on the telephone's call button. She swallowed and quietly asked, "Daddy?" Her mind started to fill in the empty space after she spoke; she wondered if he would call her names or just get right to disowning her. After what seemed like an eternity, he began to speak.

"Nadine, are you really doing this?" His voice was calm, but she could hear a tremor of fury working under the surface. "You're making a goddamn spectacle out of yourself, girl. You come out of there right now and end this foolishness, or I—"

"No, Daddy," Nadine said. She shocked herself not only by the firm denial, but by interrupting the man for the first time in her life. Hell, it was probably the first time in *his* life that he had been interrupted by anyone, let alone his daughter. She went on, "I've been wronged, and I'm not just going to sit down and take it. Do you understand that? You may not agree with who I am or even this job that I'm trying to save. But you have to understand that all I'm doing is standing up for my beliefs, and I won't stand down. You wouldn't want me to."

There was another pause, no sound except for the sound of her father's breathing. Goosebumps rose on her arms, and she hugged herself against the sudden chill. Her father's silence was the most terrifying thing she had ever heard, but she refused to be the one who broke it. It was up to him to hang up, to give in. Twice she started to apologize and twice she bit down on her tongue to keep from saying anything aloud. *Let him break the standoff. Let him...*

"Your mother said you'd say that."

She blinked. She had won. Dear God in heaven, she had stood up to her father, and she had won.

He continued, "All of this, the...the broadcast and the call-in thing. You're just doing what you think is right. Your mom said I would be proud of anyone else. And you know...it hurts that I only turned my back on you because you were my daughter. I didn't realize it had gotten to that point with us. My fault, I suppose. God knows you tried to be civil." He coughed and continued, "Forget what I said a minute ago, Nadine. You don't let anyone pull you out of that booth before you're ready. You hear me?"

"Yes, sir," Nadine said, tears burning in her eyes.

"I'm proud of you, Dean."

She sobbed and managed to get out, "Thank you, Daddy."

"I'll...I'll see you."

"Yeah, Daddy. I...I have to go back on the air."

"Okay. I'm sorry I made you cry."

She laughed through her tears. "It's okay, Daddy. I love you, Daddy."

"I love you, too, Nadine."

Nadine barely managed to push the button to disconnect the call before she put her head down on the desk. She wept, big body-shaking sobs that prevented her from hearing the door open. A hand landed in the middle of her back, and she jumped, her pulse racing in panic until she realized it was Miranda leaning over her shoulder. Miranda gently pried Nadine out of the chair and traded places with her. Nadine let herself be guided onto Miranda's lap and buried her wet face against the woman's neck.

With some difficulty, Miranda pulled the microphone close and hit the on-air button. In a smooth, professional radio voice, she said, "We apologize for the delay. We're experiencing a brief technical difficulty. Please stay tuned, and Nadine will be back after *Eleanor Rigby* by the Beatles."

She pushed the microphone away, started the song, and turned her full attention to Nadine. Nadine let herself be held, shaking from the force of her tears. Miranda smoothed a palm down Nadine's hair and whispered a soft, comforting murmur in her ear. Nadine could not make out the words, but the loving tone went straight to her soul.

When the sobs died down at last, Miranda said, "Who was it? Who the hell hurt you?"

"No," Nadine whispered. She realized that Miranda had gotten the wrong idea and shook her head quickly. Her stomach ached, her chest ached, but she managed a smile. Turning her head, she kissed Miranda's neck. "Thank you, but no. I'm...they're happy tears, I swear." She pulled back and kissed Miranda's mouth, her tears flowing once more as her heart soared.

When the storm of tears calmed a little, Nadine explained the call. She could feel the tension in Miranda's body begin to relax as she revealed what her father had said. Miranda shifted them both so Nadine was no longer in her lap and got them both a can of soda out of the fridge. As she sat down, she shook her head. "Your father accepts you. That's...that's huge, Dean."

"I don't know about accepting me," Nadine corrected, blowing her nose in a tissue. "He never said he was okay with me being gay, and he never forgave me for abandoning the family business. He just said he understood my reasons and supported me standing up for my rights. Still...big day."

Miranda nodded. "Big day indeed." She toasted Nadine and touched their cans together.

Nadine smiled and said, "I'm going to take some more calls." She answered the first line, "This is KELF and you're on with the Pixie."

"My name is Kevin Dawes, and I've been in a relationship with the same man for fifteen years," the caller said, his voice trembling with emotion. "We were in an openly gay marriage for ten of those years until we moved to Squire's Isle. We came out to a couple of people when we first got here and saw their reactions change in a heartbeat. We knew we'd never be accepted, so we went in the closet and firmly shut the door. We've been hiding ever since, but no more. Thanks, Nadine."

"Thank you for calling, Kevin. May I ask your partner's name or...?"

"His name is Alex."

"Hi, Alex. Kevin, is there anything you'd like to hear?"

"Yeah, I'd like to hear *Thank You (Falettinme Be Mice Elf Agin)* by Sly and the Family Stone."

"Ooh, I love that song. It's appropriate, and it has Elf in the title. Thanks for calling, Kevin."

She pulled the CD from the shelf and looked at Miranda. "Thank *you* for being here for me. I needed the shoulder."

"Any time," Miranda promised.

"KELF, hello. You're on with the Pixie."

"Hi, Nadine."

Nadine tensed and looked at Miranda. "Kate, hello."

"I've been listening to your entire show. I'm home now, they...they released me about an hour ago. I am so damned proud of you, babe."

"Thank you, Kate," she said. She was touched that Kate had taken the time to call in. It was a good sign their friendship might survive the end of their relationship. "Are you feeling well?"

"I am. I wanted to call and..." Kate cleared her throat. "You can play this on the air, Nadine. My name is Kathryn Price. I'm a reporter for the Squire's Isle *Register,* and it was my article that caused all of these problems for Nadine. And I want to admit to the town, to my employers, to everyone listening right now that...I am a lesbian."

Nadine closed her eyes, honored by Kate's sacrifice. "Are you okay, Kate?"

"I'm fine," Kate replied softly. "I'm going to be just fine. Thank you, Nadine."

"Thank *you,* Kate. I love you."

"Love you," Kate said.

She disconnected the call and felt Miranda's hand on her thigh. She smiled and turned for the hug she knew was waiting. If there was one thing she already knew about Miranda Powell — the woman was big on giving out hugs.

"You're on with the Pixie."

"You're going to Hell, you know," the male caller cried indignantly. "All gays are—"

"If I'm going to hell, you can finish your thought when you run into me down there. All right, chief?" Nadine asked. Miranda covered her mouth to keep from laughing on the air. Nadine shook her head and pressed the phone line button. "Next caller, please."

"KELF, talk to me."

"You know what the problem with America is?"

Nadine kept her finger over the disconnect button. "No. What's the problem with America, sir?"

"That with divorce, broken homes, children growing up with single-parent families, we're making such a big deal out of someone loving someone else. If you're happy, more power to you. As long as you're in love, I could care less who it's with."

"Thank you very much for calling, sir. Can I play anything for you?"

"You're on the air with the Pixie."

"Hello, Miss Butler. My name is Amelia Judah. I work at the library, and I'm not calling about the overdue book you have out."

"I appreciate that, Mrs. Judah. And, uh, I'll...I'll get that to you as soon as possible."

"Good girl. I was listening to your show, and I realized it's partially the library's fault you're in this pickle. When the subject of inappropriate content was raised, I volunteered to read the book in question. I have to admit, I found it not to my liking. But I did *not* find anything objectionable, and I didn't support taking it off the shelves."

"Thank you for being honest, Mrs. Judah."

"Well, I could hardly do anything else, dear. I'd have to look it up to get the entire quote, but it starts, 'First they came for the Socialists, and I did not speak out because I was not a Socialist.' And it ends, 'Then they came for me, and there was no one left to speak out for me.' You can't, and shouldn't, go quietly. Good girl, Miss Butler. And seeing as how you're under the threat of unemployment, we'll waive the five-cent overdue charge on your book. Granted you get it in before next week."

"I'll do my level best, Mrs. Judah." She was relieved to have the support and just a little amused by the woman's insistence on reminding her about the overdue book. "Thank you very much for your call and for reminding us of that wonderful quote. Can I play anything for you?"

Creedence Clearwater Revival, Jackson Browne, and Pink Floyd broke up the rest of the calls. Nadine leaned back and talked to Miranda while the music played. She put her feet in Miranda's lap, and Miranda lightly massaged Nadine's feet as they spoke. Halfway through an Aerosmith song, Nadine suddenly realized they were being more intimate together than she and Kate had ever been. While the revelation made her sad, it also gave her hope for the future. She grinned and pinned Miranda's fingers between her feet.

"Cut that out," Miranda chuckled.

"Sorry."

"No, you're not." This was said with a smile that Nadine found beautiful.

"No, I'm not," Nadine confessed. "I love how comfortable I am with you. I've known you for all this time and we're friends, right?"

Miranda nodded. "I don't have many friends, but I've counted you as one of mine for a while. Even if I never really showed it before this week."

Nadine nodded her understanding and toyed with the tab of her soda can. "I think this is how it's supposed to be. Love and relationships. You can't just grab someone, take them home, end up with them the rest of your life. That's what I was trying to do with Kate. You need a basis of some sort if you really want to make it last."

"I don't believe that," Miranda said.

"No?"

"No. I think you *can* stumble over the person you're supposed to be with. You don't need an existing relationship just to make your romance work. Otherwise Simon would have to marry Willa."

Nadine frowned in confusion. "I thought Simon *was* married to Willa."

Miranda shook her head. "No, of course not. But while I don't think it's necessary? I certainly think a basis of friendship helps." She smoothed her hands down Nadine's ankles and caressed her calves.

Nadine blushed at the blatant groping, but did nothing to dissuade her.

"Oh, Dean..." Miranda said a moment later after glancing at the clock.

Nadine turned, and her good mood evaporated. It was three minutes to five o'clock. She pulled her feet from Miranda's grasp and turned to face the microphone. She felt equal parts relief, dread, and sadness. It was like the last day of school and the end of summer all at the same time. Silencing the song that had been playing, she pulled the microphone closer.

"Well, ladies and gentlemen, it's almost five o'clock," Nadine said. "That will be it from me. For now, maybe for good. I wanted one last show, I wanted what I was promised — that I could come on here, play some music, and say what I wanted to say. So many people stood up to help make sure that happened, I'd be lost without them. Miranda Powell, Joe Hogan, Billy..." She glanced at Miranda, who shrugged. "I...I'm sorry, Billy, I don't know your last name. Amy Wellis, the cookies were delicious.

"I want to thank everyone who called in, everyone who came out today, and those who will be inspired by this show to come out in the future. Coming out was one of the greatest things that's happened to me. It's changed my life, and I can honestly say I think it's changed me for the better." She felt Miranda's hand on her shoulder and reached up to hold it. "Thank you to my listeners. Thank you to everyone who believed in me and who believes in me still. Thank you, Clifton Gail, for standing up for yourself and for being behind me.

"We've only got a couple of minutes left. I was promised one show and that's all I'll take up. Hoagie is right downstairs, and I'll be sending him up on my way down. I'm going to clean up the booth for him so he can abandon his watchtower downstairs. And I'm pretty sure Hoagie doesn't have any diatribes he wants to go off on, so it should be pure music and contests and all that stuff I know you guys love."

Nadine bit her thumb and blinked away tears. When she was sure she could speak again, she went on, "All I ever wanted was to be a disc jockey. I wanted to be paid to play music and talk to people who loved it as much as I did. No matter how it ends, I got to live my dream. What else can anyone ask for? Thank you. To everyone who has ever listened to me, to anyone who has ever cared about some little girl sitting in a booth playing music. This song is for everyone in December Harbor and everyone on Squire's Isle. I think it sums up what I wanted to say pretty nicely. This is...this has been Nadine Butler. Your KELF Pixie. S-s-signing off. Good-bye, everyone."

She hit a button, and *Imagine* by John Lennon began to play.

Looking over the console for a moment, Nadine ran her hand over the assorted buttons and controls. She leaned back in the chair and took in the view out of the window — the small sailboats, the tree-lined shore that made up the northern rim of the harbor, and the clear blue winter sky. The booth was tiny, it was dark, and it had a not-very-unpleasant odor to it, but it was home. It had been her favorite place in the world ever since she was a little girl. To say good-bye to it was almost too much. She ran her hand over the edge of the table and pushed the microphone out of the way. It took her a moment to realize she was grieving. This was her home, and it was being taken from her.

Miranda stood and held out her hand. Nadine took it and let Miranda pull her to her feet. She gathered the cookies while Miranda put her jacket back on, and they walked from the booth hand-in-hand. Nadine leaned against Miranda's shoulder and said, "What a show."

"What a show," Miranda echoed with a smile. Nadine squeezed her hand.

As they came downstairs, Billy crossed the lobby to intercept them. When he saw Nadine, his face broke into a wide smile. "Hey, Miss Butler." He caught himself and said, "I mean, Miss Nadine. You made it."

"I sure did, Billy." She paused and hoped it was not too rude to be blunt before she continued, "Billy, I'm so sorry I have to ask this, but what is your last name?"

"Joseph, ma'am."

Nadine slipped her hand out of Miranda's and walked over to him. She kissed him once on each cheek and solemnly said, "Thank you for protecting me today, William Joseph."

He bowed his head and shuffled his feet back and forth. Giving her an embarrassed smile, he unlocked the door. Nadine renewed her grip on Miranda's hand. They walked out of the building together; the world exploded in a cacophony of noise that made Nadine flinch. On their left, Amy and her Coffee Table Book patrons sent up a cheer. From directly ahead of them, a group of protesters shouted a chorus of sneers and name-calling. Eleanor Nelson was standing off to one side with her oh-so-holy church group.

Eleanor lifted her hands to give the crowd a rhythm when she began to chant: "Homos must go! Homos must go!" Thrusting their placards in the air, the crowd joined in with her.

Sheriff Rucker and Deputy White's patrol cars were parked tail-to-nose at the curb. Both officers were standing in the street between the station and the mob. White had his arms crossed over his chest, his back to the mob. He looked irritated. Rucker had his hand on his belt, not quite on his holster but close enough to draw the eye to it.

When Nadine reached Hoagie, she offered him her free hand and helped the big man to his feet. His knees popped as he rose, and he brushed off the seat of his pants. Grinning, Hoagie said, "Looks like you made it, Pixie. Wish I could've been there to hear it."

"Trust me," Miranda said. "Someone somewhere recorded every word."

Hoagie's grin widened. "Nadine, I've been thinking...why don't you come back up and sit in on my show? Special guest co-host, that sort of thing. I'd take a backseat and you could..."

"Hoagie, no," Nadine interrupted. "Thank you, and I love you for thinking of it, but...but no. I don't want you to get into trouble. All I wanted was the last show I was promised, and I've got it. Thanks to you." She kissed his cheek and patted his muscular forearm. "I'm satisfied. Really."

He shifted his feet and said, "Well. So long as you're sure..."

"The offer means the world to me, Hoagie, but it wouldn't be the same. I'd feel like I was cheating."

"I understand that," he said. He kissed her cheek. "Take care of yourself, Nadine. Don't be a stranger."

Miranda guided Nadine to the bike rack and looked over her shoulder at the crowd. "Are you sure you don't want a ride? You could always come back and get your bike when things have calmed down a little."

"Nope. I'm not changing my habits just because of a couple of closed-minded idiots. The sooner they see I won't be scared away, the sooner they'll stop trying."

Hoagie had already gone back into the station and Rucker was crossing the street, no doubt to tell her that he and White were leaving. Nadine pulled her key from the pocket of her jeans and was about to unlock her bike's chain when someone yelled out her name. She lifted her head and turned in the direction of the voice. Miranda and Rucker turned their bodies in response to the call, too, and, for one split second, they left Nadine exposed to the crowd.

She never saw what hit her, but she did hear the impact. Strangely enough, it seemed to come from behind her ears rather than in the middle of her face where she was hit. The impact made a quiet *thock*, a solid yet somehow hollow sound that was followed by a snap. Nadine screamed, more in surprised fright than pain, and covered her face as she fell backwards. Warm liquid — *it can't be blood, it can't be blood,* she told herself — trickled down her nose. The liquid ran stinging into her eyes, and she screwed them shut as tightly as she could. Nadine lay on the ground, curled into a ball with her arms protecting her head. A drumbeat of pain throbbed through her skull. She heard Miranda frantically yelling for someone to call an ambulance. As the shriek of sirens burst through the confusion, she began to sob.

Chapter Twelve

When it came time to decide between pursuing the fleeing mob and helping Nadine Butler, Rucker turned away from the pursuit, jerking a thumb over his shoulder as he passed his deputy. White needed no further directions; he jumped into the squad car and peeled off after the protestors, who had panicked and scattered in the shocked moments following the attack. Rucker dropped to his knees next to Nadine and pulled a white handkerchief from his pocket, folding it into a pad. He carefully eased Nadine's hands away from her face, wincing when he saw the bloody slash between her eyebrows. Covering the wound with the handkerchief, he pressed down to staunch the bleeding. "What the hell happened?" he asked.

"I don't know," Miranda said, her distress obvious. "She just fell down. She...she just fell. Jesus!"

He glanced around the scene, noting the pieces of her eyeglasses; a chunk of concrete from the construction site on the corner lay a few feet away. He was furious at himself for underestimating how far the mob would go. "Keep her still," he ordered Miranda. He lifted her eyelid with his thumb and checked her pupils with the flashlight on his keychain. "Nadine? Nadine, can you hear me?"

She moaned quietly and slurred, "What..."

"Good girl," Rucker said. "We're just going to wait for the..."

As if on cue, the sound of sirens filled the air. Moments later, the ambulance pulled around the corner, and Rucker stood to wave them down. Two medics — Miranda wondered if they were the same ones who had helped Kate — jumped from the ambulance as soon as it came to a halt. They pushed Miranda aside and knelt next to Nadine in the street.

"She lost consciousness," Rucker informed them.

The medics fitted Nadine with a cervical collar, put a dressing on her bleeding face wound, and lifted her onto a gurney.

By now, Nadine was more alert and protested, "No, I'm-I'm fine. I'm fine, you can let me go..."

"You've received a head injury," Rucker said. "Let's just be on the safe side here."

The medics loaded her into the back of the ambulance. One of them asked Miranda, "Are you riding with her?"

She looked at Rucker, and he motioned her on. "Go. I'll see if Randy caught any of those cowards."

Miranda climbed into the back of the ambulance and let Rucker shut the door on her. When the van pulled away, Rucker returned to the spot where Nadine had fallen. He picked up the chunk of concrete that had hit her and scanned the now-empty street. He couldn't believe the people in his little town could go to such lengths over something so damned trivial. He wrapped the rock in a handkerchief from his pocket — there was a chance it could eventually be used as evidence — and walked to his patrol car.

Some time later, Nadine opened her eyes and immediately wished she had kept them shut. The fluorescent lights above the bed were on, the light it cast burning like napalm across her face. Her head was throbbing, both at the temples and between her eyes. When she brought her hand up to probe the site of the most pain, she found a piece of gauze between her eyebrows instead of the familiar bridge of her glasses. For a moment, Nadine was confused, then she remembered the attack outside the station. Her heart jumped, but it was obvious from the antiseptic smell that she was in the hospital, and Nadine relaxed a trifle. She was not in a personal room but a curtained space. The emergency room, maybe. That was good. Whatever had happened was not bad enough that she had needed to be admitted. She turned her face out of the sun and cracked an eyelid to look for a call button. A doctor appeared at her bedside before she managed to find what she was looking for.

The doctor checked her chart and said, "Glad to see you're awake."

Nadine squinted. Without her glasses, the world was a miserable blur. The doctor's voice was vaguely familiar, but she blamed that on her job; she had probably spoken to half the people on the island, if not more. She asked, "What happened?"

"It seems you were hit in the face with a rock. Piece of concrete sidewalk, according to the sheriff. Can you tell me who the President is?"

"Unfortunately," Nadine said with a smile. She named the President, and the doctor marked it down on the chart. The doctor continued with the interrogation until she was satisfied Nadine had not suffered serious memory loss.

"Other than a pair of shiners and the massive headache, yeah, I think you'll be just fine." The doctor slipped a penlight from her coat pocket and said, "Look here." She shone the light into Nadine's right eye, held it, and then dropped it back down. She repeated the gesture with the left eye and nodded at whatever she saw. "Pupils equal and reactive. Any nausea? Dizziness? Double vision?"

Nadine shook her head very carefully.

The doctor went on, "You lost consciousness for less than a minute at the scene, according to the sheriff. X-rays showed no fractures, so I'm confident you'll be fine. As for the wound, your glasses saved you from needing stitches. There will be kind of an ugly mark for a while, but when it's healed you won't even have a scar. I'm going to prescribe some Ibuprofen for the headache. Do you have someone who can stay with you tonight?"

"Yes, I can ask someone." Nadine knew that either Kate or Miranda would be willing to stay with her.

"I'll need to speak with them to make sure they know what to do. No alcohol for at least twenty-four hours. Avoid strenuous activity. If you sleep, make sure whoever's watching you wakes you up every couple of hours to check you out."

"Okay," Nadine said.

The doctor started to walk away and paused. She pulled the curtain back around the bed and returned to stand in front of Nadine. "On a personal note, I listened to your show most of the day," the woman confessed. "I would have called in, but...I saw what had happened to you and started worrying about patients refusing treatment. I couldn't come out publicly, but when you showed up here, well...I do hate having to do it under these circumstances, but I'm gay."

Nadine had to smile. "I know."

The doctor blinked in apparent bewilderment "What? How could you?"

"I'm not sure without my glasses, but you *are* Doctor Tom, aren't you?"

"Yes."

"You treated my girl...I mean, my former girlfriend. Kate Price? When I showed up at the hospital, you treated me like a spouse, not a concerned friend. I had my suspicions then, but...well. Suffice to say, I'm not exactly surprised."

Dr. Tom cocked an eyebrow. "Well. I guess I am talking to the town expert."

Nadine groaned, "Oh, God, I'm going to be the town's poster lesbian, aren't I?"

"We'd prefer to keep you here for twenty-four hours for observation, but if you insist on leaving, there's no reason to force you to stay. Just be sure to come back tomorrow so we can see how you're progressing," Dr. Tom said.

"I will, definitely. Even if I don't want to, someone will drag me in."

"And if your symptoms worsen, come straight to the ER. Don't wait."

"I will."

Dr. Tom smiled. "In the meantime, some of your friends are in the waiting room. Should I let them in?"

"Just Miranda for now."

"Would've been my choice, too. Just a moment."

The doctor left. Nadine listened to the sounds of the ER filtering in — urgent voices, the clatter of gurney wheels, footsteps, mechanical beeping and buzzing. She closed her eyes, sick of seeing the world as a fuzzy half-image. She heard someone yell at a doctor, something metallic clanging on the floor, and another anonymous someone grumbling about how expensive their crappy coffee was. *I hope Miranda comes soon*, she thought, stifling a yawn.

She did not realize she had almost fallen asleep until she felt a hand on her elbow and Miranda quietly saying, "Dean? Are you awake, hon?"

Nadine opened her eyes. Miranda was a blurred blob, but she was relieved to see her anyway. "I'm fine. Headache like you wouldn't believe, but...yeah. And it doesn't help that I can barely see anything..."

"Would these help?" Miranda asked. She held up Nadine's glasses. The rock had broken them in half at the bridge, but someone had wrapped the broken halves with tape to hold them together. "I had to do something while I was waiting. Billy picked them up and brought them from the station, and a nurse gave me the tape. I, uh, I hope you don't mind looking like a dork."

"Thank you," Nadine said. The small gesture was heart-warming and made her feel loved and cherished. She touched the tape and slipped the glasses back on. Looking up, she blinked as Miranda and everything else swam into focus. The frame felt remarkably fragile balanced on her nose, and the lenses were scratched from their collision with the pavement, but all in all, she was enjoying a much nicer picture of the world.

"It's much better, thank you," Nadine repeated. She took Miranda's hand, using her as balance so she could slip off the bed.

"Did the doctor say it was all right to move?" Miranda asked.

"Checked me out, said I was fine," Nadine said. "She wanted to admit me for twenty-four hours, but...I just want to go home. I want this day to be over."

"Okay," Miranda said. Nadine wrapped her arm around Miranda's waist out of instinct. Neither of them pulled away from the intimacy of the new position. It was comforting to have a strong, warm body to lean against. "Did Rucker catch whoever threw that piece of concrete?" Nadine asked.

"No. The crowd broke up as soon as you went down. Deputy White went after them and handed out a bunch of citations for misdemeanors like disturbing the peace, but no one owned up to throwing the rock."

Nadine sighed, "Probably too much to hope for, voluntarily turning themselves in. Cowards."

Miranda nodded "You up to walking?"

"With some help, yes." Nadine clapped her hand over Miranda's. There was a wheelchair parked near the edge of the curtain, and Miranda eased Nadine into the seat. Nadine settled comfortably in the seat and let Miranda wheel her out of the curtained-off area.

Miranda took her to a small waiting room. As opposed to the dim and dreary waiting room upstairs, the ground-floor space had a picture window and two lamps that flooded it with light. Nadine was grateful her friends were able to wait for her in relative comfort and smiled when she saw Kate coming toward her.

The woman looked like she had shed ten years since the last time Nadine had seen her. She was dressed in a white blouse and blue slacks, her hair done up in a French twist. She had put on make-up and, other than the slight worry in her eyes, looked a hundred percent better.

Nadine leaned forward and Kate leaned down for a hug. Nadine said, "You should be in bed."

"Look who's talking," Kate scoffed. "Matilda called me and told me you'd been hurt."

"Who's Matilda?" Hoagie asked.

"Inside joke," Kate smiled. She kissed Nadine's eyebrow and said, "I'm glad you're okay. Do you need a ride or...?"

"Um..." Nadine looked from Kate to Miranda.

Miranda said, "I'll give her a ride home if she wants."

"Yeah," Nadine said, nodding.

Kate's smile widened. She hugged Nadine again, whispering in her ear, "Looks like I was right, huh?"

"Shh," Nadine admonished. She kissed Kate's cheek and went on, "I'm glad you're doing better."

Kate nodded. Nadine turned to Hoagie and Billy. She embraced them both and poked Hoagie in the chest with a finger. "Shouldn't you be on the air?"

Hoagie shook his head. "I got Simon to come in and cover for me."

Miranda and Nadine both blurted in simultaneous disbelief, "You talked to Simon?"

"Yeah," Hoagie said. He looked at them, frowning. "I talk to him all the time. The hard part is getting that guy to shut up. Why? What's wrong?"

Nadine laughed, which was not a good idea, as it set off a new wave of pain in her head. "Nothing, Hoagie. Nothing at all." She reached up and squeezed the hand Miranda had rested on her shoulder. "Let's go home. I've had a really, really long day."

Hoagie glanced at their interlaced fingers and raised an eyebrow. "Whoa...wait a minute. You? And you? Are the two of you...?"

"Yes, Hoagie," Miranda said. "I'm gay, too."

He glared at Billy, as if this was his fault, and said, "See? I knew I shouldn't have supported this. All the eligible women, gone! Right from under my nose, in one fell swoop!"

Nadine wrapped her free arm around Hoagie's waist and said, "Aw, you big lug. We can double-date sometime. I'm sure at least a couple of the women on the island are bisexual."

"Gotta be one or two," Miranda agreed.

"Oh, hardy-har-har," Hoagie said, sniffing in mock disdain. "Bill, my man, we've got a couple of lesbian vaudeville comediennes. Going to take your act on the road, ladies?"

Nadine carefully shook her head. "No way, Hoagie. I'm home to stay."

Hoagie gave them a ride back to the station so Miranda could pick up her car. Nadine put her bike in the lobby where it would stay safe until she was able to come back and retrieve it, then curled up on the passenger seat of Miranda's car, resting the side of her face against the cool window glass.

"Do you want to just go home?" Miranda asked, starting the engine. "You haven't eaten anything all day."

"I'm not hungry. Just...yeah, just take me home. I'll be fine on the couch."

Miranda frowned. "What?"

"I don't have a bed."

"Then I'm not taking you home."

"Miranda, it's fine..."

"No, it's not. You have a head injury." She pulled out of the parking garage and said, "I'm taking you to my place. The doctor talked to me before I left. You may not get a lot of sleep, but at least you'll be...not getting it in a comfortable place. Or something like that."

"Are you sure?" Nadine murmured.

"You've had a hell of a day already. Any day that ends in the hospital requires a nice comfy bed at the end of it. It's my new rule." She turned her attention back to the road and went on, "So it's final. No arguments."

"Fine," Nadine murmured. "No arguments." Despite her grumbling, it felt very nice to have someone to care for her this way. Kate would have helped her, but she would not have been the taskmaster Miranda was set on being. The fact that Miranda cared enough to be strict was a new and welcome dimension to their relationship. She tucked her hand under her cheek, closed her eyes, and drifted.

After arriving at the condo community, Miranda walked Nadine into the house and directed her to the bedroom. The sun had gone down, leaving the sky beyond the window a deep crimson-yellow smear that darkened to magenta on the horizon. In a haze of pain and exhaustion, Nadine only received the vaguest impression of the room's furniture and décor. She did see a large queen-sized bed flanked by apparently antique wooden nightstands, but all she cared about was the mattress underneath her when Miranda sat her down. Nadine watched with disembodied interest as her shoes were untied and slipped off her feet.

"Want to keep your socks?" Miranda asked.

"Not really," Nadine said. It hardly mattered, but as long as Miranda was offering to keep touching her...

Miranda glanced at Nadine's blouse and cleared her throat. "Um...you could probably take care of..." She made a gesture that encompassed the rest of Nadine's clothes.

"Yeah," Nadine said. "Probably."

They stared at each other for a moment. Miranda finally broke the staring contest, looking toward the dresser in the corner. "There are some pajamas in there. Probably...they'd be too big for you."

Nadine was four inches shorter than Miranda and would most likely be swimming in her clothes. She smiled at the offer. "Okay. Thank you, Miranda. For everything."

Miranda kissed Nadine's lips, a brief peck that was tender instead of passionate. "No problem," she whispered. "I'll be in the living room if you need anything. Anything at all. I'll see you in about an hour." She walked out the room, leaving the door open a crack.

When Miranda was gone, Nadine got undressed and put on a pajama shirt that covered her to mid-thigh. She decided not to wear the pajama pants, which were too baggy. Scooting under the sheets, she lay down, closing her eyes and letting the darkness take her away into a deep, untroubled sleep.

True to her word, Miranda gently shook Nadine awake an hour later. They spoke in hushed tones while Miranda went over the doctor's checklist. She left the bedside lamp off, reading only by the light spilling from the corridor through the open bedroom door. When she determined Nadine was not nauseated or confused, she left the room again with another promise to come back in one more hour.

Nadine woke on her own forty-five minutes later. It was dark outside, and the house was silent around her. She touched the sheets and rolled onto her back. She could smell Miranda on the sheets, on the pillows, and all around her. It was a very pleasant way to wake up. She yawned and felt only a twinge of pain between her eyes, the tender new scab pulling a bit.

Finally, Nadine kicked back the blankets and climbed out of bed. She tugged the hem of her pajama shirt down to cover herself as she stumbled to the bathroom.

In the living room, Miranda sat on the edge of the couch finishing up the latest in a series of phone calls. She heard the toilet flush and tensed, unused to hearing that sound in her house. It took only a moment to remember why she was not alone, and she smiled. Nadine was awake. Miranda turned her attention back to the caller. "No, it's all right," she said into the phone. "No, it's nothing. Thank you for calling me, and I'm sorry for getting back to you so late. Yes, everything seems to be fine. Okay. Okay, you too. Bye."

"Am I interrupting?" Nadine asked, coming into the room.

"No," Miranda said. "I was just..." She turned around, and the words died in her throat. Nadine was leaning against the hallway wall, wearing only a white pajama top that left her legs exposed. The bottom buttons were undone, and Miranda spent a moment trying to determine if what she could see at the juncture of Nadine's thighs was a shadow or something else, something more provocative...she turned away and blushed, refusing to complete the thought.

"Should I not have worn this?" Nadine asked. She had tucked the cuffs of the too-long sleeves into her palm. She looked puny in the giant shirt, her hair mussed from sleep, and Miranda just wanted to grab her and hold her and make sure she knew everything was all right.

Miranda finally said, "No. That's, uh...a good choice. Come over here and sit down for a minute."

Nadine walked over and sat on the couch next to Miranda. She rubbed her brow and looked at the sprawl of papers that was scattered around the faintly humming laptop on the coffee table. "What is all this?"

"Work. Does your head still hurt? I have some Tylenol..."

"It's fine," Nadine said. "I'll live with it a while before I knock it out with pills. What are you doing?"

Miranda turned back to her laptop. "Well, it seems that during your broadcast today, I missed a bit of work. And before you apologize, I'd much rather spend the day in your booth with you. It was...it was the time of my life."

Nadine smiled sleepily. When she crossed her legs, Miranda was distracted by a flash of thigh and cleared her throat. "Anyway, I was catching up on some of my voicemail," she went on. "When Clifton Gail called in, he neglected to mention that he was friends with Joe Lack. They had a talk, and I'm happy to say that Joe Lack's Pizza is again offering to promote your show."

"Lucky me," Nadine said, shrugging. "What does he have to lose? It doesn't cost anything to promote a non-existent show."

Miranda pressed on, playing it coy. "I also received calls from Chin's and Duck Soup. They're both considering advertising on your show again."

"Miranda, I love you for doing all of this, but...you know I don't have a show any more."

"You don't understand," Miranda said, becoming slightly frustrated by Nadine's obtuseness. "After you got hit with a rock, it was like...well, you might as well have gotten shot."

"Gee, thanks," Nadine said.

"Deputy White cited a handful of people, but far less than there actually were in that crowd. He only had five or six citations on record when I called him earlier. Most of the people they've spoken to claim they were at work or home all day. The ones who were proven to be at the radio station have all pointed the finger at Eleanor Nelson as the ringleader. The deputy thinks they're afraid of being grouped in with rock-throwing homophobes and are trying to cover their tracks."

Nadine smiled. "The homophobe part, they don't mind so much. The rock-throwing part, though..."

"Sheriff Rucker can likely make a case for aggravated assault, maybe even attempted murder at whoever threw the rock," Miranda said. "He's looking into getting Ms. Nelson charged with incitement to riot. None of those people wants to go to jail, whatever their beliefs. And nobody wants to be associated with violence, either.

"So scoff if you will, but Chin's and Duck Soup called *me* asking about advertising again. Your show has proven you have supporters in this town. They're afraid of losing business by turning their backs on you. Your show today has done more good than we could have hoped."

Nadine's expression was pained. "I know it's just the headache talking, but...I don't *have* a show, Miranda."

"No, not tonight," Miranda said. "But tomorrow? Who knows?"

"Dugan won't back down. Remember what Hoagie told us when he drove us back to your car? Dugan wanted me arrested for that stunt I pulled today. You've got a silver tongue, Miranda Powell, but I don't foresee you talking him out of that."

"We'll see," Miranda said. "Right now, we've got seventy-five percent of your sponsors back. Tomorrow, I'll start calling the others. Now that I know what buttons to push, I'll see if we can get every damned one of them crawling back with their tails between their legs, then we'll see about getting your show back."

"Kind of putting the cart before the horse, aren't you?"

"Dugan won't give us the horse until we prove we have something for it to pull."

Nadine grinned and leaned toward Miranda. They kissed, slowly and tenderly. Nadine shifted and faced Miranda fully, deepening their kiss. Miranda opened her eyes when they parted; her gaze traveled down to the shadowy place between Nadine's thighs.

She closed her eyes. Her mouth was dry, her palms clammy, and her heart was trying to knock its way out of her chest. "Um...you still want to do the waiting thing, right?"

"I do," Nadine whispered. She sounded more than a little sad that she was the one making them wait. She kissed Miranda's cheek and repeated more firmly, "I do."

"Then maybe — and don't take this the wrong way — maybe you could put on some damned pants!"

Nadine laughed and moved her hands to her lap. "You pervert."

"Exhibitionist."

"Voyeur."

"Put your pants on, woman."

Nadine got off the couch and went into the bedroom, presumably to get dressed. Miranda watched her go, admiring the way the pajama top bunched around Nadine's ass. She picked up a folder and fanned herself with it, sagging against the back of the couch.

Miranda did not mind waiting, not for someone like Nadine, but if she was not careful, the waiting was liable to kill her.

Once Nadine had found her jeans and swapped out her blood-stained shirt for one of Miranda's, they fixed dinner together in the fully stocked kitchen. Miranda decided on chicken Caesar salad from ingredients in her fridge and smiled sheepishly at Nadine's awe. "It's just food."

"You're talking to a woman who eats leftovers three days out of the week. Believe me, this is gourmet."

They divvied up the tasks, Nadine taking care of sautéing the strips of chicken while Miranda prepared the boiled eggs, dressing, and bowls of romaine lettuce. When the chicken was done and cooled, they added it to the salads and carried their bowls to the kitchen table.

Through the living room window, the stone security wall only partially blocked an impressive view of Mount Blaine, the island's majestic peak. As always, Miranda enjoyed the scenery. The island was not mountainous by any stretch of the imagination, but the slope did stand out impressively against the full moon.

They ate quietly, occasionally laughing about something that had happened during Nadine's last show, but soon fell into comfortable silence again. When half their salads had disappeared, Miranda twirled her fork and asked, trying for a casual tone, "So do you think this would count as a date?"

Nadine chewed her mouthful of salad and swallowed before she answered thoughtfully, "Yes. But only because we prepared it together. Automatic date right there."

Miranda smiled and put her utensil down. "I love the way you look at things. It's...it's gotta be why you're so popular. You're just..." She struggled to find the right words. "I-I-I don't know," she blurted, flustered. "You really make me feel good when I listen to you, Dean."

"I love when you call me Dean."

Miranda blushed. Finally, after gnawing her bottom lip, she felt compelled to ask, "And you are absolutely sure that you want to wait for the sex part of the relationship?"

"Absolutely sure," Nadine said, a trace of sadness in her voice.

Miranda nodded sadly. She understood Nadine's reasons, but she had never exactly been the picture of self-restraint. Delayed gratification was not part of her vocabulary. Still, for Nadine, she was willing to make the sacrifice. "Okay. Just making sure."

"Of course, making out on the couch after dinner doesn't constitute sex in my book."

Miranda's eyes widened. "Mine either."

They rushed to finish the meal.

Miranda touched her when the lights were out, tracing Nadine's lips with soft fingertips. Nadine kissed the fingers one by one, then leaned in and mouthed the sweet spot behind Miranda's ear, making the woman squirm. The mellow blue moon shining through the window was the only illumination Nadine needed. She offered her mouth to Miranda's exploration, slow and slick and wonderful, igniting a slow burn in the pit of her belly. Nadine was the one to finally call it quits, gently easing away from Miranda. "I should..." she gasped, breathless and trembling.

"Yes, quickly," Miranda panted, her cheeks gilded by moonlight.

Nadine could not resist stealing another kiss. "I think I'm going to fall in love with you soon."

"It's about time you caught up."

Nadine smiled in the darkness and said, "I'm going to bed."

"Go, before I run after you panting like a dog."

Nadine slid off the couch and walked to the hallway. "You don't need pajamas or...?"

"I'm fine," Miranda said, her voice cracking. "Good night, Nadine."

"Good night, Miranda."

Nadine paused in the bedroom doorway and glanced into the darkened living room. She half-expected to see Miranda's silhouette coming down the hall after her, but nothing stirred at that end of the house. She fought the urge to tell Miranda to come to bed with her, ached for Miranda to join her, but she knew waiting was for the best. Reluctantly, Nadine closed the door and went to bed alone.

Nadine awoke the next morning to the smells of bacon and coffee, two of her most favorite things. She opened her eyes and rose from the bed, pushing aside her blankets and struggling into her jeans before she left the bedroom. Stumbling to the kitchen, she blinked at the meal Miranda was in the midst of preparing. The woman was at the stove, her back to the door. A half-empty egg carton stood next to the pan, and the wrapper from the bacon was sticking out of the trash. The smells that had drawn Nadine to the kitchen were nearly overwhelming now, and her mouth started to water.

Miranda finally saw her standing in the doorway and smiled. "Hi, Dean. Did you sleep well?"

"Like a rock," Nadine said, giving the woman a wry smile in return. Her forehead was still throbbing a little, but thankfully did not hurt badly enough to make her grab for the pill bottle. She walked up behind Miranda and embraced her from behind. Lifting herself onto her tiptoes, she kissed the back of Miranda's neck. "You said you loved me."

"Did I?"

"It was a roundabout way of saying it."

"Oh."

"I talk for a living, remember."

Miranda playfully said, "You *used* to talk for a living. You're the one who keeps saying you don't have a show anymore."

"That's Thomas Dugan, actually," Nadine grumbled.

"Right," Miranda said. She slipped out of Nadine's embrace and said, "Hope you like scrambled eggs. They're all I know how to make."

Nadine replied, "I adore them, and this all smells delicious. But...d-do I have time to shower first?"

"Yeah, go, go," Miranda said, flapping a hand at her. "I'll save you some bacon. The towels are in the cabinet by the bathroom door."

Nadine thanked her and hurried off. The whole situation was so cozily domestic that she could not help but laugh when Miranda called after her, "Save me some hot water!"

Kate wore dark sunglasses and a hat with a brim wide enough to hide her face when she left the house. It was not shame that made her hide her face; she finally knew what Nadine was talking about when she said she felt liberated. Vanity was why she had wrapped herself up like the invisible woman. She hated how pale she looked after her time in the hospital. She hated the way she was sure that people looked at her with pity, the words "suicide attempt" on their lips.

She had been given a few days off to "recover from her bout with the flu", as the city editor had emphasized. However Kate was unable to just sit in the apartment, especially not on the couch she now planned to sell or burn, so she went out and simply wandered around town for a while. After a while, she ducked into Coffee Table Books to escape the wind and get something to eat.

Ordering one of the big plate-sized cookies and a coffee from the chirpy girl behind the counter, Kate took a seat in a booth by the window. There were only a handful of customers in the shop, but it was the slow time between ferries. She unraveled her scarf and watched people walking by on the pavement outside.

Something tapped her coffee cup, and Kate jumped, unaware anyone was next to the table.

"Ooh, sorry," Amy said. "Didn't mean to startle you there." She held up a coffee pot. "Top you off?"

Kate relaxed and nodded, even though she had barely taken a sip yet. "Hi, Amy."

"Hi, stranger." Amy poured about a drop into the cup and set the pot down on the table. "How are you doing?"

"Better, I suppose." She was surprised to find she was not offended by Amy's question. If anything, she was touched by the show of concern. "I'm not thinking about it anymore. I'm still going to see a counselor, though. Once or twice a month, maybe..."

Amy frowned. "Thinking about what?"

Kate's hand twitched. "You said 'how are you doing?' That's what everyone has been saying to me lately, it seems like."

"What are you talking about?"

"I tried to..." Kate's voice trailed off, and she cleared her throat. Since everyone she had spoken recently already knew the sordid story, it was the first time she had been forced to admit what she had done out loud. She lowered her head and spoke quietly, ashamed of the words. "I overdosed on pills on Monday. They got me to the hospital..."

From the expression on Amy's face, Kate could tell she was the one person on the island who had missed the news. "Oh, my God!" Amy exclaimed. "Are you all right?"

"Fine," Kate said, nodding. "Like I said. But I don't feel like that anymore. It was...ironically, I think it was the wake-up call I needed." She smiled and added. "I'm really sorry. I just assumed everyone had heard or...you know, could tell by looking at me."

"Well, I spend a lot of my time in the kitchen. Not a lot of time for gossip. As for how you look...you look gorgeous to me."

Kate looked up and saw a flirtatious sparkle in Amy's eyes. Maybe the jealousy she had felt from Nadine hadn't been so out of place after all. She had to admit, Amy was attractive. She impulsively leaned forward and asked, "Would you like to get dinner sometime?"

Nadine walked back into the kitchen after about fifteen minutes. "Your shower is heaven on earth," she said, running her fingers through her wet hair.

Miranda turned, her smile fading as she stared at Nadine's shirt.

Nadine glanced down and asked, "What is it? What..."

Miranda pointed a finger at the rusty stains of dried blood on the shirt's collar.

"Oh. Sorry," Nadine said, sounding contrite. "I grabbed the wrong shirt, mine instead of yours. Force of habit, I guess."

"I don't suppose I could get you to take your shirt off," Miranda said, attempting a weak smile.

Nadine started to unbutton her blouse.

Miranda panicked and quickly said, "I was joking, Nadine, you don't..."

"It's okay," Nadine said. "Can I wear your T-shirt again until I can get a change?"

"Yes," Miranda sighed. She breathed a sigh of relief when Nadine retreated back into the bedroom to finish undressing. Seeing the blood on the woman's shirt brought back recollections of the hellish day before — the mob of protestors, the sudden attack, the helpless shock of seeing Nadine fall down with blood on her face...she had been so sure that some asshole had shot Nadine. Miranda shuddered at the memory and refused to acknowledge it. Everything had worked out fine; there was no need to stress herself with might-have-beens.

She scooped a portion of scrambled eggs onto a clean plate, added some bacon, and was pouring a glass of orange juice when Nadine returned. Miranda looked her over and smiled. The T-shirt was a bit baggy, but on the whole, Nadine looked good. "Much better," she said, kissing Nadine's temple. "Head okay?"

"Head okay." Nadine picked up the plate of food. "Wow. If that whole 'manager of a local radio station' gig falls through, you can get a job over at Yolk Folks."

"If it means I don't have to deal with Thomas Dugan anymore, I'll go get an application today." Miranda kept her tone light, but she was dead serious. If it got Dugan out of her life, she would have been willing to clean out animal pens at the Seattle Zoo.

They sat down together and ate breakfast at the table in the sunny niche off the kitchen. Nadine squinted against the morning brightness streaming through the window. "I wondered what was so special about this place," she murmured. "I mean, it's not that big. But the view..."

"And the security," Miranda added.

Nadine nodded, examining her plate. "Can I get something out of the fridge?"

Miranda nodded. She watched as Nadine retreated into the kitchen. When Nadine came back, she had a squeeze-bottle of ketchup; she added a small pool of the stuff next to her scrambled eggs.

Disgusted, Miranda made a face and said, "Oh, that's it. The relationship is off."

Nadine stuck her tongue out and defiantly took a bite. "So," she said, chewing and swallowing the mouthful before she continued. "What's on the agenda for today?"

"Today, we blackmail Tom Dugan to get you your job back."

A glob of yellow egg tinted with red ketchup froze halfway to Nadine's mouth.

Miranda smiled smugly, content to keep her secret for the moment, and dug into her own breakfast.

Nadine walked with Miranda into the KELF office. The front doors, damaged by the crowd the day before, were already being repaired. There were no protesters today on the sidewalk. There was no reason, since Nadine was officially fired.

Nadine had read in the paper that Eleanor Nelson had become a scape-goat for the attack on the station. People the police had spoken to admitted to protesting but all claimed they had no idea how the situation had gotten so out of hand so quickly. Members of the mob who could be identified were threatened with charges of accessory to aggravated assault, reckless disregard, property damage, and unlawful assembly, not to mention other misdemeanors, and the subject of jail time was being discussed by the district attorney's office. Pending criminal charges plus the additional threat of civil liability was enough to turn some of them into State's witnesses against Eleanor. An arrest was believed to be imminent.

Despite the backpedaling from Nadine's other detractors, Thomas Dugan remained obdurate.

She and Miranda had stopped at her apartment so she could change into something sensible and business-appropriate for the confrontation to come. She had finally decided on a powder blue pantsuit and an old pair of glasses that were slightly too big for her face but at least were not held together with masking tape. She felt like a little girl playing pretend, a feeling amplified by the fact that she had no idea what Miranda was up to.

Nadine followed Miranda into the building and smiled at Sue as she passed the receptionist's desk.

"Good to see you, Miss Powell," Sue called. "*Lovely* to see you, Miss Butler!"

When they were on the stairs, Miranda turned and whispered, "I just get 'good'. You get 'lovely'?"

"I'm nicer than you are."

Miranda rolled her eyes and continued up to the main offices. Thomas Dugan was already there, seated at the conference table. As Miranda made her way over, he frowned and pointed at Nadine. "What, pray tell, is *she* doing here? She is *persona non grata* in this station as long as I own it."

"Nice one," Hoagie said as he approached from the direction of the bathrooms. "You got word of the day toilet paper or something?"

"Hoagie," Nadine admonished, stifling a chuckle. She went over and embraced him tightly. "What are you doing here so early?"

"Bargaining chip," Hoagie said. He winked at her, refusing to elaborate, and took a seat to Dugan's right. Miranda and Nadine sat next to each other. Miranda opened her briefcase and withdrew the papers Nadine had seen her working on the night before. She stacked them on the table in front of her. Dugan leaned forward. Clasping his hands in front of him, he gazed calmly at the assembled group.

When they were all in place, Miranda stood up. "Mr. Dugan, we're here today to respectfully ask you to reinstate Nadine Butler at her full salary."

"No." Dugan snorted and shook his head. He started to get to his feet. "Is that all? Are we done here?"

Miranda did not waver. "Sit down, Mr. Dugan, please."

Dugan sighed and returned to his seat with obvious reluctance.

"Your reason for firing Nadine was sound," Miranda went on. "In a business such as this, you cannot justify employing someone who is costing your station money. Nadine had no sponsors; you couldn't very well keep her around. But as of last night, Gail's Seafood Shack, Joe Lack's Pizza, Chin's Chinese Buffet, Duck Soup Restaurant, and Yolk Folks have all pledged to sponsor her show again. By the end of business today, I assure you that she will be fully backed by her original sponsors and by the people and businesses of this town."

"She took over my radio station," Dugan said, his tone indicating he knew exactly what kind of corner he was being backed into. "She turned it into her own personal soap box."

"Yes, sir," Miranda said. "But do you think she was just shouting in the wind yesterday? I got a few statistics that I think you'll be interested to see." She pushed the papers toward him and said, "This is a breakdown of the calls that came through the switchboard yesterday. Eighty percent were in favor of Nadine. Only fifteen percent were against her staying on the air."

Hoagie scoffed. "I guess all of her detractors were too busy throwing rocks to bother calling in."

"The majority of listeners," Miranda continued, ignoring Hoagie's comment, "are in Nadine's corner. Do you really want to alienate that much of your core audience?"

"She took over my radio station," Dugan repeated. "You expect me to just ignore that?"

"No, sir. Last week, I put in a request that she be given a raise. I hereby withdraw that request. If Nadine is hired back, her salary will remain the same as it was before. Consider it a penalty for unauthorized content on her show."

Dugan glared at Nadine. "I could still fire her for that unauthorized content."

Hoagie muttered something uncomplimentary under his breath and leaned back in his chair, which creaked in protest.

"You could, Mr. Dugan," Miranda said crisply, "but then you'd have to find two replacements. If Nadine doesn't come back, I'll clear out my desk and leave with her."

Nadine's eyes widened. No wonder Miranda had kept the plan to herself; she never would have gone along with this. "Miranda..."

"Nadine," Miranda warned. She gave Nadine a look that said she knew what she was doing.

Nadine did not like it, but she did not really have a choice. She glanced at Hoagie, who also nodded, and swallowed back further protests. *Might as well see how this plays out*, she thought. *And what does Hoagie have to do with getting my job back?*

Dugan seemed unfazed. "I'll be sorry to see you go, Ms. Powell, but the sad truth is that station managers are a dime a dozen. I'll find another one before too long." His lips curled in a superior, arrogant smirk as he tried to stare her down.

"And in the meantime, who would run your station?" Miranda demanded.

The corners of Dugan's mouth wavered.

"And talent would be even harder to replace." Everyone turned to look at Hoagie, who was buffing his fingernails on his shirt. "With Nadine gone, I'm the biggest celebrity this station has," he went on, "and if she goes, I go."

"That leaves you with a void from eleven in the morning until Leah comes on at nine," Miranda informed Dugan. "A void that is usually filled by two very popular disc jockeys. If listeners start to abandon the radio station — and why wouldn't they, if their favorite disc jockey disappears? — the advertisers won't have any reason to stick with KELF. I put in a call to a station in Seattle, and they would be thrilled to have Nadine on-staff regardless of this local tempest in a teapot. There's a big lesbian and gay community over there that I'm sure would love to help her achieve celebrity status."

Surprised, Nadine stared at Miranda. This was news to her.

"If this station's signal got a little boost," Miranda continued, "who's to say that it wouldn't reach all the way out here?"

"I hear KTOT is starting to come in real clear from the mainland," Hoagie said. "I was thinking about listening to them sometime. I guess if I leave here, I'll have the opportunity."

Dugan's face had gone pale, and he was shifting uncomfortably in his chair. Miranda picked up the files she had put down in front of him and pushed away from the table. "Think about it," she said. "I know you have the weekend DJ filling in for Nadine today. But you better think long and hard about how permanent you want that arrangement to be."

Miranda straightened her back and continued, "*Now* we're done." She motioned for Nadine and Hoagie to stand up, and they walked toward the stairs.

They had not gotten halfway across the bullpen before Dugan hollered, "All right! All right, wait a damn minute. Come back here."

Nadine looked at Miranda, completely shocked by Dugan's change of heart. Miranda smiled at her and turned on her heel to go back to the negotiating table.

It took another hour's worth of discussion before Miranda convinced Dugan that reinstating Nadine was his idea. He finally "decided" her punishment should be a week off without pay for her little on-air stunt, as well as a freeze on her salary for the following year. Nadine, thrown for a loop by this show of generosity, accepted the punishment gracefully. Having her job back with little more than a slap on the wrist was more than she could have dreamed. Before they made it official, however, she asked for one small addition to the terms. Dugan reluctantly accepted her request.

Chapter Thirteen

By 11:15 in the morning, Kate and Amy had been sitting together talking in Coffee Table Books for nearly three hours. KELF was playing, as usual, through the ceiling-mounted speakers. When the music ended and the DJ began speaking, Amy looked up and shook her head. "It feels so bizarre to not hear Nadine right now."

"Good almost afternoon, everybody," the male DJ said smoothly. "My name is Ben Jones, and I will be filling in for Nadine Butler in this slot for the time being. The temperature is a nice and comfortable sixty-four degrees right now, but I know you don't want to hear about the weather. We have a special guest in the booth right now, so I'm going to turn the mic over so she can tell you a bit of really good news. Nadine?"

Amy paused, a cookie halfway to her mouth, and glanced at the speakers, her brows rising.

Surprised, Kate turned as well and asked, "Did he just say...?"

Nadine's voice came through loud and clear. "Hello, boys and girls and miscellaneous. You're not hearing things, and you're not listening to a recording. I am Nadine Butler, the Pixie, and I am live on the air once more."

The entire store exploded in loud applause and whistles of delight. Kate was happy with the reply, but not surprised. She had known for a long time just how loved Nadine Butler was by her fans.

"It turns out the squeaky wheel does occasionally get the grease," Nadine said, "and the supporters I mentioned yesterday rose my squeak to a roar. I am happy to report that following a week's suspension for my unauthorized broadcast content, I am returning to the airwaves on Monday rested, refreshed, and ready to go. So be good to each other between now and then and be good to Ben. He's just a weekend DJ; he's doing the best he can."

There was a scuffling noise, and Nadine added, "Ow! Okay, he just hit me. Roast the fool."

"Get outta my booth!" Jones exclaimed.

"*My* booth!"

"Not this week, it isn't!"

"I'll be back!"

"That was Nadine, the Persistent Pixie there, and as she said, I am only going to be here until Monday," Jones said, "so I might as well make the best of it. I'm going to have a contest for dinner for two at Duck Soup Restaurant if you can give me the correct answer to this question..."

Kate sat back in the booth with a sigh of relief. Hearing Nadine on the radio again, knowing she was no longer in danger of losing her job, was a weight off her shoulders. It was like she had been given permission to stop feeling guilty. It was like she was being given permission to move on.

She smiled at Amy, who smiled back at her.

That night, Miranda invited Nadine out to Gail's Seafood Restaurant for a celebratory dinner. They arrived not long after the last ferry of the evening churned into the harbor and had to ease their way through the small crowd of tourists swarming the boardwalk. Nadine tightened her hand around Miranda's and did not release it until they were inside the restaurant.

"What's wrong?" Miranda asked softly.

"Crowds. I'm uncomfortable when there are large groups of people lurking about."

Miranda kissed Nadine's forehead, just over the square of gauze between her eyes, being careful to avoid bumping into her glasses. They had not seen any more protesters, but the station had received a handful of nasty letters that afternoon. "Do you want to go home and eat in?"

"No," Nadine said defiantly. "I want to sit at a table and have dinner with my girlfriend."

Miranda smiled and took Nadine's hand again. They walked up to the hostess stand and waited. The restaurant was partially lit with a handful of glass lights along the back wall, but most of the light came from the old-fashioned lanterns in the center of each occupied table. The wood-paneled walls and low ceiling gave the room an undeniably romantic air. A young woman wearing a black tuxedo stepped up to the podium and smiled in welcome. "Good evening, welcome to Gail's. Do you have a reservation?"

"Powell, for two," Miranda said.

The hostess checked her book and smiled. "Right this way." She pulled two menus from the slot next to the podium and turned on her heel, walking across the restaurant while Miranda and Nadine followed behind. Nadine fought the urge to pull her hand from Miranda's; she struggled to remain at the woman's side and not two paces apart. They could walk hand-in-hand, she told herself; they could be on a date. Her love life did not have to be a secret any longer.

The hostess guided them to a small two-person table next to the window. It overlooked the boardwalk and, more importantly, the harbor and the gently swaying masts of sailboats tucked away for the night in their slips. The moon was high in the night sky, reflecting off the dark water like a stream of milk. Nadine and Miranda took their seats. The hostess lit the lantern on their table, handed them each a menu, and said, "Your waitress will be with you shortly."

"Thank you," Miranda said. She was seated with her back to the wall and could see most of the restaurant. A few patrons had turned their heads when they passed, and a few more were taking occasional peeks over their shoulders at their table.

"How many people are staring?" Nadine asked.

"None," Miranda said firmly. "It's mostly just quick glances."

Nadine smiled and looked down at her open menu. The waitress approached and introduced herself, took their drink orders, and promised to return once they had a chance to look over their menus.

Miranda's hand tensed around her menu when she saw a man push his chair back from his table and stand. The man began walking toward them. Her mind flashed back to the hate mail. Simply because the mob had been broken up did not mean the person who had thrown the rock had been apprehended. Hate still existed. Eleanor Nelson's church was trying to mount a campaign to get the charges against her dropped, and they might succeed. Most folks on the island just wanted the furor to die down so it could be decently forgotten.

Miranda breathed, "Dean, someone's coming."

Nadine moved slightly to her right and peered at the approaching man out of the corner of her eye. She went slightly rigid but did not seem too alarmed.

He stopped next to the table and smiled sheepishly. "Um. Hi. I hate to interrupt your evening, but you're Nadine Butler, aren't you?"

"I am."

"I'm a really big fan of yours. I just wanted to let you know I was ready to throw my radio out the window when I heard what had happened. Really good to know you'll be back. Well...anyway, I wanted to...say that. Again, sorry for interrupting."

"Thank you. What's your name?"

"Steve."

"It's really nice to meet you, Steve. Thanks for listening."

He nodded, smiled at Miranda, and headed back to his own seat.

Nadine grinned and said, "I still have fans."

"You always had fans," Miranda assured her. She reached across the table and took Nadine's hand. She did not have to pretend it was anything but a loving gesture. She did not have to pull her hand back, afraid of people seeing it and jumping to conclusions. This is what Nadine had meant about feeling free. The night belonged to them, not the Eleanor Nelsons of the world, and Miranda was determined to make the most of it.

Later that week on Friday, Miranda left work early and walked directly to the ferry lanes. She met Nadine, who had parked Miranda's car on the front row. Nadine moved over to let Miranda get in behind the wheel. They shared a hello kiss and, when the loading horn blew, drove onto the five o'clock ferry.

Their tickets to the theater were for forty-five minutes after docking, so Miranda drove like a woman possessed to get there on time. After the show, she took Nadine for a leisurely dinner at a small family restaurant, then they went sightseeing in downtown Seattle. They finally called it a night when Nadine was spending more time covering her yawns than pointing out the sights.

As they checked into the hotel, Nadine hesitated when the clerk asked if they wanted one room or two. Nadine looked willing to make it *The Night*, but remained silent. Miranda smiled knowingly, "We'll need two rooms."

When they were alone in the elevator, Miranda explained, "You weren't sure." She touched Nadine's cheek and went on, "You should be absolutely positive before we spend the night together."

Nadine smiled and kissed her before the elevator doors opened.

A few days later, Nadine was back at work and Miranda was back behind her desk. They were forced to reduce their dates to the occasional take-out dinner and making out on Nadine's couch. They always ended it before it got too far, but Nadine admitted it was becoming harder and harder for her to say goodbye to Miranda at the end of the evening.

Two Fridays after their trip to the mainland, Nadine invited Miranda to her apartment for a "home-cooked" meal. The day before their date she ordered the meal, making sure it would arrive in time for her to transfer everything from containers to bowls and plates. The next afternoon, Nadine went straight home from work, met the deliveryman from Harbor Lights Restaurant, and proceeded with her ruse.

When the food was laid out and the apartment was filled with the delicious smell of sautéed sea bass and rice, Nadine went to the bathroom to shower and change clothes. She was fine until she heard a rap on the door, which made her heart beat double-time in nervous anticipation. Smoothing down her dress, she made sure the table was set and went to the front door. "Hel...oh, wow," she stammered in admiration.

Miranda smiled. Her hairstyle had obviously been shaped by a gifted stylist's hand. The gorgeous black dress she wore formed a teardrop shape, flowing from the neck and then spreading out across her curves like glistening ink. Her shoulders were bare and, when she did a mock runway turn, Nadine saw that her back was completely bare as well. The dress was fastened behind her neck in the vintage Halston style.

Nadine cleared her throat and finally found her voice. "Wow," she repeated. "So this is what 'speechless' feels like."

Miranda's smile widened, and she glanced down at herself. "You like?"

"Yeah," Nadine breathed. "Yeah, yeah, yeah. I...I should change."

Miranda shook her head. "Are you crazy? That's the dress."

Nadine blushed. She had been sure Miranda would not remember, but she was wearing the dress she had worn to work one hot summer day, only tonight, her chest and shoulders were not hidden by a T-shirt. "Is it like you pictured?" she asked.

"Better," Miranda said.

Nadine stepped aside and said, "Come in."

Miranda walked into the apartment and pecked Nadine's lips. "Something smells delicious." She sniffed the air. "Oh, and there's seafood, too."

Nadine let out a chuckle and closed the door. She took Miranda's hand and said, "We'll eat in a minute, but there's something I want to show you first." She was nervous, shaking slightly as she took a step backward.

"Okay."

She led Miranda across the living room to the hallway that led to the three back rooms in the apartment. Once they were in the hallway, Nadine hesitated. She had been so sure all day, but now it felt corny and staged. She turned to face Miranda and said, "I'm just showing you this. I'm not trying to pressure you or imply that anything is going to happen."

"Okay," Miranda repeated, her expression full of curiosity.

Nadine opened the bedroom door and stepped back. "Tada!" she said, gesturing. The mass of boxes and old clothes had vanished, replaced by a brand-new queen-sized bed. The royal blue comforter was pulled back at one corner to reveal pristine white sheets, the pillows sitting against the headboard like plump marshmallows.

Nadine worried her bottom lip with her teeth. She was nervous of what Miranda would say, in equal parts afraid that she would take the invitation and that she would ignore it. "I bought a bed," she said.

"I can see that," Miranda said softly. Her eyes were bright, her lips curled upward in an amused and affectionate smile. "Why did you...?"

"I've been thinking about...you know...*The Night*. And I hated knowing that every night you were here wouldn't be *The Night* because I didn't want to consummate our relationship on the couch. So, I...um, I bought a bed."

"I love it," Miranda said. She turned Nadine around and bent down to kiss her.

Nadine let herself be pressed against the doorframe and slid her hands up Miranda's arms. When she had her fingers linked behind Miranda's head, she broke the kiss and said, "Of course, when I said I wasn't trying to pressure you, I didn't mean tonight couldn't be *The Night*, just that I...you know, wasn't...I wasn't..."

"I think it is *The Night*," Miranda interrupted as she claimed Nadine's lips again.

"Really?" Nadine said against Miranda's mouth.

"Mm."

They moved into the bedroom. Nadine gasped, "Good. I was about to tackle you in the foyer."

Sitting down on the edge of the bed, Miranda drew Nadine down beside her before pulling back a little, resting her hands on Nadine's shoulders. Each inhaled breath shook Nadine until she felt like her bones were rattling. Her hands shook where they were curled around Miranda's hips.

Miranda kissed Nadine's cheek and asked, "Have you slept in this bed yet?"

"No," Nadine said. She was elated and scared, nervous, eager for this moment. Her heart raced.

"Then we're going to christen it?" Miranda asked. She stood up and moved in front of Nadine, lifting her skirt past her knees so she could straddle Nadine's legs. Nadine's gaze trailed down the smooth material of Miranda's dress, pausing to take in the long length of the woman's legs that had just been exposed. She felt her mouth go dry.

"And it won't ruin the dinner you slaved over?" Miranda went on.

"We both know that it's take-out," Nadine replied. She lifted Miranda's skirt a little higher. Nerves were fading, becoming overwhelmed by raw lust. No, that wasn't right. It was lust with Kate. This was something far more dangerous.

This was love, or at least the beginning of it.

Her hands slipped up the smooth flesh of Miranda's legs until she reached her panties. She looked up, asking permission, and hooked her fingers in the thin cotton. Miranda put a hand on Nadine's shoulder for balance as Nadine pulled the underwear down. Nadine kissed Miranda's belly through her dress and let the panties fall. Miranda stepped out of them and brushed them aside with one foot.

Miranda bent and kissed Nadine's brow. She slipped Nadine's glasses off and laid them aside, then slid her lips down to her ear and licked the curve, making Nadine shiver. Miranda whispered, "Lie down."

Nadine let herself be guided down to the mattress, which felt as if it was ten times softer than it had been in the showroom. Miranda put a knee on the mattress. The bed sank slightly under her weight as she crawled up to settle beside Nadine. Stroking Nadine's hair back from her face, Miranda said, "You are so lovely."

Nadine turned on her side and slid her hands down Miranda's bare back. Slipping her hands beneath the edge of the skirt, she cupped Miranda's ass and pulled her closer. They kissed again, a meeting of mouths that made her hungry for more. Miranda sank down onto Nadine, pinning her to the mattress. To Nadine, it felt like being wrapped in a sheet of cotton — Miranda's gentle weight on top of her, the blanket and mattress below, surrounded by warmth and the heady scent of Miranda's perfume.

As they continued to kiss, Miranda moved her hands down Nadine's body in a heated caress, tugging the hem of her dress higher with every pass. "I thought this would never happen," Miranda said. "I never thought you could want me."

Nadine kissed the curve of Miranda's neck. "I want you, Miranda. I want you so much."

She lifted her arms over her head, her heart racing, and her breath caught in her throat as she was undressed. Miranda tossed the flimsy dress aside and looked down at her, brushing her hands over the material of Nadine's bra, unhooking the clasp in the front. She pushed the soft cups to one side and cupped Nadine's breasts, making her exhale sharply. Her nipples hardened against Miranda's palms, and she arched into the touch. She felt like a virgin, as if she had never been in bed with a woman before.

The brush of Miranda's dress against her skin was driving her mad. She slipped her hands around Miranda's neck and, with trembling fingers, undid the knot. Miranda tugged the loosened top half of the dress down and sat up, now bare to the waist. Nadine exhaled again, half sigh and half whimper, and brushed her fingertips across Miranda's pebbled nipples. Miranda closed her eyes and gently rocked her hips as Nadine's hands flattened on her belly, fingers circling her navel.

Nadine could not take the suspense any longer. Her body ached; her heart was full to bursting. She blinked away tears and pleaded, "Miranda...please."

Miranda crossed her arms and pulled the dress off over her head before bowing over Nadine. Miranda was tender, slow, letting Nadine get used to a position before she moved. She used Nadine's quiet whimpers as a guide, keeping her lips on Nadine's throat while she slowly brought her to climax with clever fingers. Nadine kept her eyes open, staring into Miranda's passion-flushed face. When Nadine trembled and sagged back into the mattress, flushed and sated, she drew Miranda's face to hers and kissed her, fumbling a hand between her thighs. Miranda spread her legs, offering herself, and whispered Nadine's name like a mantra throughout her orgasm. Afterwards, she settled over Nadine's naked body, breast to breast, and kissed her slowly. Her hair was tangled, stuck to the sweaty skin of her forehead and cheeks.

"Wow," Nadine breathed against Miranda's lips.

"Wow," Miranda agreed. She looked up and saw tears on Nadine's cheeks. She hooked her finger under Nadine's chin and kissed the tears away. Nadine shivered, and Miranda said, "Was it okay?"

"So okay," Nadine whispered. She kissed Miranda's lips and said, "I love you."

"I love you, too."

Nadine nuzzled Miranda's cheek and said, "Are you hungry?"

"I could eat."

Nadine sniffled and smiled. "Our food is probably cold by now."

"S'okay," Miranda said. She rose and slid lower on the mattress. She kissed Nadine's nipple and looked up, eyes twinkling. "I wasn't thinking of eating food."

Nadine's eyes widened.

Later that night, Nadine returned from a visit to the bathroom and paused in the doorway. Miranda was on her side, her body curled around a void about the size of Nadine's body. Nadine stood for a moment, watching her new lover sleep. It was a simple thing, but she had never felt the need to watch Kate sleep. She had never felt compelled to stare at any of her lovers like this, to drink them into her heart and soul until she was saturated with a weight of tenderness.

As she was about to walk to bed, Miranda's arm stretched, her hand feeling around the empty mattress. Miranda did not wake, but she shifted and whispered, "Dean."

"I'm here," Nadine replied, sliding under the covers. She was pulled close, Miranda's naked body spooning around hers. A warm mouth pressed a sleepy kiss to the back of her neck. Nadine took Miranda's limp hand where it was resting between her breasts and brought it up to kiss the knuckles.

"I'm here," she repeated, her heart full.

Several weeks later, Miranda's condo had undergone a major transformation. Boxes stood stacked in the hallway, clothes lay in dry-cleaning bags on the chair next to the dresser. A row of books stood along the wall waiting to be put away. Nadine tilted her head to look around the mattress. "You got that end?" she asked.

Miranda knelt and pushed aside a box of clothes. "Okay, you've got a clear path."

The mover lifted the mattress and his partner turned it so they could get out of the bedroom door. Nadine stepped into the room from the hallway and said, "Miranda, I...whoops." She moved to the side and let the movers carry the mattress away. She watched them go and went on, "I was going to ask about the bookshelf. Do you want to alphabetize them together or put in your stuff, then mine?"

"Put 'em all together," Miranda said.

"Okay." Nadine motioned over her shoulder at the disappearing end of the mattress. "I didn't know you were getting rid of your bed."

"Yeah. We don't really need two beds. Now that I'm out, we don't even need a decoy bedroom." Miranda pulled Nadine close and kissed her neck, making it a noisy, spluttering raspberry of a buss that had the smaller woman squirming. "I don't have to tell people you're just my roommate, Live-in Lover."

Nadine giggled and wriggled out of Miranda's embrace. "Stop it. I was just going to say that your bed was so beautiful. We could give my bed to Goodwill or something. I've only had it for about a month."

"Yeah, but it's seen a lifetime of action in those few weeks."

Nadine smiled shyly. "I feel weird, though. This is your bed. You've had it for years."

"Yep," Miranda said. "Almost ten years in fact. Lot of history. Lot of one-night stands, lot of memories of relationships that went wrong, but the bed in your apartment only has one memory — you and me. Us. That's my bed they're taking out; I'm replacing it with *our* bed."

"In that case," Nadine said, blushing, "I'll stop giving you grief about it."

Miranda smiled. She had hesitated asking Nadine to move in with her. It had seemed so sudden, an impulse that she became sure was going to turn out to be a bad idea. But now that it was done, now that the majority of Nadine's stuff had made it across town, it felt extremely good. It felt right. She knelt down and gathered a handful of books to add to her fireplace display.

Live-in Lover.

She chuckled and put Nadine's brand-new copy of *Sparks of Love* on the top of the stack.

Two months later, Nadine was riding her bike down Spring Street when she spotted a familiar navy pea coat on the sidewalk. She angled toward the pedestrian and whistled as she rode up behind her. "Kate!"

Kate turned and smiled in recognition. "Dean!"

Nadine straddled her bike and leaned over the handlebars to give her ex-girlfriend a hug.

"How are you?" Kate asked. "I haven't seen you since you moved out!"

"I know! It feels like ages!" Nadine noticed Kate's hairstyle and said in surprise, "Look at *you*, though. What happened to all your hair?"

Kate reached up and fluffed the pageboy cut. "You like? I've wanted short hair for ages, but Amy suggested it."

"Oh, I see." Nadine winked. "How are things with you two?"

"Fantastic," Kate said, a slight blush rising in her cheeks. "I think we've really got something there."

Nadine beamed. "That's wonderful, Kate! I am so happy for you."

"And Melinda?"

"Miranda," Nadine corrected. It seemed Kate was still playing the name game, but she knew it was just good-natured teasing. "She's wonderful. We're still arguing about who will do what chores, but we're getting there. I've almost worn her down on dishes duty."

"Hang in there," Kate laughed. They embraced again, and Kate pecked Nadine's cheek. It was a move that, not very long ago, would have caused both of them anxiety and forced them to look around to see who might be watching. The very casualness of the gesture now struck Nadine as something of a miracle.

"Amy wants to have you two over to her place for dinner sometime soon," Kate said.

"That sounds very doable. I'll see when Miranda can get free."

"Okay." Kate checked her watch and went on, "Ooh, you better get going..."

"Yep. No rest for the weary. It was good seeing you again, Kate. Give me a call sometime?"

"You've got it."

They parted ways. Nadine was grateful their friendship had survived intact. Kate had always been a great friend; it was the sex part that had proven to be emotionally unsatisfying. Now she had the best of both worlds — a friendship with Kate and a wonderful romance with someone she loved with all her heart.

Nadine rode the rest of the way to the station with a smile on her face. She chained the bike up in front and looked across the street at her parents' photography shop. The lights were on, but she could not see either of them behind the counter.

Since the day her father called into the show, she and Miranda had been invited to dinner at her childhood home. It was the first time she had been inside since she was twenty, packing some things for college. Her father had remained cold, but she could see the cracks in his stoic façade. He spoke to her, acted sociable to Miranda, but seemed aloof and distracted the entire time. Nadine attributed this to a lack of social skills rather than any lingering bad feelings. Old habits died hard, but at least he was trying. Nadine remembered she had kissed him on the cheek that night, and he had shaken Miranda's hand as they were leaving.

Nadine walked inside the station. Sue said hello and handed her a few phone messages. She was still getting calls from people coming out of the closet. The majority of calls, however, were from people pledging their continued support of her. A couple of people had admitted to her they were part of the mob outside the station and had apologized. From what she could tell, they were not really violently homophobic. They were just afraid of something they did not understand, and the mob had been an easy outlet for that fear. It had been Eleanor Nelson and her Bible-thumpers that had raised it to a criminal endeavor.

She shuffled through the messages and thanked Sue before she headed upstairs.

Miranda had left their home before Nadine was even awake, so she had not seen her lover at all that day. Nadine dumped her messages and satchel at her desk and went to Miranda's office door. She saw the woman was on the phone, so she waved to get her attention.

Miranda smiled and blew a kiss across the office to her.

Billy, who was pushing his mop bucket past when Nadine caught the kiss, snapped at her, "Now, there'll be none of that, Miss Nadine. This is a place of business."

Nadine shook her head. "You're just jealous."

"Yer darn tootin'," he said as he continued on his way.

Nadine went to the door of the booth and waited patiently for Simon and Willa to finish their show. The red on-air light went dark, and she went inside. Willa looked at her and tensed. She was still uncomfortable around Nadine, still offered her the cold shoulder, but she was willing to be professional toward her. Though Willa had never admitted it, Nadine suspected she had been nearby when the rock was tossed. There was a fear in Willa's eyes every time they met Nadine's; she imagined it was a fear of getting found out, a fear that people would know what she had done. Nadine often wondered if Willa, in a fit of anger, had thrown the rock without thinking. She would never ask, though. She would not even be able to pretend civility if she knew for a fact that Willa had attacked her with no provocation.

She feigned a cold courtesy with Willa when their jobs made it necessary. Nadine forced a smile. "Good show today?" she asked.

"It was," Willa said. Her words were clipped, her tone icy. "Have a nice day, Nadine."

"You, too. Bye, Simon."

The man offered her a wave as he slipped out of the booth.

Nadine slid into the chair Willa had been using and waited until Buffalo Springfield stopped singing *For What It's Worth*. As she inhaled the familiar smell of the booth and looked out of the window at her three-by-five view of the world, she smiled and felt peace settle over her. She had always felt happy on the air, but now it was something more. She knew this was where she belonged. This small booth was her home and she would never take it for granted again.

She pulled the microphone forward and said, "Good morning, Squire's Isle. Willa and Simon are gone, but your beloved Pixie is here in their place. So sit back, relax, grab something good to eat, and get ready for six hours of non-stop great music and maybe even a couple of giveaways. Coming up in the next hour, I'm going to be playing some ELO, Roy Orbison, and Tom Petty, and the rest of it is up to you fine folks. Call in with your requests, and I'll do my best to get them all on for you.

"My name is Nadine Butler, the Pixie, and I am going to be here with you for the rest of your work day. We'll start playing all those great hits soon, but first we have to get a few dreaded commercials out of the way. So stick with me. We'll be right back."

Geonn (pronounced like John) Cannon was born and raised in Oklahoma, but recent events have led him to believe he belongs somewhere on the water. He's a cat person with two of the beasts in his house, a Sagittarius with brown hair and hazel eyes and has a bad habit of writing. He would have been an actor if he hadn't been terrible at acting, and an ice cream man if hadn't been afraid of eating all his profits. He enjoys reading and writing but can't get the hang of arithmetic.

For more nonsense about Geonn, including news about future releases, please visit www.geonncannon.com.